FEARLESS

DIANA PALMER

FEARLESS

HQN™

ISBN-13: 978-0-373-77300-8
ISBN-10:   0-373-77300-5

FEARLESS

This edition published by arrangement with Harlequin Books S.A.

® and TM are trademarks of the publisher. Trademarks indicated with ® are registered
in the United States Patent and Trademark Office, the Canadian Trade Marks Office
and in other countries.

www.HQNBooks.com

Printed in U.S.A.

In memoriam:
James M. Rea, Attorney-at-Law
My first boss

1

"I WON'T GO," GLORYANNE Barnes muttered.

Tall, elegant Detective Rick Marquez just stared at her, his dark eyes unyielding. "Hey, don't go. No problem. We've got a body bag just your size down at the medical examiner's office."

She threw a wadded up piece of paper across the desk at him.

He caught it with one lean hand and raised an eyebrow. "Assault on a peace officer…"

"Don't you quote the law to me," she shot back, rising. "I can cite legal precedents from memory."

She came around the desk slowly, thinner than she usually was, but still attractive in her beige suit. Her skirt flowed to midcalf, above small feet in ankle-strapped high heels that flattered what showed of her legs. She perched herself on the edge of the desk. Her high cheekbones were faintly flushed from temper, and something more worrying. She had very long, light blond hair which she wore loose, so that it fell in a cascade down her back almost to her waist. She had pale green eyes and a wide forehead, with a perfect bow of a mouth under her straight nose. She never wore makeup and didn't need to. Her complexion was flawless, her lips a natural mauve. She wouldn't win any beauty contests, but she was attractive when she smiled. She didn't smile much these days.

"I won't be any safer in Jacobsville than I am here," she said, trotting out the same old tired argument she'd been using for the past ten minutes.

"You will," he insisted. "Cash Grier is chief of police. Eb Scott and his ex-mercenary cronies live there, as well. It's such a small town that any outsider will be noticed immediately."

She was frowning. Her eyes, behind the trendy frames of the glasses she occasionally wore in place of contact lenses for extreme nearsightedness, were thoughtful.

"Besides—" he played his trump card "—your doctor said…"

"That's not your business." She cut him off.

"It is if you drop dead on your desk!" he said, driven to indiscretion by her stubbornness. "You're the only witness we've got to what Fuentes said! He could kill you to shut you up!"

Her lips made a thin line. "I've had death threats ever since I got out of college and took a job here as an assistant district attorney," she replied. "It goes with the work."

"Most people don't mean it literally when they threaten to kill you," he returned. "Fuentes does. Do I really have to remind you what happened to your co-worker Doug Lerner two months ago? Better yet, would you like to see the autopsy photos?"

"You don't have any autopsy photos that I haven't already seen, Detective Marquez," she said quietly, folding her arms across her firm, small breasts. "I'm not really shockable."

He actually groaned out loud. His hands moved into his pockets, allowing her a glimpse of the .45 automatic he carried on his belt. His black hair, almost as long as hers, was gathered in a ponytail at his nape. He had jet-black eyes and a flawless olive complexion, not to mention a wide, sensuous mouth. He was very good-looking.

"Jason said he'd get me a bodyguard," she said when the silence grew noticeable.

"Your stepbrother has his own problems," he replied. "And your stepsister, Gracie, would be no help at all. She's so scatterbrained that she doesn't remember where she lives half the time!"

"The Pendletons have been good to me," she defended them. "They hated my mother, but they liked me."

Most people had hated her mother, a social-climbing anti-social personality who'd been physically abusive to Glory since her birth. Glory's father had taken her to the emergency room half a dozen times, mumbling about falls and other accidents that left suspicious bruises. But when one bout of explosive temper had left her with a broken hip, the authorities finally stepped in. Glory's mother was charged with child abuse and Glory testified against her.

By that time, Beverly Barnes was already having an affair with Myron Pendleton and he was a multimillionaire. He got her a team of lawyers who convinced a jury that Glory's father had caused the injury that her mother had given her, that Glory had lied out of fear of her father. The upshot was that the charges against Beverly were dropped. Glory's father, Todd Barnes, was arrested and tried for child abuse and convicted, despite Glory's tearful defense of him. But even though her mother was exonerated, the judge wasn't convinced that Glory would be safe with her. In a surprise move, Glory went into state custody, at the age of thirteen. Her mother didn't appeal the decision.

When Beverly subsequently married Myron Pendleton, at his urging, she tried to get custody of Glory again. But the same judge who'd heard the case against Glory's father denied custody to Beverly. It would keep the child safe, the judge said.

What the court didn't know was that Glory was in more danger at the foster home where she'd been placed, in the custody of a couple who did as little as possible for the six children they were responsible for. They only wanted the money. Two older boys in the same household were always trying to fondle Glory, whose tiny breasts had begun to grow. The harassment went on for several weeks and culminated in an assault that left her bruised and traumatized, and afraid of anything male. Glory had told her foster parents, but they said she was making it up. Furious, Glory dialed the emergency number and when the police came, she ran out past her foster mother and all but jumped into the arms of the policewoman who came to check out her situation.

Glory was taken to the emergency room, where a doctor, sickened by what he saw, gave the police enough evidence to have the foster parents charged with neglect, and the two teenage boys with assault and battery and attempted sodomy.

But the foster parents denied everything and pointed out that Glory had lied about her mother abusing her. So she went back to the same house, where her treatment became nightmarish. The two teenage boys wanted revenge as much as the spiteful foster parents did. But they were temporarily in juvenile detention, pending a bond hearing, fortunately. The foster parents weren't, and they were furious. So Glory stuck close to the two younger girls, both under five years old, whom she had been made responsible for. She was grateful that they required so much looking-after. It spared her retribution, at least for the first few days back at the house.

Jason Pendleton hated his stepmother, Beverly. But he was curious about her young daughter, especially after a friend in law enforcement in Jacobsville contacted him about what had happened to Glory. The same week she was sent back to the foster home, he sent a private investigator to check out her situation. What he discovered made him sick. He and his sister, Gracie, actually went themselves to the foster home after they'd read the investigator's covertly obtained police report on the incident—which was, of course, denied by the custodians. They pointed to Glory's attempt to blame her mother for the abuse that had sent her father to prison, where he was killed by another inmate within six months.

The day the Pendletons arrived, the two teenage boys who had victimized Glory were released to the custody of the foster parents, pending trial. Glory had been running away from the teenagers all day. They'd already torn her blouse and left bruises on her. She'd been afraid to call the police again. So Jason found Glory in the closet in the bedroom she shared with the two little girls, hiding under her pitiful handful of clothes on wire hangers, crying. Her arms were bruised all over, and there was a smear of blood on her mouth. When he reached in, she cowered and shook all over with fear.

Years later, she could still remember how gently he picked her up and carried her out of the room, out of the house. She was placed tenderly in the backseat of his Jaguar, with Gracie, while Jason went back into the foster home. His deeply tanned, lean face was stiff with bridled fury when he returned. He didn't say a word. He started the car and drove Glory away.

Despite her mother's barely contained rage at having Glory in the same house where she lived, Glory was given her own room between Gracie's and Jason's, and her mother was not allowed near her. In one of their more infamous battles, Jason had threatened to have his own legal team reopen the child abuse case. He had no doubt that Glory was telling the truth about who the real abuser was. Beverly had stormed out without a reply to Jason's threats. But she left Glory alone.

It became a magical time for the tragic young girl, belonging to a family which valued her. Even Myron found her delightful company.

After Beverly died unexpectedly of a stroke when her daughter was fifteen, Glory's life settled into something approaching normalcy. But the trauma of her youth had consequences that none of her adoptive family had anticipated.

Her broken hip, despite two surgeries and the insertion of a steel pin, was never the same. She had a pronounced limp that no physical therapy could erase. And there was something else; her family had a history of hypertension, which Glory inherited. No one actually said that the stress of her young life had added to the genetic predisposition toward it. But Glory thought it did. She was put on medication during her last year in high school. Severely overweight, shy, introverted and uncomfortable around boys, she was also the target of bullies. Other girls made fun of her. They went so far as to put false messages about her on the Internet and one girl formed a club devoted to ridiculing Glory.

Jason Pendleton found out about it. The girls were dealt with, one charged with harassment and another's parents threatened with lawsuits. The abuse stopped. Mostly. But it left Glory feeling alone and out of place wherever she went. Her health, never good, caused many absences during the time of turmoil. She lost weight. She was a good student and made excellent grades, despite it. She went on to college and then to law school with the support of her stepsiblings, and graduated magna cum laude. From there, she went to the San Antonio District Attorney's office as a junior public prosecutor. Four years later, she was a highly respected assistant prosecutor with an impressive record of convictions against gang members and, most recently, drug smugglers. Her weight problem was in the past now, thanks to a good dietician.

But in her private life, she was alone. She had no close friends. She couldn't trust people, especially men. Her traumatic youth in foster care had predisposed her to be suspicious of everyone, especially anyone male. She had male friends, but she had never had a lover. She never wanted one. Nobody got close enough to Glory Barnes to hurt her.

Now this stubborn San Antonio detective was trying to force her to leave her job and hide in a small town from the drug lord she'd prosecuted for distributing cocaine.

Fuentes was the newest in a long line of drug lords who'd crossed the border into Texas, enlarging his drug territory with the help of his street gang associates. One of them, with the promise of immunity from Glory, had testified in the trial and despite his millions, the drug czar had been facing up to fifteen years in federal prison for distribution of crack cocaine. A hung jury on that case had let him walk.

After she lost the drug case against him, she'd been sitting in the hall when Fuentes came out of the courtroom. He couldn't resist bragging about his victory. Fuentes sat down beside her and made a threat. He had worldwide connections and he could have anybody killed, even cops. He had, he said, taken out a persistent local deputy sheriff who'd harassed him by hiring a contract killer only two weeks ago. Glory would be next if she didn't lay off investigating him, he'd added with an arrogant smile. Sadly for him, Glory had been wearing a court-sanctioned wire at the time. His arrest had come the very next day.

His fury had been far-reaching. Someone had actually fired a gun at Glory when she walked out of the courthouse two days ago, missing her head by a fraction of an inch. She'd turned to look for her bus when her assailant fired. It had been such a close call that Detective Marquez was determined not to risk her a second time.

"Even if he gets me, you've still got the tape," she argued.

"The defense will swear it's been tampered with," he muttered. "It's why the D.A. didn't put it in evidence."

She swore under her breath. Her color was higher than usual, too.

As if on a signal, the door opened and Haynes walked in with a glass of water and a pill bottle. Sy Haynes was Glory's administrative assistant, a paralegal with a sharp tongue and the authority of a drill sergeant. "You haven't taken your capsule today," she muttered, popping the lid on the medicine bottle and shaking one capsule into Glory's outheld hand. "One close call a month is enough," she added, referring to what Glory's doctor had termed a possible mild heart attack arising from the pressure of the trial. A stress test had detected a problem that might require surgery if Glory didn't take her medicine and keep to her low-fat diet and adopt a low-stress lifestyle.

Marquez wanted her to leave town and she didn't want to go. But what her doctor had said to her was something she wasn't willing to share with Marquez or Sy. He'd told her that if she didn't get out of town, and into some sort of sedentary lifestyle, she was going to have a major heart attack and die at the prosecutor's table in her courtroom.

She swallowed the capsule. "The damned things include a diuretic," she said irritably. "I have to go to the bathroom every few minutes. How am I supposed to prosecute a case when I have to interrupt myself six times an hour?"

"Wear a diaper," Haynes replied imperturbably.

Glory gave her a glare.

"The D.A. doesn't want you to die in the courtroom." Marquez pressed his advantage now that he had backup. "He might not get reelected. Besides, he likes you."

"He likes me because I have no private life," she retorted. "I carry case files home with me every night. I'd miss yelling at people."

"You can yell at the workers on the Pendletons's organic truck farm in Jacobsville," Marquez assured her.

"At least I do know something about farming. My father had a little truck farm…" She closed up like a flower. It still hurt, after all these years, to remember the pain of seeing him taken away in an orange jumpsuit, cringing when she sobbed and begged the judge to let him go.

"Your father would be proud of you," Haynes interjected. "Especially now that you've cleared his name of that child abuse charge."

"It won't bring him back," she said dully. Her eyes narrowed. "But at least they finally found the man who killed him. He'll never get out now. If he ever goes up before the parole board, I'll be sitting there with pictures of my father at every hearing for the rest of my life."

They didn't doubt it. She was a vengeful woman, in her quiet way.

"Come on," Marquez coaxed. "You need a rest, anyway. It's peaceful in Jacobsville."

"Peaceful," she nodded. "Right. Last year, there was a shootout in Jacobsville with drug dealers who moved hundreds of kilos of cocaine into the city limits and kidnapped a child. Two years before that, drug lord Manuel Lopez's men were stormed on his property in Jacobsville in a gun battle where his henchmen had stockpiled bales of marijuana."

"Nobody's been shot at for two months," Marquez assured her.

"What if I'm recognized by any leftover drug smugglers?"

"They won't be looking for you on a farm. San Antonio is a big city, and you're one of dozens of assistant district attorneys," he pointed out. "Your face isn't that well known even here, and certainly not in Jacobsville. You've changed a lot since you went to school there. Even if someone remembers you, it will be for the past, not the present. You'll be a quiet little woman from San Antonio with health problems watching over several fields of vegetables and fruit, thanks to your friends, the Pendletons."

He hesitated. "One more thing. You can't admit that you're related to them, or even that you know them well. Nobody in Jacobsville, except the police chief, will know what you really do for a living. We're giving you a cover story that can be checked out by any suspicious people. It's foolproof."

"Didn't they say that about the Titanic's design?"

"If she goes, I have to go with her," Haynes said firmly. "She won't take her medicine if I'm not there pushing it under her nose every day."

Before Glory could open her mouth, Marquez was shaking his head.

"It's going to be hard enough to help Glory fit in," he told Haynes. "If she takes you with her, a gang member who might not recognize you alone might recognize the assistant who goes to court with her most of the time. Most of the gangs deal in drug trafficking."

Glory grimaced. "He's right," she told her assistant sadly. "I'd love for you to go with me, but it's risky."

Haynes looked miserable. "I could wear a disguise."

"No," Marquez said quietly. "You're more useful here. If any of the other attorneys find out something about Fuentes, you're in the perfect position to pass it on to me."

"I guess you're right," Haynes said. She glanced at Glory with a rueful smile. "I'll have to find a new boss while you're gone."

"Jon Blackhawk over at the FBI office is looking for another assistant," Marquez suggested.

Haynes glared at him. "He'll never get another one in this town, not after what he did to the last one."

Marquez was trying to keep a straight face. "I'm sure it was all a terrible misunderstanding."

Glory let out a chuckle in spite of herself. "Some misunderstanding. His assistant thought he was very attractive and asked him over to her place for dinner. He actually called the police and had her charged with sexual harassment."

Marquez let out the laugh he'd been holding back. "She was a beautiful blonde with a high IQ and his own mother had recommended her for the job. Blackhawk phoned his mother and told her that his latest assistant had tried to seduce him. His mother asked how. Now she's outraged over what he did and she won't speak to him, either. The girl was her best friend's daughter."

"He did drop the sexual harassment charge," Glory pointed out.

"Yes, but she quit just the same and went online to tell every woman in San Antonio what he did to her." He whistled. "I'll bet he'll grow gray hair before he gets a date in this town."

"Serves him right," Haynes muttered.

"Oh, it gets worse," Marquez added with a grin. "Remember Joceline Perry, who works for Garon Grier and one of the other local FBI agents? They gave Jon's work to her."

"Oh, dear," Haynes murmured.

Joceline was something of a local legend among administrative assistants. She was known for her cutting wit and refusal to do work she considered beneath her position. She would drive Jon Blackhawk up the wall on a good day. God only knew what she'd do to him after the other secretary quit.

"Poor guy," Glory murmured. But she grinned.

Haynes glanced at Glory with a worried look. "What are you going to do on the farm? You wouldn't dare go out and hoe in the fields, would you?"

"Of course not," Glory assured her. "I can can."

"You can what?" Haynes frowned.

"You have heard of canning?" Glory replied. "It's how you put up fruits and vegetables so that they don't spoil. I can do jam and jelly and pickles and all sorts of stuff."

Marquez raised an eyebrow. "My mother used to do it, but her hands aren't what they used to be. It's an art."

"A valuable skill," Glory said smugly.

"You'll need to wear jeans and look less elegant," Marquez told her. "No suits on the farm."

"I lived in Jacobsville when I was a child," Glory reminded him with a forced smile, without going into detail. Marquez was old enough to have known about Glory's ordeal. Of course, a lot of people didn't, even there. "I can fit in."

"Then you'll go?" Marquez persisted.

Glory sat back against the desk. She was outnumbered and outgunned. They were probably right. San Antonio was a big city, but she'd been in the same apartment building for two years and everyone who lived there knew her. She'd be easy to find if someone asked the right questions. If she got herself killed, Fuentes would walk, and more people would be butchered in his insane quest for wealth.

If her doctor was right—and he was a very good doctor—the move right now might save her life, such as it was. She couldn't admit how frightened she was about his prognosis. Not to anyone. Tough girls like Glory didn't whine about their burdens.

"What about Jason and Gracie?" she blurted out suddenly.

"Jason's already hired a small army of bodyguards," Marquez assured her. "He and Gracie will be fine. It's you they're worried about. All of us are worried about you."

She drew in a long breath. "I guess a bulletproof vest and a Glock wouldn't convince you to let me stay here?"

"Fuentes has bullets that penetrate body armor, and nobody outside a psycho ward would give you a gun."

"All right," she said heavily. "I'll go. Do I have to ramrod this farm?"

"No, Jason's put in a manager." He frowned. "Odd guy. He isn't from Texas. I don't know where Jason found him. He's…" He started to say that the manager was one of the most unpleasant, taciturn people he'd ever met, despite the fact that the farm workers liked him. But it might not be the best time to say it. "He's very good at managing people," Marquez said instead.

"As long as he doesn't try to manage me, I guess it's okay," she said.

"He won't know anything about you, except what Jason

tells him," he assured her. "Jason won't have told him about why you're there, and you can't, either. Apparently the manager's just had some sort of blow in his life, too, and he's taken the job to get himself over it."

"A truck farm," she murmured.

"I know where there's an animal shelter," Marquez replied whimsically. "They need someone to feed the lions."

She glared at him. "With my luck, they'd try to feed me *to* the lions. No, thanks."

"This is for your own good," Marquez said quietly. "You know that."

She sighed. "Yes, I suppose it is." She moved away from the desk. "My whole life, I've been forced to run away from problems. I'd hoped that this time, at least, I could stand and deliver."

"Neat phrasing," Marquez mused. "Would you like to borrow my sword?"

She gave him a keen glance. "Your mother should never have given you that claymore," she told him. "You're very lucky that the patrol officer could be convinced to drop the charges."

He looked affronted. "The guy picked the lock on my apartment door and let himself in. When I woke up, he was packing my new laptop into a book bag for transport!"

"You have a sidearm," she pointed out.

He glowered at her. "I forgot and left it locked in the pocket of my car that night. But the sword was mounted right over my bed."

"They say the thief actually jumped out the window when

he brandished that huge weapon," Glory told Haynes, who grinned.

"My apartment is on the ground floor," Marquez informed them.

"Yes, but you were chasing the thief down the street in your…" She cleared her throat. "Well, you were out of uniform."

"I got arrested for streaking," Marquez muttered. "Can you believe that?"

"Of course I can! You were naked!" Glory replied.

"How I sleep has nothing to do with the fact that the guy was robbing me! At least I got him down and immobilized by the time the squad car spotted me." He shook his head. "I told the arresting officer who I was, and he asked to see my badge."

Glory put her hand over her mouth to stifle a giggle.

"Did you tell him where it was?" Haynes asked.

"I told him where he could put it if he didn't arrest the burglar." He moved restlessly. "Anyway, another squad car pulled up behind him, and it was an officer who knew me."

"A female officer," Glory told Haynes, with glee.

Marquez's high cheekbones actually seemed to flush. "The burglar's tote came in handy," he murmured. "At least I got to ride back to my apartment. But the story got out from the night shift, and by the next afternoon, I was a minor celebrity."

"What a pity you didn't get caught by the squad car's camera," Haynes giggled. "They could have featured you on that TV show, *Cops.*"

He glared at her. "I was robbed!"

"Well, he didn't actually get to keep anything he took, did he?" Haynes asked.

"He fell on my new laptop when I tackled him," Marquez scoffed. "Trashed the hard drive. I lost all my files."

"Never heard of backing up with hard copy, I guess?" Glory queried.

"Who expects to have someone break into a cop's apartment and rob him?"

"He does have a point," Haynes had to admit.

"I guess so."

Marquez looked at his watch and grimaced. "I have to be in court this afternoon to testify for a homicide case," he told them. "I can tell my boss that you're going to Jacobsville, right?"

She sighed. "Yes. I'll go tomorrow morning, first thing. Do I need a letter of introduction or anything?"

"No. Jason will let the manager know you're coming. You can stay in the house on the property."

She hesitated. "Where is the manager staying?"

"Also in the house." He held up a hand. "Before you say it, there's a housekeeper who lives in the house and cooks for the manager."

That relaxed her, but only a little. She didn't like strange men, especially at close quarters. She decided that despite the summer heat, she'd pack thick cotton pajamas and a long robe.

JACOBSVILLE SEEMED MUCH smaller than she remembered it. The main street was almost exactly the same as it had been when she lived nearby. There was the pharmacy where her father had gone for medicine. Over there was the café which Barbara, Marquez's mother, had run for as long as she could remember. There was the hardware store and the feed store and the clothing boutique. It was all the same. Only Glory herself had changed.

As she turned onto the narrow paved road that led to the Pendletons's truck farm, she began to feel sick at her stomach. She'd forgotten. The house was the same one she'd shared with her mother and father, until her mother's explosive temper had shattered Glory's young body and their family. Until now, she hadn't thought about how difficult it might be, trying to live there again.

The old pecan tree in the front yard was still there. She spotted it before she saw the mailbox beside the narrow paved driveway. Years ago, there had been a tire swing on the tree.

The real surprise was the house. The Pendletons must have spent some money remodeling it, because the old clapboard house of Glory's youth was now an elegant white Victorian with gingerbread woodwork. There was a long, wide front porch which contained a swing, a settee and several rocking chairs. Far behind the house was a huge steel warehouse where workers were putting boxes of fresh corn and peas and tomatoes and other produce from the large fields on all sides of the house and warehouse. The fields seemed to stretch for miles into the flat distance.

She pulled up in the graveled parking lot under another

pecan tree and cut off the engine. Her small sedan contained most of her worldly goods. Except for her furniture, and she hadn't even considered bringing that along. She was keeping her apartment in San Antonio. The rent was paid up for six months, courtesy of her stepbrother. She wondered when she'd get to go home.

She opened the door and got out, just in time to see a tall, jean-clad man with jet-black hair and a mustache come down the front steps. He had a strong face and an athletic physique. He walked with such elegance that he seemed to glide along. He looked foreign.

He spotted Glory and his taut expression grew even more reserved. He moved toward her with a quick, elegant step. As he came closer, she could see that his eyes were black, like jet, under a jutting brow and dark eyebrows. She had the odd feeling that he was the sort of man you hope you never meet in a dark alley.

He stopped just in front of her, adding up her inexpensive car, her eyeglasses, her windswept blond hair in its tight bun and her modest clothing. If he was measuring, she thought, she'd fallen short.

"May I help you?" he asked coldly.

She leaned heavily on the car door. "I'm the canner."

He blinked. "Excuse me?"

She swallowed, hard. He was very tall and he looked half out of humor already. "I can can."

"We don't hire exotic dancers," he shot back.

Her green eyes widened. "Excuse me?"

"The can-can is a dance, I believe?"

"Is it, really?" she asked with a mischievous glance. "Would you like to demonstrate it, and I'll give you my opinion of whether it's a dance or not?"

Incredible, she thought. Until now, she hadn't really believed that a man's eyes could explode with bad temper...

2

THE MAN'S JAW CLENCHED. "I am not in the mood for games," he said in coldly accented English.

"First you talk about dancing, now you're on about games," she said. "Really, I don't care about your private life. I was sent here to help with the canning. Jason Pendleton offered me the position."

His eyes were really smoldering now. "He what?"

"Gave me a job," she replied. She frowned. "Are you hard of hearing?"

He took a step toward her and she moved further toward the hinges. He looked ferocious. "Jason Pendleton offered you a job, here?"

"Yes, he did," she replied. Perhaps humor wasn't a very good idea at the time. "He said you needed someone to help put up his organic fruit. I can make preserves and jellies and I know how to can vegetables."

He seemed to be struggling with her presence. It was obvious that he wasn't happy about her coming here. "Jason said nothing about it to me."

"He told me he'd phone you tonight. He's in Montana at a cattle show."

"I know where he is."

Her hip was throbbing. She didn't want to mention it. He was irritated enough already. "Would you like me to sleep in the car?" she asked politely.

He seemed to realize where they were, as if he'd lost his train of thought. "I'll have Consuelo get a room ready for you," he said without enthusiasm. "She's been putting up the jellies and preserves herself. It's a new line. We have a processing plant for the vegetables. If the fruit line catches on, we'll add it into the plant. Consuelo said the kitchen here is plenty large enough to do for a sampling of products."

"I won't get in her way," she promised.

"Come on, then. I'll introduce you before I leave."

Was he going to quit already, then, to keep from having to work with her? she wanted to ask. Pity he had no sense of humor.

She reached back into the car for her red dragon cane. She had an umbrella stand full of the helpful devices, in all sorts of colors and styles. If one had to be handicapped, she reasoned, one should be flamboyant about it.

She closed the door, leaning on the cane.

His expression was inexplicable. He scowled.

She waited for him to comment about her disability.

He didn't. He turned and walked, slowly, back to the house, waiting for her to catch up. She recognized that expression. It was pity. She clenched her teeth. If he offered to help her up the steps, she was going to hit him right in the knee with her cane.

He didn't do that, either. He did open the door for her, grudgingly.

Great, she told herself as she walked into the foyer. We'll communicate in sign language from now on, I guess.

He led the way through a comfortable living room with polished bare wood floors, through what seemed like pantries on both sides of the narrow passage, and into an enormous kitchen with new appliances, a large table and chairs, a worktable, and yellow lace curtains at all the windows. The floor was linoleum with a stone pattern. The cabinets were oak-stained, roomy and easy to reach. There was a counter that went from the dishwasher and sink around to the stove. The refrigerator was standing alone in a corner. It must have offended the cook and been exiled, Glory thought wickedly.

A small dark woman with her hair in a complicated ponytail down her back, tied in four places with pink ribbon, turned at the sound of footsteps. She had a round face and laughing dark eyes.

"Consuelo," the tall man said, indicating Glory, "this is the new canner."

Consuelo's eyebrows arched.

"I told him I can can and he called me an exotic dancer," Glory told the woman.

The other woman seemed to be fighting laughter.

"This is Consuelo Aguila," he introduced. "And this is…" He stopped dead, because he didn't know who the new arrival was.

Glory waited for him to get on with it. She wasn't inclined to help out.

"You didn't ask her name?" Consuelo chided. She went to Glory, with a big smile. "You are welcome here. I can use the help. What is your name?"

"Gloryanne," came the soft reply. "Gloryanne Barnes."

The tall man raised both eyebrows. "Who named you?"

Her eyes grew solemn. "My father. He thought having a child was a glorious occasion."

He was curious about her expression. She seemed reluctant to add anything more.

"Do you know who he is?" Consuelo asked her, indicating the tall man.

Glory pursed her lips. She shook her head.

"You didn't even introduce yourself?" Consuelo asked the man, aghast.

He glowered at her. "She won't be working with me," he said flatly.

"Yes, but she's going to live in the house…?"

"I don't mind sleeping in my car," Glory said at once, very pleasantly.

"Don't be absurd," he growled. "I have to go to the hardware store to pick up some more stakes for the tomato plants," he told the small, dark woman. "Give her a room and tell her how we work here."

Glory opened her mouth to protest his attitude, but he whirled and strode out of the room without another word. The front screen door banged loudly as he went out it.

"Well, he's a charmer, isn't he?" Glory asked the older woman with a grin. "I can hardly wait to settle in and make his life utterly miserable."

Consuelo laughed. "He's not so bad," she said. "We don't know why he took over when Mr. Wilkes resigned. The boss—that's Mr. Pendleton, he lives in San Antonio—told us that Rodrigo had lost his family recently and was in mourning. He came here to pick up his life again."

"Oh, dear," Glory said quietly. "Sorry. I shouldn't have been so sarcastic toward him."

"It rolls off his back," the woman scoffed. "He works like a tiger. He is never cruel or harsh with the men who work in the fields. He is a cultured man, I think, because he loves to listen to DVDs of opera and classical music. But once, we had a worker get into a fight with another man, and Rodrigo intervened. Nobody saw him move, but in the flash of a light, the aggressor was lying on his back in the dirt with many bruises. The men don't give Rodrigo any reason to go after them, since that happened. He is very strong."

"Rodrigo?" Glory sounded out the name. It had a quiet dignity.

"Rodrigo Ramirez," she replied. "He worked on a cattle ranch down in Sonora, he said."

"He came from Mexico?"

"I think he was born there, but he does not speak of his past."

"His accent is very slight," Glory mused. "He speaks Spanish, I guess."

"Spanish, French, Danish, Portuguese, German, Italian and, of all things, Apache."

Glory was confused. "With a talent like that, he's managing a truck farm in Texas?"

Consuelo chuckled. "I, also, made this observation. He led me to believe he once worked as a translator. Where, he did not say."

Glory smiled. "Well, at least this is going to be an interesting job."

"You know the big boss, Jason Pendleton?"

Glory nodded. "Well, sort of," she amended quickly. "I was more friendly with his sister," she confided.

"Ah. Gracie." Consuelo chuckled again. "She came with him once. There was a cat with a broken leg lying beside the road, a stray that hung around here. Gracie picked it up, blood and dirt and all, and made Jason take her to the nearest vet. She was wearing a silk dress that would cost me two months wages, and it didn't matter. The cat was what mattered." She smiled. "She should marry. It would be a very lucky man, to have a wife like that."

"She doesn't want to get married," Glory said. "Her real father was a hell-raiser."

"Hers and Jason's, you mean..."

Glory shook her head. "You see, Jason and Gracie aren't related. Her father died when she was in her early teens. Her stepmother married Jason's father. Then her stepmother died and Jason's father married again." She didn't add that Jason's stepfather was also her own stepfather. It was complicated.

Consuelo took off her apron. "I must show you to the guest room." She turned, and only then noticed the cane, half hidden behind Glory's jean-clad leg. Her eyebrows met. "You should have told me," she fussed. "I would never have let you stand like that while I gossiped! It must be painful."

"I didn't notice. Really."

"The room is downstairs, at least," Consuelo said, leading the way past the pantry shelves, into the living room, and through a far door that led to another hall, which ended in a bathroom opening into a small, blue-wallpapered room with white trim.

"It's lovely," Glory told her.

"It's small," Consuelo said. "Rodrigo chose it for himself, but I told him he needed more room than this. He has two computers and several pieces of radio equipment. A hobby, he said. There is a small desk in the study that he uses, but he prefers his bedroom when he's doing the books."

"He's antisocial?"

"He has nothing to do with women," Consuelo replied. She frowned. "Although, there was a pretty blonde woman who came here to see him one day. They seemed very close. I asked. But he ignored the question. He does not talk about himself."

"How odd."

"You are not married, or engaged?"

Glory shook her head. "I don't want to marry. Ever."

"You don't want children?"

Glory frowned. "I don't know that I should try to have them," she said. "I have a...medical problem. It would be dangerous." She sighed. "But since I don't trust men very much, it's probably just as well."

Consuelo didn't ask any more questions, but her manner with Glory was gentle.

The truck farm was huge. There were many fields, each with a separate crop, and the plantings were staggered so that something was always ready to harvest. The fruit trees were just being picked. Peaches and apricots, nectarines and kiwi fruit were first to harvest. The apple trees were varieties that produced in the fall. In between were berries, dewberries and raspberries and blackberries and strawberries.

"I'm going to be busy," Glory exclaimed when Consuelo pointed out the various surrounding fields.

"We both are," the older woman replied. "I was thinking about giving up this job. It's too much for one woman. But two of us, we can manage, I think. The jams and jellies and pickles will add a lot to our revenue if they sell. They're popular with tourists. We also stock them at the local florist shop, and they're put in gift baskets. We have a processing plant for the organic vegetables and an online shop that our warehouse operates. They ship orders. But this is early days for our specialty canning. I've only managed to do the usual things, fruit preserves and jellies. I would love to do small batches of organic corn and peas and beans as well, but they mostly do those at the processing center in bulk. Besides, those require the pressure cooker to process and more time than I have had since Rodrigo took charge. He is a dynamo, that man."

"Pressure cookers make me nervous," Glory began.

"We've all heard terrible stories about how they can explode," Consuelo chuckled. "But this is a new age. They all have failsafe controls nowadays. Anyway, we won't use them here. Let me show you what we're working on. It's an easy job."

EASY. THE WORK WAS. Glory's hip pained her, and she spent some of her time on a heating pad. But Consuelo found her a stool and she adjusted to the new physical demands of her job.

Rodrigo, however, was not easy. He seemed to have taken an instant dislike to Glory and was determined to say as little to her as possible in the course of a day.

He seemed to think she was a useless person. He was impersonally tolerant of her disability, but he often looked at her as if he suspected that her brain was locked away in a fleshy cabinet and was only taken out occasionally to be polished. She wondered what he'd think if he knew what she did for a living and why she was actually down here. It amused her to consider his reaction.

One day, he brought a new man into the house and told Consuelo that he would be overseeing the men while Rodrigo had to be away over the weekend. Glory didn't like the newcomer at all. He seemed to never look anyone in the eye. He was small and swarthy and he made a point of staring at Glory's body when he spoke to her. Already uneasy around men she didn't know, this one was causing her some real problems.

Consuelo noticed, and she got between the man and Glory when he became too friendly.

"I cannot imagine what was in Señor Ramirez's mind when he hired that Castillo man as an assistant," Consuelo muttered to Glory when they were alone in the kitchen. "I don't like having him around here. He's spent time in jail."

"How did you know that?" Glory asked. She knew the answer, but she wondered if Consuelo was just sensing the man's past or if there was a reason for the remark.

"The muscles in his arms and torso are huge, and he has tattoos everywhere." She mentioned one particular tattoo that marked him as a member of one of the more notorious Los Angeles street gangs.

Glory, who knew about gang members all too well, was surprised and impressed by the woman's knowledge.

"What is he doing here?" Glory asked aloud, pondering.

"I would not dare to ask," came the solemn reply. "Señor Pendleton should be told, but it would be worth my job to mention it outside the house. We will have to trust that Rodrigo knows what he is doing."

"There's a strange bird," Glory remarked. "Rodrigo. He's very cultured and quite intelligent. I'm sure he could write his own ticket in management anywhere he wanted to work. He seems out of place on a truck farm."

Consuelo chuckled. "I would not ask that one anything which was not necessary for the performance of my job," she replied. "From time to time, something upsets him. He is eloquent with bad words, and he does not tolerate sloppy work or tardiness. One man he scolded for drinking on the job was fired the same day. He is a hard taskmaster."

"Yes, I thought he seemed that sort of man. He's not happy."

Consuelo looked at her and nodded. "You are perceptive. No, he is not. And I think that he is not usually a moody person. He must have loved his family very much. I notice how he is with my son, Marco, when he visits me."

"You have children, then?" Glory asked gently.

Consuelo smiled. "Yes, a boy. He has just turned twenty-one. I adore him."

"Does he live nearby?"

Consuelo shook her head. "He lives in Houston. But he comes to see me when he can. Especially when there's a soccer game on cable—he can't afford it, but Rodrigo had it put in here so that he doesn't miss the games."

"Soccer?" Glory's green eyes lit up. "I love soccer!"

"You do?" Consuelo was excited. "Which team do you like best?"

Glory smiled sheepishly. "Mexico. I know I should support

our own team in this country, but I love the Mexican team. I have a flag of the team that hangs in my living room during the World Cup and the Copita."

"I probably should not tell you that I am related to a player on that team."

"You are?" Glory exclaimed. "Which one?"

Before she could answer, Rodrigo walked in. He stopped in the doorway, scowling at Glory's radiance when she smiled. "What did I interrupt?" he asked curiously.

"We were talking about soccer," Consuelo began.

He glanced at Glory. "Don't tell me you watch it?"

"Every chance I get," she replied.

He made a sound in his throat, like a subdued chuckle. He turned to Consuelo. "I'm going to be away for the weekend. I'm leaving Castillo in charge. If you have any problems with him, let me know."

"He does not…" Consuelo began, glancing at Glory.

"He doesn't bother us," Glory interrupted with a speaking glance.

"Since you have no contact with him, I can't imagine why he should," he told her. "If you need me, you have my cell phone number."

"Yes," Consuelo said.

He walked out without another word.

"Why didn't you let me tell him?" Consuelo asked worriedly.

"He'd think I was complaining to you," Glory said simply. "If Castillo gives me any trouble, I'll take care of him myself."

She smiled gently. "You shouldn't think that my hip slows me down very much," she said softly. "I can take care of myself. But thank you for caring."

Consuelo hesitated, then she smiled. "Okay. I'll let you handle it your way."

Glory nodded, and went back to work.

CASTILLO DIDN'T BOTHER them. But he did have a long conversation with a man in a white van. Glory watched covertly from the kitchen window, making sure she wasn't visible to him. The van was old and beat-up and the man driving it was as muscular and as tattooed as Castillo. She made a mental note of the van's license plate and wrote it down on a pad, just in case.

She shouldn't have been so suspicious of people, she told herself. But she knew a lot about drug smuggling from the cases she'd prosecuted, and she had something of a second sense about the "mules" who transported cocaine and marijuana and methamphetamine from one place to another. Many of the "mules" were in street gangs that also helped distribute the product.

She and Consuelo were kept busy for the next couple of weeks as the fruit started to come in. They had baskets and baskets of it, picked by the workers and spread around the kitchen. If Glory had wondered why there were two stoves, she didn't have to ask any longer. Both were going night and day as the sweet smell of preserves and jams and jellies wafted through the house.

Slowly Glory had become accustomed to seeing Rodrigo

in the kitchen at mealtimes. He slept upstairs, so she didn't see him at night. Sometimes she heard him pacing up there. His room was apparently right over hers.

She served Rodrigo bacon and eggs and the homemade biscuits she'd made since she was ten, because Consuelo had to go to the store for more canning supplies, including jars and lids. She poured coffee into a cup and put that on the table as well. She'd long since eaten herself, so she went back to peeling a basket of peaches.

RODRIGO WATCHED HER COVERTLY. She had her hair in its usual braid. She was wearing old blue jeans and a green T-shirt that showed very little skin. She wasn't a pretty woman. He found her uninteresting. Not that it mattered. Now that Sarina was married, and she and Bernadette were no longer part of his life, not much did matter. He'd hoped that the reappearance of Bernadette's father, Colby Lane, would make no difference to the close ties he had with the woman and child. But in scant weeks, Colby and Sarina were inseparable. They had been married years ago and it seemed that the marriage was never annulled. It was like death to Rodrigo, who'd been part of Sarina's family for three years. He couldn't cope. It was why he'd taken on this assignment. It was both covert and dangerous. He was known to the big drug lords, and his cover was paper thin since he'd helped put away Cara Dominguez, successor to famous, and dead, drug lord Manuel Lopez.

Rodrigo was an agent for the Drug Enforcement Administration. He and Sarina, a fellow agent, had worked out of the Tucson division for three years. Then they'd been asked to go undercover in Houston to ferret out a smuggling enterprise. They'd been successful. But Colby Lane, who'd helped set up the smugglers, had walked off with Sarina and Bernadette. Rodrigo had been devastated.

Sarina had promised Colby that she'd give up her DEA job and go to work for Police Chief Cash Grier here in Jacobsville. So Rodrigo had asked for this undercover assignment, to be near her. But Sarina had been persuaded by the DEA to work with Alexander Cobb in the Houston office on another case. Colby hadn't liked it. Rodrigo had liked it less. She was in Houston, and he was here. Colby had remained at Ritter Oil Corporation in Houston as assistant of security for the firm, while Sarina settled back in with the Houston DEA office. Bernadette was back in Houston finishing out the school year in a familiar place.

Sarina had come here to tell him the news. It had been painful, seeing her again. She knew how he felt; she was sorry for him. It didn't help. His life was in pieces. She was concerned that his cover was too flimsy and he stood to be killed if the drug lords found him out. It didn't matter. There was a price on his head in almost every other country in the world from his days as a professional mercenary. This country was the only place left where he wasn't in danger of being assassinated. On the other hand, his line of work was likely to get him killed.

"You don't talk much, do you?" Rodrigo asked the woman peeling peaches beside him.

She smiled. "Not a lot, no," she replied.

"How do you like the job, so far?" he asked.

"It's nice," she replied. "And I like Consuelo."

"Everyone does. She has a big heart."

She peeled another peach. He finished his coffee and got up to get a refill for himself. She noticed. "I don't mind doing that," she said. "It's part of my job to work in the kitchen."

He ignored the comment, added cream to his coffee, and sat back down. "How did you hurt your leg?"

Her face closed up. She didn't like remembering. "It was when I was a child," she said, circumventing the question.

He was watching her, very closely. "And you don't talk about it, do you?"

She looked him in the eye. "No. I don't."

He sipped coffee. His eyes narrowed. "Most women your age are married or involved with someone."

"I like my own company," she told him.

"You don't share things," he replied. "You don't trust anyone. You keep to yourself, do your job and go home."

Her eyebrows arched. "Are we doing a psychological profile?"

He laughed coolly. "I like to know something about the people I work with."

"I'm twenty-six years old, I've never been arrested, I hate liver, I pay my bills on time and I've never cheated on my income tax. Oh," she added, "and I wear size nine shoes, in case it ever comes up."

He chuckled then. His dark eyes were amused, alive, intent on her face. "Do I sound like an interrogator?"

"Something like that," she said, smiling.

"Consuelo says you speak Spanish."

"Tengo que hablarlo," she replied. *"Para hacer mi trabajo."*

"¿Y qué es su trabajo, pues, rubia?" he replied.

She smiled gently. "You speak it so beautifully," she said involuntarily. "I was taught Castilian, although I don't lisp my 'c's."

"You make yourself understood," he told her. "Are you literate?"

She nodded. "I love to read in Spanish."

"What do you like to read?"

She bit her lower lip and gave him an odd look. "Well…"

"Come on."

She sighed. "I like to read about Juan Belmonte and Joselito and Manolete."

His eyebrows arched toward his hairline. "Bullfighters? You like to read about Spanish bullfighters?"

She scowled. "Old bullfighters," she corrected. "Belmonte and Joselito fought bulls in the early part of the twentieth century, and Manolete died in the ring in 1947."

"So they did." He studied her over his coffee mug. "You're full of surprises, aren't you? Soccer and bullfighting." He shook his head. "I would have taken you for a woman who liked poetry."

IF HE'D KNOWN HER, and her lifestyle, it would have shocked him that she'd even considered doing manual labor, much less read poetry. She was amused at the thought.

"I do like poetry," she replied. And she did.

"So do I," he said surprisingly.

"Which poets?" she fished.

He smiled. "Lorca."

Her lips parted on a shocked breath. "He wrote about the death of his friend Sánchez Mejías in the bull ring."

"Yes, and was killed himself in the Spanish Civil War a few years later."

"How odd," she said, thinking aloud.

"That I read Lorca?"

"Well, considering what he wrote, yes. It's something of a coincidence, isn't it?"

"What poets do you read?" he returned.

"I like Rupert Brooke." In fact, as she looked at Rodrigo she was remembering a special poem, about death finding the poet long before he tired of watching the object of the poem. She thought involuntarily that Rodrigo was good to look at. He was very handsome.

He pursed his lips. "I wonder if we could possibly be thinking of the same poem?" he wondered aloud.

"Which one did you have in mind?" she probed.

"'Death will find me long before I tire of watching you,'" he began in a slow, sensuous, faintly accented tone.

The peach she was peeling fell out of her hands and rolled across the kitchen floor while she stared at the man across the table from her with wide-eyed shock.

3

RODRIGO STARED AT HER curiously. She was a contradiction. She seemed simple and sweet, but she was educated. He was certain that she wasn't what she appeared to be, but it was far too soon to start dissecting her personality. She interested him, but he didn't want her to. He was still mourning Sarina. Anyway, it amused him that she liked the same poems he did.

She got up slowly and picked up her peach, tossing it away because Consuelo had waxed the floor that morning and she was wary of getting even a trace of wax in her fruit. She washed her hands again as well.

"I'm glad to see that you appreciate the danger of contamination," Rodrigo said.

She smiled. "Consuelo would have whacked me with a

broom if she'd caught me putting anything in the pot that had been on her floor, no matter how clean it is."

"She's a good woman."

"She is," Glory agreed. "She's been very kind to me."

He finished his coffee and got up. But he didn't leave. "One of the workers told me that Castillo made a suggestive remark to you when you went to ask him for replacement baskets for some berries that had molded."

She gave him a wary look. She'd had words with Castillo over his foul language. He'd only laughed. It had made her very angry. But she didn't want to get a reputation for tale-telling. There was more to it than that, of course. Her mother hadn't been the only person who'd been physically abusive to her. The two teenage boys in the foster home had harassed and frightened her for months and then assaulted her. As a result of the violence in her past, she was uneasy and frightened around men. Rodrigo had been away when the new employee had made suggestive remarks, and Glory and Consuelo would have been no match for a man with the muscles Castillo enjoyed displaying, if Glory had antagonized him.

"You're afraid of him," Rodrigo said quietly, watching her reaction to the statement.

She swallowed. Her hand contracted on the knife. She didn't want to admit that, even though it was true. She was afraid of men. It hurt her pride to have to admit it.

"Was it a man, who did that to you?" he asked unexpectedly, indicating her hip.

She was too emotionally torn to choose her words. "My mother did it," she replied.

Whatever reply he'd expected, that wasn't it. "God in heaven, your mother?" he exclaimed.

She couldn't meet his eyes. "Yes."

"Why?"

"She was killing my cat," she said, feeling the pain all over again. "I tried to stop her."

"What did she hit you with?"

The memory was still painful. "A baseball bat. My own baseball bat. I played on my school team just briefly."

His indrawn breath was audible in the silence that followed. "And the cat?"

The memory hurt. "My daddy buried it for me while I was in the hospital," she managed huskily.

"*Niña*," he whispered huskily. "*Lo siento*."

She'd never had comfort. It had been offered, and refused, several times during traumatic periods of her life. Sympathy was weakening. It was the enemy. She tried valiantly to stem the tears, but she couldn't stop them. The tenderness in Rodrigo's deep voice made her hungry for comfort. Her wet eyes betrayed that need to him.

He took the knife and the peaches from her, set them aside and pulled her up tight into his arms. He held her, rocked her, while years of sorrow and grief poured out of her in a blinding tide.

"What a witch she must have been," he murmured into her soft hair.

"Yes," she said simply, remembering what came after her accident. The arrest of her father and his conviction, the foster homes, the assault...

She should have been afraid of him. The memory of the boys overpowering her in her foster home haunted her. But she wasn't afraid. She clung to him, burying her wet face in his broad chest. His arms were strong and warm, and he held her in a gentle but tight nonsexual way. It was a landmark in her life, that comfort. Jason had held her when she cried, of course, but Jason was like a loving big brother. This man was something entirely different.

He smoothed her hair, thinking how it helped to feel another human body close against his. He grieved for the loss of Sarina and Bernadette, and deep inside he remembered his anguish when the drug lord, Manuel Lopez, had killed his only sister. He knew grief. He began to understand this woman a little. She was strong. She must be, to have survived such an ordeal. He suspected there were more traumatic things in her past, things she'd never told another living soul.

After a minute, she moved away from him. She was embarrassed. She dabbed at her eyes with the hem of her apron and turned to pick up the peaches and the knife.

"We all have tragedies," he said quietly. "We live with them in silence. Sometimes the pain breaks free and becomes visible. It should not embarrass you to realize that you are human."

She looked up at him with red eyes. She nodded.

He smiled and glanced at his watch. "I have to get the men started. Breakfast was very nice. Your biscuits are better than Consuelo's, but don't tell her."

She managed a watery smile. "I won't."

He started out the door.

"Señor Ramirez," she called.

He turned, his eyebrows arched.

"Thank you," she managed.

"You're welcome."

She watched him go, twisting inside with unfamiliar emotions. She couldn't remember any man, except for Jason, holding her like that in her adult life. It had been wonderful. Now she had to put it right out of her mind. She didn't want anyone close to her emotionally. Not even Rodrigo.

THE NEXT WEEK, SHE was surprised to find a police car in the front yard. She went to the front porch and paused as the town's police chief, Cash Grier, bounded up the steps.

She hadn't seen him before, and she was surprised by the long ponytail he wore. She'd heard that he was unconventional, and there were some interesting rumors about his past that were spoken in whispers. Even up in San Antonio, he was something of a legend in law enforcement circles.

"You're Chief Grier," she said as he approached her.

He grinned. "What gave me away?" he asked.

"The badge that says 'Police Chief,'" she replied, tongue-in-cheek. "What can I do for you?"

He chuckled. "I came to see Rodrigo. Is he around?"

"He was," she replied. "But he hasn't come in for lunch, or called." She turned and opened the screen door, leaning heavily on the cane. "Consuelo, do you know where Mr. Ramirez is?"

"He said he was going to the hardware store to pick up the extra buckets he ordered," she called.

Glory turned back to the chief, and found him eyeing her cane. She became defensive. "Something bothering you?" she asked pertly.

"Sorry," he said. "I didn't mean to stare. You're young to be walking with a cane."

She nodded, her green eyes meeting his dark ones. "I've been using it for a long time."

He cocked his head, and he wasn't smiling. "Your mother was Beverly Barnes, wasn't she?" he asked coldly.

She drew in her breath.

"Marquez's mother runs the local eatery," he replied. "I know about you from her. She and Rick don't have any secrets."

"Nobody is supposed to know why I'm here," she began worriedly.

He held up a hand. "I haven't said anything, and I won't. I gather you include Rodrigo in those people who aren't supposed to know why you're here?"

"Yes," she said quickly. "Especially Rodrigo."

He nodded. "I'll watch your back," he told her. "But it would be wise to have Rodrigo in on it."

She couldn't imagine why. The manager of a truck farm wouldn't know what to do against a drug lord. "The fewer people who know, the better," she told him. "Fuentes would love to hang me out to dry before the trial. I know too much."

"Marquez told me. He said he had to fight you to get you to come down here in the first place. The thing is, Fuentes probably has confederates that we don't know about."

"Here?" she asked.

"Very likely. I have a few contacts on the wrong side of the law. Word is that he's hiring teenagers for his more potent areas of vengeance. They go to juvenile hall, you see, not prison. I understand that he's recruiting in a Houston gang—Los Serpientes. If you see any suspicious activity here, or any new young faces hiring on, I want to know about it. Night or day. Especially if you feel threatened at all. I don't care if it's after midnight, either."

"That's generous of you," she said, and she smiled.

"Not really," he sighed. "Tris, our baby girl, keeps us awake all hours just lately. She's teething, so you probably wouldn't even have to wake us up."

"Your wife is very famous," she replied shyly.

He chuckled with pride. "Yes, but you'd never know it to see her pushing baby Tris in a cart in the Sav-A-Lot Grocery Store," he assured her.

Grocery store. The store had a van. Something niggled in the back of her mind. She remembered something. "There was a van," she said suddenly. "This man Castillo that Mr.

Ramirez just hired to be his assistant was talking to some man in a battered old white van. Something changed hands—money or drugs, maybe. It was suspicious, so I wrote down the license plate number."

"Smart girl," he said, impressed.

"I put it on a pad in the kitchen. Would you like to come in and have coffee? Consuelo's made a nice peach pie for supper."

"I love coffee and pie," he assured her.

"Come in, then."

He followed her into the kitchen, where Consuelo greeted him, but with obvious suspicion. He got the number from Glory while Consuelo was out of the room.

"Consuelo doesn't like policemen," she confided. "I don't know why. I mentioned something about the extra patrols that were coming past the house, and she was belligerent."

"Could be the immigration investigations," Cash murmured. "They've stepped up in the new political climate."

"What about the extra patrols?" she asked suddenly.

He glanced toward the doorway to make sure Consuelo wasn't around. "One of Ramirez's employees has a rap sheet. We've been keeping a low profile, but we're keeping an eye on him." He grinned. "Nice work, getting that tag number."

She chuckled. "I feel like an undercover narc or something," she murmured as he got up to leave.

He laughed. "I can't tell you why that's amusing, but one day you'll see. Thanks for the coffee and pie."

"You're very welcome." She hesitated. "Can you tell me which employee you've got your eye on?"

He sighed. "You've probably guessed that already."

She nodded. "Castillo has tats and muscles like a wrestler. It doesn't take much guesswork. I've seen his type come through my office for years."

"So have I," he said.

"Do you know Mr. Ramirez well?" she asked suddenly.

"Not really," he said deliberately. "I've seen him around. But I actually came today to check with him about one of your employees who may be in the country illegally."

She wondered which employee. "Should I ask him to phone you when he comes in?" she asked.

"Do that, if you don't mind."

"I'll be glad to." She leaned on her cane, frowning. Another thought provoked her next question. "That illegal," she said slowly. "You don't think it's Angel Martinez, do you?" she added, recalling the sweet little man who was always so courteous to her when he came into the house with Rodrigo. She was fond of him.

His eyebrows arched. "Why do you say that?"

She shifted her weight. Her hip was hurting. "It's just that he and his wife, Carla, have three children. They're so nice, and they're happy here. They come from a village in Central America where there was a paramilitary group. Somebody in the village identified one of the rebels to the government authorities. The next day, Angel took Carla and the children to a healer in another village because one of the children had a sore eye. When they got back, everybody in the village was dead, laid out like firewood on the ground."

He moved closer. "I know what life in those villages is like," he said with surprising sympathy. "And I know what good people the Martinezes are. Sometimes enforcing the law is painful even for professionals."

His sympathy made her bold. "I know an attorney in San Antonio who specializes in immigration cases," she began.

He sighed, noting her expression. "And I know one of the federal attorneys," he replied with resignation. "Okay. I'll go make some phone calls."

She beamed up at him. "I knew you were a nice man the minute I saw you."

"Did you? How?" he asked with real curiosity.

"The ponytail," she told him. "It has to be a sign of personal courage." It was overt flattery.

He laughed. "Well! I'll have to go home and tell Tippy that the secret's out."

She grinned.

His expression became solemn. "Castillo is dangerous. Don't get brave when you're on your own here."

"I realized that early on," she assured him. "He has no respect for women."

"Or men," he added. "Watch your back."

"I will."

He waved on his way down the steps.

RODRIGO WAS CURIOUS ABOUT the conversation Glory had with Chief Grier. Too curious.

"Did he say anything about the illegal immigrant he's

looking for?" he asked over bowls of soup at the supper table with Consuelo.

Glory hesitated. She didn't quite know Rodrigo enough to trust him with information of a potentially tragic case.

Consuelo grinned at him. "She's afraid you might blow the whistle on Angel," she said in a stage whisper.

Glory flushed and Rodrigo burst out laughing.

"I would never have suspected you of having anarchist leanings," he chided Glory.

She finished a spoonful of soup before she answered him. "I'm not an anarchist. I just think people make snap decisions without all the facts. I know that immigrants put a strain on our economy." She put the spoon down and looked at him. "But aren't we all Americans? I mean, the continent is North America, isn't it? If you're from north, central or south America, you're still an American."

Rodrigo looked at Consuelo. "She's a socialist," he said.

"I am not classifiable," she argued. "I just think that helping people in desperate need is supposed to be what freedom and democracy are all about. It isn't as if they want to come here and sit down and let us all support them. They're some of the hardest working people in the world. You know yourself that you have to force your hired hands to come out of the fields. Hard work is all they know. They're just happy to live someplace where they don't have to worry about being shot or run out of their villages by multinational corporations looking for land."

He hadn't interrupted her. He was watching her with

narrow, intent eyes, unaware that his soup spoon was frozen in midair.

She raised her eyebrows. "Is my mustache on crooked?" she asked mischievously.

He laughed and put the spoon down. "No. I'm impressed by your knowledge of third world communities."

She wanted so badly to ask about his own knowledge of them, but she was shy of him. The memory of the fervent embrace she'd shared with him made her tingle all over every time she pictured it. He was very strong, and very attractive.

He finished his coffee, glancing at her. "You're dying to know, aren't you?" he asked with a bland expression.

"Know what?"

"Where I come from."

Her cheeks went pink. "I'm sorry. I shouldn't pry…"

"I was born in Sonora, in northern Mexico," he told her. He skipped the part about his family and their illustrious connections, including their wealth. He had to remember his concocted history. "My parents worked for a man who ran cattle. I learned the business from the ground up, and eventually managed a ranch."

She felt strongly that he wasn't telling the whole story, but she wasn't going to dig too deeply. It was too soon. "Did you get tired of the ranch?"

He laughed. "The owner did. He sold his holdings to a politician who thought he knew all about cattle ranching from watching reruns of *High Chapparel,* that old television Western."

"Did he really know all about it?" she fished.

"He lost the cattle in the first six months to disease because he didn't believe in preventative medicine, and he lost the land two months after that in a poker game with two supposed friends. No ranch, no job, so I came north looking for work."

She frowned. Jason Pendleton wasn't the sort of man who socialized with day laborers, she thought, even though he wasn't a snob. "How did you meet Jason...I mean, Mr. Pendleton?" she corrected.

He caught the slip, but let it pass. "We were both acquainted with a man who was opening a new restaurant in San Antonio. He introduced us. Jason said that he needed someone to ramrod a truck farm in a little Texas town, and I was looking for work."

Actually he'd approached Jason, with the help of a mutual friend, and explained that he needed the job temporarily to provide his cover while he tried to shut down Fuentes and his operation. Jason had agreed to go along with it.

Their next conversation, the day Glory arrived, had been about Glory going to work on the truck farm. Jason had told him nothing about Glory, least of all that she was his stepsister, but he hadn't liked Rodrigo's remark about Glory being crippled and it was evident. Rodrigo had the feeling that Jason was overly fond of Glory—perhaps they were even lovers. It had been a taut conversation.

Rodrigo was tempted to ask Glory about her relationship with Jason, but he didn't want to rock the boat.

"Well, your English is a hundred times better than my Spanish," she sighed, breaking into his thoughts.

"I work hard at it."

Consuelo was stirring cake batter. She glanced at Rodrigo curiously. "That Castillo man is going to be trouble, you mark my words."

He leaned back in his chair and looked at her. "We've been over this twice already," he said quietly. "You want your son to work here and take his place. But Marco doesn't know how to manage people." He said it in an odd tone, as if he was holding something back.

She glowered at him. "He can so manage people. He's smart, too. Not book smart, but street smart."

Rodrigo looked thoughtful. His eyes narrowed. "All right, then. Have him come and talk to me tomorrow."

Consuelo's dark eyes lit up. "You mean it?"

"I mean it."

"I'll call him right now!" She put down the bowl of unfinished batter and left the room, wiping her hands on her apron as she went.

"Is he as nice as she is? Her son, I mean?" Glory asked.

Rodrigo seemed distracted. "He's a hard worker," he replied. "But he has some friends I don't like."

"I'll bet I have some friends you wouldn't like," she retorted. "It's the boy who'll be working here, not his friends."

He cocked an eyebrow. "Outspoken, aren't you?"

"From time to time," she confessed. "Sorry."

"Don't apologize," he replied, finishing his coffee. "I like to know where I stand with people. Honesty is a rare commodity these days."

She could have written a check on that. She was lied to day by day on the job, by criminals who swore innocence. It was always somebody else's fault, not theirs. They were framed. The witnesses were blind. The arresting officers were brutal. They weren't getting a fair trial. And on and on it went.

"I said," Rodrigo repeated, "will you and Consuelo have enough jars and lids, or should we get more?"

She started. She'd been lost in thought. "Sorry. I really don't know. Consuelo brings them out. I haven't really paid attention to how many we've got."

"I'll ask her on the way out. If Castillo gives you any more lip, tell me," he said, pausing in the doorway. "We don't allow harassment here."

"I will," she promised.

She watched him go into the other room, heard the murmur of his deep voice as he spoke to Consuelo. He really was a handsome man, she thought. If she hadn't been carrying so many emotional scars, she might have looked for a way to worm herself into his life. It was odd that a man like that would still be single at his age, which she judged to be mid-thirties. It was none of her business, she reminded herself. She only worked here.

TWO DAYS LATER, A late model SUV pulled up in the driveway. A slender, pretty blonde woman got out and darted up the steps. She was wearing blue jeans and a pink tank top. She looked young and carefree and happy.

Consuelo was busy washing jars and lids before they started on the next batch of peaches when there came a knock at the door. Glory went to answer it, leaning heavily on the cane. She'd had a bad night.

The young woman grinned at her. "Hi," she said in a friendly tone. "Is Rodrigo around?"

For some inexplicable reason, Glory felt her heart drop. "Yes," she said. "He's at the warehouse overseeing the packing. We're stocking it with fruit preserves and jellies for the Internet business."

"Okay," she said. "Thanks."

If it had been anyone else, Glory would have gone back to the kitchen. But the woman fit the description Consuelo had mentioned, and she was curious. She watched as the other woman approached the big warehouse out back. Rodrigo spotted her and his whole face became radiant. He held out his arms and she ran into them, to be swung around and kissed heartily on the cheek.

If Glory had needed reminding that Rodrigo was handsome enough to attract almost any woman he wanted, that proved it. She turned and went back into the house. It hurt her that Rodrigo wanted someone else. She didn't dare question why.

He didn't bring the visitor into the house. They stood together under a big mesquite tree, very close, and spoke for a long time. Glory wasn't spying. But she was looking out the window. She couldn't help it. That those two had shared a close relationship was impossible not to notice.

Finally Rodrigo took the blonde's hand in his and led her back to the SUV, helping her up into her seat. She smiled and waved as she drove away. Rodrigo stood looking after the truck, his smile gone into eclipse. His hands dug into his jean pockets and the misery he felt was evident even at a distance. He looked like a man who'd lost everything he loved.

Glory went back to her canning, pensively. She wondered what had gone wrong for Rodrigo that he and the blonde woman weren't together.

She asked Consuelo, against her better judgment.

"Who is that blonde woman who comes to visit Rodrigo?" she asked, trying to sound casual.

Consuelo gave her a stealthy look. "I don't know," she said. "But it's obvious that she means something to Rodrigo."

"I noticed," Glory replied. "She seems very nice."

"He's fond of her, you can tell." She set the timer on the pressure cooker. "But if you look close," she added gently, "you can tell that it's only fondness on her part. She likes him, but she isn't in love."

"He is," Glory blurted out.

Consuelo glanced at her curiously. "You're perceptive."

Glory smiled. "He seems like a good person."

"He's the best. We all like him."

"I noticed that he seems…"

Before she could finish the sentence, the back door opened and a tall, handsome young man with wavy black hair, dark eyes and an olive complexion came in through the back door without knocking. He was wearing jeans and a pullover shirt, and broadcasting gang colors and tattoos.

Glory didn't dare voice that summary. She wasn't supposed to know about gang symbols. But she did. This young man belonged to the infamous Los Serpientes gang of Houston. She wondered what in the world he was doing in the kitchen.

Before she could ask, he grinned and hugged Consuelo, swinging her around in a circle and laughing the whole time.

"Hi, Mom!" he said in greeting.

Consuelo hugged him back and gave him a big kiss on both cheeks. She turned, her arm around his muscular waist. "Glory, this is my son, Marco!" she announced.

4

CONSUELO'S SON? GLORY had to hide her consternation. The young man was good-looking and personable, but he was unmistakably a gang member. She was worried that Rodrigo might not know. He came from Mexico, from a ranch in a rural area that probably didn't have any gang activity.

"This is Glory." Consuelo introduced her son to the younger woman.

"Hi," he said, smiling. "Nice to meet you."

"Same here," Glory replied, and tried to smile normally.

"Where's the boss?" he asked Consuelo.

"Out in the warehouse," she told him. "You be nice," she added firmly.

"I'm always nice," he scoffed. "He'll love me. You just wait and see!"

He winked at his mother, gave Glory a brief glance and went out the back door whistling.

"Isn't he handsome?" Consuelo asked. "He looks just as his father did, at that age."

Glory had been curious about Consuelo's husband. She never mentioned him.

"Is his father still alive?" she asked delicately.

Consuelo grimaced. "He's in prison," she said bluntly, watching for Glory's reaction. "They said he was smuggling drugs across the border. It was all lies, but we had no money for a good defense attorney, so he went to prison. I write to him, but he's in California. It's a long way, and expensive even to take the bus there." She sighed. "He's a good man. He said the police had him mixed up with a man he knew, but he got arrested and charged just the same."

Glory sympathized, but she wasn't convinced. The state had to have a certain level of evidence before it proceeded to charge anyone. No prosecutor wanted to waste taxpayer money pursuing a case he couldn't win.

"Marco looks just like him," Consuelo continued, smiling as she washed more canning jars and lids. "But he trusts people too much. He was arrested last month in Houston and charged with trespassing," she added curtly. "Stupid cops! He was just lost, driving around a strange neighborhood, and they assumed he was involved in a drive-by shooting, can you imagine?"

Drive-by shootings and gang wars over drug turf were commonplace in Glory's world, but she didn't dare mention it. As for the police mistaking a lost motorist for a drive-by shooter, that was unlikely. It was obvious that Consuelo thought her son was the center of the universe. It would do no good to point out that an innocent boy wouldn't be likely to sport gang paraphernalia and tattoos. It was fairly obvious that Consuelo didn't have a clue as to her son's true nature.

"He's very good-looking," Glory said, feigning innocence.

"Yes," Consuelo said, smiling absently. "Just like his father."

Glory had lost track of the good-looking muscular boys who'd passed through her office on their way to prison. The whole culture of low-income teens seemed to glorify doing time, as if it were a status symbol for young men. She recalled a social crusader who went into the poor sections of town trying to convince gang members to give up their lives of crime and become useful members of society. In other words, give up the thousands of dollars they made running drugs or manufacturing them to work behind a counter in a fast-food store for minimum wage.

Someone who had never seen the agonizing poverty that produced criminals had no idea how difficult it was to break out of the mold. She'd lost track of the number of poor mothers with absent husbands trying to raise multiple children alone on a minimum wage salary, often with health problems as well. The older children had to help take care of the younger ones. Frustrated by their home lives, when they lacked attention there, they found it in a gang. There were so many gangs. Many were international. Each had its own colors, tattoos, hand signals and methods of wearing clothing to express their particular affiliations publicly. Most police departments had at least one officer whose specialty was the gang culture. Glory knew the basics, because she'd had to prosecute gang members for drug peddling, homicides, burglaries and other felonies. She never stopped feeling rage at the conditions that produced the crime.

She glanced at Consuelo. "Is Marco your only child?" she asked suddenly.

Consuelo hesitated, just for a heartbeat, before she turned. "Yes," she replied. She noted Glory's curiosity. "I had health problems," she added quickly.

Glory smiled convincingly. "He's a very nice young man," she replied. "He doesn't seem the least bit spoiled by being an only child."

Consuelo relaxed and returned the smile. "No. He certainly wasn't spoiled." She went back to her canning.

Glory filed the conversation away. She didn't know of one single family among the immigrants who had less than three children. Many deplored contraception. Perhaps it was true that Consuelo had health problems. But it was curious that she had only one child, and that she seemed so intelligent when she was working at a job that didn't require much education.

That went double for Rodrigo, the educated bit. Glory couldn't figure him out. He seemed the least likely person to be working as a manual laborer. It disturbed her that he'd given jobs to men like Castillo and Marco. Neither of the young men looked like farm hands. They were too savvy.

What if, she asked herself, Rodrigo was himself on the wrong side of the law? The question shocked her. He seemed so honest. But, she recalled, she'd prosecuted at least two people whose integrity was attested to by a veritable parade of character witnesses. But the criminals were only adept at putting on an act. A very convincing act, at that. Very often, people could be the exact opposites of their assumed roles.

Rodrigo might even be an illegal himself. Glory's step-brother, Jason Pendleton, was sympathetic to all sorts of people. He might have felt sorry for Rodrigo and given him the job out of sympathy.

What if Rodrigo was illegal, and mixed up in drug trafficking? She felt sick inside. What would she do? Her duty would be to turn him in and make sure he was prosecuted. She, of all people, knew the anguish drug dealers could cause parents. She knew the source of the drug money as well—upstanding, greedy businessmen who wanted to make a fortune fast, without putting too much effort into it. They didn't see the families whose lives were torn apart by the effects of crystal meth or cocaine or methodone. They didn't have to bury promising children, or watch their loved ones suffer through rehabilitation. They didn't have to visit those children in prison. The money men didn't care about all that. They just cared about their profit.

Could Rodrigo be one of those businessmen? Could he be a drug dealer, using the farm as a cover?

Her heart sank. Surely not. He was kind. He was intelligent and caring. He couldn't be mixed up in that terrible business. But what, her conscience asked, if he was? If she knew, if she had proof, could she live with herself if she didn't turn him in? Could she do that?

"My, what a long face!" Consuelo chided.

Glory caught herself and laughed self-consciously. "Is that how I look? Sorry. I was thinking about all that fruit waiting for us in the warehouse."

Consuelo rolled her eyes. "Isn't it the truth!"

They returned to casual conversation, and Glory put away her suspicions.

THAT EVENING, SHE SAT in the porch swing listening to the musical sound of crickets nearby. It was a sultry night, but not too hot. She closed her eyes and smelled jasmine on the night air. It had been a while since she'd been in a porch swing. She tried not to remember sitting beside her father on long summer nights and asking him about days past, when he was a little boy going to local rodeos. He knew all the famous bull riders and bronc riders, and often had invited them to the house for coffee and cake. Her mother hadn't liked that. She considered such people beneath her station in life and deliberately absented herself when they came to the house. She felt her father's sadness even now, years later...

The screen door opened and Rodrigo came outside. He paused to light a thin cigar before he turned toward Glory.

"The mosquitoes will eat you alive," he cautioned.

She'd already killed two of the pesky things. "If they're willing to sacrifice their lives to suck my blood, let them."

He chuckled. He walked toward her and paused at the porch rail, looking out over the flat landscape in the distance. "It's been a long time since I had time to worry about mosquitoes," he mused. "Do you mind?" he indicated the empty place beside her.

She shook her head and he sat down, jostling the swing for a few seconds before he kicked it back into a smooth rhythm.

"Have you always worked on the land?" she asked him conversationally.

"In a sense," he replied. He blew out a puff of smoke. "My father had a ranch, when I was a boy. I grew up with cowboys."

She smiled. "So did I. My father took me to the rodeos and introduced me to the stars." She grimaced. "My mother hated such people. She gave my father a bad time when he invited them to come and have coffee. But he did all the cooking, so she couldn't complain that he was making work for her."

He glanced at her. "What did your mother do?"

"Nothing," she said coldly. "She wanted to be a rich man's wife. She thought my father was going to stay in rodeo and bring home all that nice prize money, but he hurt his back and quit. She was furious when he bought a little farm with his savings."

She didn't mention that it was this house where they lived, or that the land which now produced vegetables and fruits had produced only vegetables for her father.

"Were her people well-to-do?"

"I have no idea who her people were," she admitted. "I used to wonder. But it doesn't make any difference now."

He frowned. "Family is the most important thing in the world. Especially children."

"You don't have any," she said without thinking.

His face set into hard lines and he didn't look at her. "That doesn't mean I didn't want them," he said harshly.

"I'm sorry," she stammered. "I don't know why I said that."

He smoked his cigar in a tense silence. "I was on the verge of marrying," he said after a minute. "She had a little girl. They were my life. I lost them to another man. He was the child's biological father."

She grimaced. His attitude began to make sense. "I'll bet the little girl misses you," she said.

"I miss her, as well."

"Sometimes," she began cautiously, "I think there's a pattern to life. People come into your life when you need them to, my father used to say. He was sure that life was hardwired, that everything happened as it was planned to happen. He said—" she hesitated, remembering her father's soft voice, at his trial "—that we have to accept things that we can't change, and that the harder we fight fate, the more painful it becomes."

He turned toward her, leaning back against the swing chain with his long legs crossed. "Is he still alive—your father?"

"No."

"Any sisters, brothers?"

"No," she replied sadly. "Just me."

"What about your mother?"

Her teeth clenched. "She's gone, too."

"You didn't mourn her, I think."

"You're right. All I ever had from her was hatred. She blamed me for trapping her into a life of poverty on a little farm with a man who could hardly spell his own name."

"She considered that she married down, I gather."

"Yes. She never let my father forget how he'd ruined her life."

"Which of them died first?"

"He did," she said, not wanting to remember it. "She remarried very soon after the funeral. Her second husband had money. She finally had everything she wanted."

"You would have benefited, too, surely."

She drew in a slow breath and shifted her weight. "The judge considered that she was dangerous to me, so, with the best of intentions, she put me into foster care. I went to a family that had five other foster kids."

"I know a little about foster homes," he said, recalling some horror stories he'd heard from comrades who'd been in state custody, however briefly. Cord Romero and his wife, Maggie, came immediately to mind.

"I think life with my mother might have been easier, even if it had been more dangerous," she murmured.

"Were you there a long time?"

"Not too long." She didn't dare say any more. He might have heard the Pendletons talk about their stepsister. "What was your childhood like?"

"Euphoric," he said honestly. "We traveled a lot. My father was, ah, in the military," he invented quickly.

"I had a friend whose father was, too. They traveled all over the world. She said it was an experience."

"Yes. One learns a great deal about other cultures, other ways of life. Many problems in politics arise because of cultural misunderstanding."

She laughed. "Yes, I know. We had a man in an office I worked for who was Middle Eastern. He liked to stand very close to people when he was talking to them. Another guy in the office was a personal space maniac. He backed right out a window one day trying to avoid letting his colleague get close to him. Fortunately it was on the first floor," she added, laughing.

He smiled. "I have seen similar things. What a mixture of people we are in this country," he murmured. "So many traditions, so many languages, so many separate belief systems."

"Things were different when I was little," she recalled.

"Yes. For me, too. Immersed in our own personal cultures, it is hard to see or understand opposing points of view, is it not?"

"It is," she agreed.

He rocked the swing back into motion. "You and Consuelo are wearing yourselves thin on this latest picking of fruit," he pointed out. "If you need help, say so. I can hire more people to help you. I've already asked Jason for permission."

"Oh, we're doing okay," she said with a smile. "I like Consuelo. She's a very interesting person."

"She is," he said.

His tone was personable, but there was something

puzzling in the way he said it. She wondered for an instant if he, too, had suspicions about his cook.

"What do you think of Marco?" he asked suddenly.

She had to be very careful in answering that question. "He's very nice-looking," she said carelessly. "Consuelo dotes on him."

"Yes." He rocked the swing again.

"She said his father was in jail."

He made an odd sound. "Yes. Serving a life sentence."

"For drug smuggling?" she blurted out incredulously, because she knew how difficult it was to send a smuggler away for life without a lot of additional felony charges.

His head turned toward her. He was very quiet. "Is that what she told you?"

She cleared her throat, hoping she hadn't given herself away. "Yes. She said he was mistaken for another man."

"Ah." He puffed on the cigarette.

"Ah?" she parroted, questioning.

"He was piloting a go-fast boat with about two hundred kilos of cocaine," he said easily. "He was so confident that he'd paid off the right people that he didn't bother to conceal the product. The Coast Guard picked him up heading for Houston."

"In a boat?"

He chuckled. "They have airplanes and helicopters, both with machine guns. They laid down a trail of tracers on both sides of his conveyance and told him to stop or learn to swim very fast. He gave up."

"Goodness! I never knew the Coast Guard worked smuggling cases," she added with pretended ignorance.

"Well, they do."

"But the product still gets through," she said sadly.

"Supply and demand drive the market. As long as there is a demand, there will certainly be a supply."

"I suppose so," she said, her voice very quiet.

He rocked the swing into motion again. It was very pleasant out here with her, he thought. But he would rather have been with Sarina and Bernadette. He was lonely. He'd never thought of himself as a family man, but three years of looking out for two other people had changed his mind. He'd even gone so far as to think about having a child of his own. Pipe dreams. All dead now.

"Is this what you planned to do with your life?" she asked suddenly. "Managing a truck farm, I mean?"

He laughed softly. "At one time, I wanted very much to be a commercial airline pilot. I have a pilot's license, although I rarely make use of it. Flying is expensive," he added quickly, in case she had some idea of how much private planes cost.

She hesitated about probing further. He was a very private person, and she sensed some irritation in his tone that she'd asked about his goals.

She stared off into the distance. "I wanted to be a ballerina when I was young," she said quietly. "I took lessons and everything."

He winced. "That must have been a painful loss."

"Yes. I'll never get rid of the limp unless they can find a

way to remake muscle and bone." She laughed shortly. "I
enjoy watching ballet productions on educational television,"
she added. "And I'd probably have embarrassed myself with
any serious dancing. I'm just clumsy. The first recital I was
in called for us to hold hands and dance past the orchestra
pit. I fell in, right onto a very big fellow playing a big tuba.
The audience thought it was all part of the routine." She
grimaced. "My mother got up and walked out of the audi-
torium," she recalled. "She never went to another recital. She
thought I did it deliberately to embarrass her."

"A truly paranoid personality," he commented.

"Yes, she was," she said quickly. "How did you know?"

"I knew a man who was the same. He thought people
were following him all the time. He was certain the CIA had
bugged his telephone. He wore a second set of clothing
under his suits, so that he could duck into a rest room and
change to throw his pursuers off the track."

"My goodness!" she exclaimed. "Did they lock him up?"

"They couldn't." He chuckled. "He headed a very dangerous federal agency at the time."

She was really curious now. "How did you find out about
it?"

He hesitated, playing for time. He was getting careless.
He was supposed to be an uneducated farm laborer. "A
cousin of mine played semipro soccer with a cousin of his,"
he replied finally.

"Nice to have a pipeline like that," she said. She laughed. "You
could have made a fortune if you'd tipped off the tabloids."

And gotten himself put on a hit list, he thought silently. The man had been a very dangerous enemy. Rodrigo had taken work in Mexico to avoid being around him until he finally retired. Having dual citizenship with the U.S. and Mexico had come in handy. It was really handy now, since there was a price on his head in almost every other country on earth. He glanced at Glory and wondered what she'd think of him if she knew the truth about his anguished past.

"Did you have pets when you were little?" she asked after a minute, just for something to say.

"Yes," he replied. "I had a parrot who spoke Danish."

"How odd," she replied.

Not really, because his father had been Danish. He didn't explain. "How about you? Did you have other pets besides the ill-fated cat?"

"Not really. I always wanted a dog, but that never happened."

"You could have one now, couldn't you?"

She could, but her work called her out at all hours. She didn't think it was fair to a dog to have to share her hectic life. Compared to what she normally did, working on this truck farm was a real vacation. She'd gone to deserted parking lots to meet informers, with the police along for protection. She'd ridden in limousines with gang bosses. She'd done a lot of dangerous things in the course of her job, and she'd made enemies. Enemies like Fuentes. If she had a pet, it would become a target, just as a boyfriend or close friend would. The people she prosecuted held life cheap compared to profit. They wouldn't hesitate to do anything in their power to harm her, including doing damage to a pet.

"I have a very small apartment," she hedged. "And my last job was working for a temporary agency. I worked odd hours."

So did he, when he wasn't pretending to run a truck farm. He'd considered taking overseas work instead of this undercover assignment, but he'd thought that Sarina and Bernadette would be living here in Jacobsville and he might get a glimpse of them from time to time. In retrospect, that had been a stupid idea. Bernadette could have blown his cover sky high without realizing it. His mind hadn't been working well just after Sarina and Colby Lane had renewed their marriage vows in a small ceremony. His heart had been broken.

"We'll have some odd hours here, for a while, as well," he said suddenly, thinking about what was coming up for his assignment.

"Putting up all the new fruit, you mean?" she asked.

He took a last puff on the cigarette and flung it out into the sand of the front yard. "No. I mean that I'll be in and out. I have some new contacts that I'm meeting. Some of them may come down to overlook the operation before they sign on with us."

"It's a very good little farm," she said absently. "I know it's hard work to grow fruits and vegetables, because I've tried to." She laughed. "My tomatoes burned up in the drought and I planted things in the wrong season. It's hard work."

"It's hard, but I enjoy it. It's relaxing work."

"Relaxing?" she exclaimed, turning slightly toward him. "It's backbreaking!"

He chuckled. "Not for me," he reminded her. "I oversee. I don't hoe or harvest."

"You have a good crew that does that," she agreed. "Is Marco going to work here?"

He hesitated. "Yes," he said. "For a while."

"Consuelo will be glad."

He leaned toward her in the dim light coming from the house. "He may bring one or two of his friends with him occasionally. If he does, stay out of their way. Don't be tempted to walk around outside, even in broad daylight."

She stared at him, pretending surprise. "Is he dangerous?"

"All men are dangerous, given the right set of circumstances," he told her flatly. "Don't ask questions. Just do what I say."

She saluted him.

He burst out laughing. "For a woman with a ragged upbringing, you cope well."

"Coping isn't a choice," she replied lightly. "We can't live in the past."

"I know," he replied, and he sounded torn.

She wanted to say something comforting, but nothing came to mind. It was too late, anyway. He got to his feet with that lazy elegance that was so much a part of him.

"I have to make an early start tomorrow. Remember, if you and Consuelo need more hands in the kitchen, we can manage one or two more people."

"Thanks," she said. "But we're doing okay."

"Good night."

"Good night."

She watched him go, aware of the faint spice of his cologne, the clean smell of his body and his clothing. He was immaculate. Certainly he didn't smell like a man who worked with his hands at hard labor.

She got up from the swing and moved slowly toward the front door. She was tired. It had been a very long day.

Sometime before morning, she woke suddenly. She didn't know why. There was a sound, a mixture of sounds, human and insistent.

She lay on her back staring up at the ceiling. A man was arguing with someone. Yelling. She didn't recognize the voice, but it wasn't Rodrigo's. She bit her lower lip. She didn't like loud voices.

After a minute, there was the sound of a car door slamming, and then an engine revving up. Gravel went flying audibly as the vehicle took off down the driveway. She'd have to ask Consuelo what was going on. It sounded as if there had been a serious quarrel.

5

When Glory dressed and went to the kitchen for breakfast, she found Consuelo sitting at the table crying.

"What's wrong?" she asked gently.

Consuelo dried her face on her apron. "Nothing," she choked. "It's okay."

"I heard someone, a man, shouting."

The older woman looked up at her with red, swollen eyes. She looked miserable. "Marco was furious because I wouldn't loan him some money. He thinks I was lying when I said I didn't have it, but I wasn't."

Glory laid a gentle hand on the other woman's shoulder. "He'll get over it. Families argue. Then they make up."

A watery smile was her reward for all that optimism. "You think he'll come back?"

"Of course," Glory assured her. She grinned. "How can he stay away from all this wonderful fruit?"

Consuelo burst out laughing. "Oh, you're good for me," she said. "What a lucky day I had when Señor Ramirez hired you!"

Glory smiled. "I like you, too. Now could we have coffee? Coffee and toast would be better, but especially coffee. I have to have my morning jolt of caffeine or I can't get both eyes to work at the same time, to say nothing of my brain."

"I was just about to make coffee," Consuelo said, jumping up. "I was waiting for the cinnamon rolls to bake."

Glory's eyes lit up. "Cinnamon rolls? Real ones? Homemade ones?"

Consuelo laughed. "Yes."

Glory slid into a chair. "What a lucky day for me, when Señor Ramirez hired you!" she said. "The closest I can come to cinnamon rolls is to buy frozen ones at the store and heat them up. You'll spoil me."

The older woman wiped her eyes and smiled. She got busy with the coffee.

LATER, IT OCCURRED TO Glory that there might have been a dark motive for Marco's need of immediate cash. She noticed that both he and Castillo spent a lot of their free time talking to each other. She wished she had some decent way to find out what they were saying. But what really bothered her was that Rodrigo was frequently involved in those conversations.

She wished she could call Marquez and talk to him confidentially about what she was learning, but she was wary of using any sort of communication around the house. Consuelo had said weeks ago that Rodrigo kept an arsenal of electronic devices in his room. He might have the ability to monitor conversations. It wouldn't do for him to get too curious about why a wage earner in his employ was having clandestine conversations with a San Antonio police detective.

MOST OF THE WORKERS spent their weekends at their own homes in a local trailer park. But on Saturday afternoon she and Consuelo were pressed into labor helping put up lanterns and streamers for a small fiesta on the farm. A mariachi band had been hired and the men had thrown together a large wooden platform for dancing.

It had been years since Glory had been to any sort of party. She got caught up in the excitement. She remembered how desperately she'd wanted to go to her junior and senior prom, but by then she was too shy and nervous around boys to feel comfortable with one. Which was just as well, because not one boy asked her out during the whole time she was in high school, thanks to the malicious Internet gossip about her.

In college, things had been a little bit different. She tried, she really tried, to make friends and be outgoing. But she learned on her first date that the world outside Jacobsville, Texas, was very different. Her date took her to have a meal in a nice restaurant, and then he tried to take her into a motel room. When persuasion and ridicule didn't work, he tried force. By then, she was living with the Pendletons. She fought her way out of the car, pulled out her cell phone and dialed Jason Pendleton's number. By the time she hung up, her erstwhile date had escaped in a spray of gravel. Shortly thereafter he transferred to another school. Jason never told Glory what he'd done to the boy. She never asked, either.

Rodrigo came out of the house just as it started getting dark. He was wearing black slacks with a white cotton shirt. He looked elegant and dangerously sensuous. Glory, in a simple white peasant dress full of handmade embroidery, had let her long blond hair down and even put on a tiny amount of makeup. She knew she'd never be able to compete with other women in any physical way, but she hoped she looked nice enough not to spoil the party.

Rodrigo came up to her at the refreshment table she and Consuelo and a couple of the workers' wives had helped fill. He smelled clean and spicy. Glory smiled at him with the excitement of the evening making her face radiant. He stared at her for a moment. She did look so much like Sarina with her hair down. She wasn't as pretty, but she had her own attractions just the same.

"We've invited all the workers," he told Glory. "A sort of thank-you for the hard work they've done this season. That goes double for the two of you, although your jobs are far from over."

"We like job security," Glory said for Consuelo, who nodded, grinning.

"Just as well," he chuckled. "We're picking more peaches next week."

There was a mutual groan.

"What was that about liking job security?" he teased.

Their answers were drowned out by the start up of the mariachi band. The deep, throbbing echo of the guitars and the trumpet drew everyone around to listen. It was an old Mexican folk song that they were playing, and as if on cue, everyone started singing it.

Rarely in her life had Glory felt so much a part of anything. She'd grown fond of the workers in the time she'd spent here. They were humble, happy, compassionate people, far more concerned with the welfare and happiness of their families than with material wealth. Jason did pay them well, she knew, but they weren't obsessed with their paychecks.

"It makes me feel good," she said when the song ended, "to see everyone so happy."

Rodrigo looked down at her. "Yes. It feels good."

She smiled shyly at him as the music began again. This time it was a slow dance. Couples began to gather on the wooden platform, close together against the faint chill of evening.

She was leaning on her cane, but she was hoping Rodrigo might ask her to dance. She could, even if only for a little while. She'd always loved to dance.

But his attention was caught by an SUV pulling up in the driveway. He went immediately to it. The driver's side door opened, and a pretty woman in a flowing white skirt and red blouse with long blond hair jumped out and hugged him. That embrace went through Glory like knives. It was that blonde woman again, the one who'd come to see Rodrigo soon after Glory's arrival here.

Rodrigo gestured toward the band, took the blonde's hand and tugged her, laughing, onto the dance floor.

Glory hated the resentment and jealousy she felt, watching them cling to each other among the gaily clad couples. She shouldn't be jealous of a man who managed her stepbrother's farms and ranches. He wasn't right for her. She refused to remember that he spoke several languages and was very intelligent. She was trying to ward off more heartache.

The blonde woman was laughing merrily as they danced. Rodrigo looked as if he'd landed in heaven. Then the maria-chis ended the slow dance and played a salsa rhythm. Rodrigo took the blonde by the waist, her hand in his, and he dem-onstrated that managing other men wasn't the only thing at which he excelled. Glory had never seen a man move like that on a dance floor. He was elegant. His steps were fluid, his movements exactly with the rhythm of the band. He inter-preted the music with a natural pulse of steps that the blonde followed effortlessly, as if they'd danced together many times before this. The other couples, entranced, backed away and stood clapping, laughing, as the duo danced to the music.

All too soon, it was over. They held each other, laughing breathlessly, as the workers crowded around them.

"What a long face," Consuelo murmured, pausing beside Glory. "What has made you so sad?"

Glory glanced involuntarily at Rodrigo and his guest. "Oh, it's that one."

"Yes." It was painful to see Rodrigo smiling, laughing. He was such a sad person around the farm. She felt sorry for him. But when she looked closely, it was apparent that it was Rodrigo who was enchanted, not the woman. She was only friendly. But what was she doing here, if she was happily married?

As if in answer to that question, the blonde suddenly looked at her watch, turned and almost ran back to the SUV, with Rodrigo close behind. They spoke for just a few minutes, then she hugged him once more, climbed back into the SUV and sped away.

Rodrigo stood there, hands in his pockets, staring after her.

"Poor man," Consuelo said sadly. "He tries to live in the past, for there is no room for him in her life now."

"She's pretty."

Consuelo's eyes popped. "And what are you, a clump of grass? There's nothing wrong with you, *niña*."

Glory's drawn face lightened a little as she met Consuelo's sympathetic gaze. She smiled. "Thanks."

She turned back to the table to get a cup of punch. The band, she thought, was really good. The music was dreamy to listen to, even if you didn't get asked to dance. The excitement she'd felt earlier was beginning to wear off. Suddenly all she wanted was to get away from everyone. She lifted her cup to her lips and sent a last, wistful glance at the wooden platform.

While she was watching the band, a lean, dark hand came over her shoulder, took the cup away and put it back on the table.

She turned, surprised. Rodrigo took the cane and propped it against the table. He wasn't smiling. His face was drawn and somber. He took one of her small hands into his big one. "Dance with me," he said in a deep, smooth tone.

Like a dreamer, she followed him slowly to the platform. He took her by the waist and lifted her onto it, and then into close, almost intimate contact with his lean, powerful body. One arm clasped her there, while his hand curled around hers and imprisoned it. She could feel his warm breath at her temple as he eased her into the sultry rhythm of the music.

Her heart ran away. She loved being held by him like this. It was as if the years dropped away and she was back in school again, excited by her first real date, hopeful of a sweet, caring relationship. She wouldn't think about the other blonde, the one he wanted, or the hunger in his eyes when the woman had left. She was only able to think about the contact with him, the strength in his body as he took her weight and lured her closer.

She felt his legs brushing against hers. The closeness made her tremble with new needs, new hungers. Her fingers dug into his back against the thin shirt. She felt the muscles respond to her helpless movement, felt his body tauten against her.

He lifted his head and looked down into her eyes, her face, and saw every raw emotion she was feeling. His hand spread on her back, coaxing her even closer. She shivered.

His dark eyes took on a strange fire. He bent, sliding his cheek against hers. "Yes, you like this," he whispered huskily. "You can't hide it, can you?"

She couldn't manage words. Her nails bit into him.

He pressed her hips slowly, sensually, into his and she shivered again. "I had forgotten how sweet this is," he whispered. "Your body clings to mine as if you were made for me. I can feel your breath against my throat, the caress of your hands at my back. If we were alone, *mi vida,* I would crush your mouth under mine and hold you so close that you would not be able to breathe unless I breathed with you."

No man had ever said such things to her, not in her whole life. She shivered again, helpless, unable to hide herself. Both her arms had gone around him under his arms, and her hands were digging into the hard muscles of his back. She felt as if every cell in her body was swollen and throbbing with passion. She ached for an end to the growing tension that made her almost sick with its intensity.

His own arms closed around her. His face buried itself in the soft, thick hair over her shoulder. "Relax," he teased softly. "You vibrate like a drum. I won't hurt you."

"I...I know that," she managed. Her voice didn't sound familiar at all.

"You think that limp makes you unattractive to men," he mused at her ear. "When it only makes you sexier. I like having you lean on me. Although I am sorry for the reason you limp."

She loved the smell of his body. She laid her cheek against

his broad, hair-roughened chest, there in the opening of his shirt. She wondered how it would feel against her bare body, and she almost gasped at the direction her thoughts were taking.

"And what forbidden dreams are producing that little whisper of dismay, eh?" he asked at her ear. He turned, pulling her even closer, and laughed softly. "Don't tighten up like that. Life is for living. It is a celebration, not a wake."

"I don't know much about celebrating," she managed in a breathless tone.

He lifted his head and looked down into her soft green eyes. "Perhaps it is time you learned," he whispered. As he spoke, his gaze fell to her pretty, soft mouth with its faint tint of pink. "And not only about celebrating," he added, as his head began to bend.

She hung there, trembling, aching, vulnerable, wanting nothing more than to feel that hard, sensual mouth crushing down on hers. Her eyes half closed. She'd been attracted to him from the very beginning. It seemed he might feel the same way. Her heart almost exploded with joy as she felt the first, brief, exquisite brush of his hard mouth over her soft one.

He moved slowly, barely tasting her, nibbling at her upper lip and then nipping it with his teeth. He laughed when she jerked away.

"So you don't like it when I bite?" he mused. "Okay. I'll do it your way." He bent again, nudging her into a secluded area where the shadows engulfed them. "Like this, then, *querida*..."

He kissed her very tenderly, hardly touching her with his mouth until her lips began to follow his. And then, breath by breath, he increased the pressure and the passion until she was moaning softly. Then he crushed his mouth down over hers, arched her into his tall, powerful body and kissed her so hard that it felt as if the world had dropped out from under her altogether. She clung to him, whimpering.

But the music was slowing. He released her abruptly, before they were noticed, or heard. He seemed preoccupied as he stared down at her swollen mouth, her flushed cheeks. His dark eyes narrowed. He held her by the waist and eased her away from him.

"What the hell am I doing?" he murmured roughly.

She knew then that it had been an impulse. Not eternal love, not even savage lust. It had just been an impulse, perhaps kindled by the presence of the woman he wanted and couldn't have. And now he looked both apologetic and uncomfortable with her. She had to find a way out for him, something that would hide her own headlong desire and spare her pride from the sting of his sudden rejection.

"Wow," she said, wide-eyed.

He blinked. "Excuse me?"

She grinned up at him. "Sorry, were you expecting a different reaction? Okay." She wiped off the smile and glared up at him, propping her hands on her hips. "How dare you treat me like a sex object!"

He was really looking odd, now.

Her eyebrows went up. "Not that approach, either? All

right. How's this?" She shook back her hair. "Honestly," she said haughtily, "you men are all alike!"

He wasn't usually so slow. The contact had gone a little to his head. She might not be a raving beauty, but she had a kissable mouth, and he liked the way she responded to him. "We are not all alike," he pointed out, eyes twinkling now.

"Yes, you are," she retorted. "Dressing in a sexy manner, wearing cologne that makes us weak-kneed, enticing us into intimate dances…"

"Guilty," he agreed, chuckling. "But I could accuse you of the same thing," he added.

She started to answer the charge, but before she could, one of the daughters of a worker, just out of high school, popped up and boldly asked Rodrigo to dance.

"Sorry," he told Glory. "But apparently, I am in demand."

"Yes, you are," the girl laughed, tugging at his hand. "Come on, Rodrigo!"

He spared a last wistful glance at Glory and let himself be led to the dance floor.

ALL TOO SOON, THE band packed up and left. The workers went back to their homes. Glory had left the party a little before everyone else. The dance had been wonderful, but her hip was killing her. She took her evening medicines and sat on her bed in her sleeveless long white cotton gown, praying for it to take effect soon. This was an old battle that she'd fought since her teens, this constant pain.

But she smiled, remembering Rodrigo's mouth on her

own, the exciting things he'd whispered in her ear. She remembered, too, that he'd been cold sober when they danced. There wasn't a trace of alcohol on his breath. Handsome, sexy Rodrigo who could have had almost any woman he wanted, and he'd chosen to dance with plain old Glory. It made her feel proud. She tried not to think that he might have been pretending with her, pretending that she was the lovely blonde woman from his past.

She was just setting her alarm clock when there was a faint tap at her bedroom door.

Puzzled, because it was very late, she walked gingerly across the carpeted floor and opened the door just a crack.

Rodrigo pushed it back, gently, and smiled at her. "You forgot to take something with you," he said.

"What?" she asked with breathless delight.

"Me."

He closed the door behind him, lifted her gently into his arms and bent to her mouth.

Kissing was addictive. She loved the tenderness he showed her, the exquisite caresses that didn't threaten, didn't frighten, but made her hungry for more.

There was more than a trace of alcohol on his breath, but she was too stunned by his sudden appearance in her bedroom to care. She was barely aware that she was suddenly lying across the bedspread with Rodrigo half beside, half over her yielded body. It felt right to lie in his arms and let him love her.

"You dress like someone's grandmother," he murmured against her mouth as his hand slid down her body.

She would have told him that no girl child wore provocative nightwear in foster care. It would have been asking for trouble. But his mouth was already over hers and seconds later, the gown was moving up as Rodrigo's hands found her soft breasts and smoothed over them.

He lifted his head to look. There was fire in his eyes now, and a faint ruddy color over his high cheekbones. "Pretty little breasts," he whispered. "Like firm apples with dusky stems..."

Before she had time to be embarrassed, his mouth had covered one of them and she was lifted completely off the bed in a shock of pleasure unlike anything she'd ever felt in her life.

Her soft cry shocked him as well. He met her wild, curious eyes while his lean hand tenderly caressed the hard crest. "You act as if this is something unknown to you," he said quietly.

She swallowed. "It is."

He didn't move. He didn't speak. His head moved a little sideways as he stared down at her, unblinking. "Glory, are you still a virgin?" he asked gently.

She bit her lower lip. It was almost a stigma of shame in the modern world, to admit to such a thing. She hesitated.

His thumb swept over her nipple in a rough caress that made her shiver. "You'd better tell me the truth," he said softly.

She drew in a long breath. She knew what would happen

when she admitted it. He'd be gone in a flash. These days, no man wanted inexperience.

"I never...I mean, I didn't feel...I haven't wanted..." she stammered, flushed.

But the expected revulsion wasn't there. He looked at her with something like reverence. The change softened his features, made his eyes darker.

"Not even this far, *mi vida?*" he whispered, indicating her bare breasts.

She grimaced and shook her head.

"Why?"

She couldn't go into her whole history. Not now. He didn't really want to know. He just wanted some explanation. "I'm not cut out for that sort of relationship," she said finally. "I...didn't want to end up like my mother. And for a long time, people seemed to think I would be like her when I grew up."

He drew his hand up to her face and traced her cheeks and her chin with a long forefinger. "Promiscuous, you mean?"

She nodded. "She slept with any man who would buy her things." It hurt to remember that, to remember her father's silent misery as his wife became the object of vicious gossip around town. His pride had suffered from it.

He smiled. "Letting a man make love to you doesn't qualify you as promiscuous," he told her. "It's a natural, beautiful thing between a man and a woman."

"My mother did it a lot."

"It's a new world from the one your grandparents grew up in."

Her eyes were solemn as she stared up at him. "Would you like a woman who went to bed with any man who asked?" she asked quietly.

He drew in an audible breath. "No," he said after a minute. "I grew up in a religious family."

"So did I," she replied. "At least, my father was religious."

He was smiling. "So you don't want to make babies until you marry."

Her whole body tingled at the way he said it. And it was visible, that reaction.

He chuckled, moving down to rest his weight on an elbow while he flicked open the rest of the buttons on his shirt and pushed it aside. "We won't go that far," he whispered. "At least, not now."

He bent to her mouth, and as he approached it, he eased down so that his bare, hair-roughened chest drew sensuously against her bare breasts. As he'd expected, it was as powerful as seduction itself. She shivered, and then moaned, and then clasped him so close that when he kissed her, it felt as though they were fused together.

He hadn't meant to let it get out of hand, but that first touch of flesh against flesh robbed him of his objectivity. It had been too long since he'd had a woman. Seeing Sarina tonight, reliving the loss of her, had made him so hungry that he'd been out of his mind. He'd been on fire when he and Sarina shared the dance floor. But even then, the earlier love play with Glory had aroused him. He couldn't stop thinking about Glory's body in his arms.

He'd had two or three beers, hoping they might calm him down and send the unwanted desire away. They hadn't. In the end, he'd come to her because he couldn't help himself. On the dance floor, he'd been sure that she wanted him. And she had. He hadn't realized that she would be so innocent. He did want to respect that innocence. It was just that it had been so long. Ages. And tonight, to his shame, he was too hungry to care about anything beyond his own fulfillment.

One long leg pushed her legs apart so that he could lever himself down against her in an intimate position. He moved slowly, feeling the power of his arousal, feeling her helpless reaction to it.

"Glory?" he whispered huskily.

"Yes?"

"Are you sure you're a virgin?"

She was in over her head. She didn't want him to stop. If this was all she could ever have in her life, it would be enough. "It doesn't matter," she whispered back into his mouth. "I want you."

"Not as much as I want you, *querida,*" he ground out.

He caught her upper thigh in his hand and dragged her hips up against his arousal, feeling the pleasure leap between them until it was like a drug in his veins. He moved against her blindly, his mouth devouring her lips.

"It isn't enough," he said harshly.

"I know."

His hand went under her, to the elastic of her briefs and began to pull it down. "I'll be good to you," he whispered.

"I'll make you so hungry that you won't feel the pain, or even remember it. I'll take you to heaven in my arms."

She couldn't answer. The air was cool against her hot skin. She felt him touching her where no one else ever had. He looked down into her eyes while he stroked her, watching her helpless reaction to the rhythmic and intimate contact that stopped her breath in her throat.

"Yes, that's it," he whispered as he increased the rhythm. "I'm going to make you explode into a thousand silky pieces, and I'm going to watch it happen to you. Then, when you're so hot that you're blind with it, I'm going to go right up inside you and give you the sweetest pleasure you've ever dreamed of having...."

She cried out as the rhythm started lifting her, lifting her, lifting her...!

Her legs opened for him eagerly. Her head was thrown back so that she could see nothing at all except the ceiling overhead. She heard the rhythmic, frantic sound of the springs in the bed moving. And then she felt his body there, hot against her, probing, pushing, penetrating as the pleasure rose so high and so hot that she cried out in a long, helpless, sobbing keen, her body lifting to his harsh, almost violent downward thrusts.

Her nails dug into him. Her voice broke.

"Look at me," he managed. "Look!"

Her eyes opened, wide and so dilated that they were almost sightless. Above her, his face was a rigid mask, choked with color, his eyes blazing as he drove for fulfillment.

"Now," he breathed. His eyes closed. "Now!"

She shuddered and shuddered as the pleasure took them both, joined them in a hot fusion that was so overwhelming that she thought she might die of it.

Her high-pitched cry was smothered by his mouth. Muffled, it reflected the frantic motion of her hips as she drained every wisp of physical delight from his body.

SHE LAY ON HER BACK, nude, satiated, throbbing with the aftereffects of passion. Her body was still moving helplessly, savoring the tiny stabs of pleasure that came with motion.

Beside her, he lay apart and unnaturally quiet.

"You bled."

She swallowed hard. He sounded very distant. "Did I?"

As passion, sated, faded away, reality came and hit him squarely between the eyes. He'd just seduced a worker in his employ, and she was a virgin to boot. His need of her had been so urgent that he hadn't been able to stop. Now he was stone-cold sober and eaten alive with guilt. They came from different worlds. She was a wage earner and he came from Spanish and Danish aristocracy. He was a decade her senior. She was uneducated and he had a degree. Worse, he was very wealthy and she could hardly afford decent clothing. And he'd taken advantage of her. He didn't feel very proud of himself.

"You said that it didn't matter, that you were innocent," he said coldly.

His voice chilled her. She'd been expecting happy ever after, and he was satisfied and wanted to make sure that she didn't accuse him of seduction. Her first time, and it had to be with a man who only wanted relief.

She was adult enough to cope. If nothing else, he'd helped get her past the nightmarish assault of her early teens. He didn't know about that. He wouldn't have understood her fear of men, a fear which had been wiped away tonight the minute he touched her under her gown. It had been a revelation.

"Well," she said heavily, "if you're planning to sue me for seduction, I have to tell you that I'll swear in court that you threw yourself at me and I couldn't help myself."

6

RODRIGO SAT UP AND STARED down at her in the darkness as if she'd lost her mind. "You what?"

"I'll countersue you," she promised, pulling the cover over her body. "All those sweet nothings you whispered in my ear, the way you flaunted your chest at me…I mean, what woman could resist a man who did everything but strip and beg to be taken to bed?"

A chuckle he couldn't choke back escaped him. "Good God." He got up and started dressing.

"That's right, blame God, too," she scoffed. "It was your own fault, and I'm not apologizing."

"I wouldn't expect you to," he assured her.

"Furthermore, I'm not marrying you. And if you get pregnant, I'll get a DNA test to prove it's not mine."

By now, he was bent over double laughing. He'd expected tears, reproaches, accusations, anything but this.

He moved to the bed, fully dressed, and sat down beside her, one arm going past her shoulder to support him as he looked down into her eyes in the dimly lit room. "But I will apologize," he said softly. "Because I meant only to kiss you. It went too far, because I had abstained for a very long time."

"Because you couldn't have her," she said wisely.

His indrawn breath was sharp.

She'd already guessed, but his reaction to the charge clinched it. He was dying for the woman he'd lost. Glory looked a little like her and, in the dark, it must have been easy for him to pretend.

"I was only standing in for her, wasn't I?" she asked sadly.

His hand moved under her head and clenched suddenly in her hair. "No," he said hotly. "I did not pretend you were her. Never could I be so heartless!"

She relaxed a little.

"I wanted you very badly," he confessed. "You have a quality of compassion that I have rarely encountered in a woman, and your body is exquisite. I enjoyed it. I hope that you enjoyed me as much. But it should not have happened."

"Why?" she asked, subdued but curious.

"We come from different worlds," he replied. "This is only an interlude, for both of us. We could hurt each other badly if we let this continue."

"I guess so," she replied.

"There is another matter. Do you use birth control?"

Her heart jumped. "No. I never had any reason to."

"And I was too far gone to consider it."

She lay very still. It was getting complicated. "I don't want a child. Certainly not one who came as an accident." It was a lie, but she had to salvage what was left of her pride. He made it clear that he wanted nothing more than her body. Actually she would have loved a child, but her health might make that impossible. Besides, Rodrigo was not going to consider marriage. She knew that already.

"Then you would go to a clinic?" he asked, and there was something chilling in his tone.

Now she faced her own system of values, and she was shocked to discover that what had seemed sensible a minute ago had suddenly become an action she could not imagine herself performing. Not even to save her own life.

"I…" She hesitated, frowning. "I…don't think I could," she said.

The hand holding her hair relaxed and was withdrawn. "How likely is it?"

"Not very," she lied.

His mind was considering possibilities. If he had a wife, and a child, perhaps he could get Sarina out of his mind and the torment would ease. It had almost destroyed him, losing her and Bernadette.

"I'll be thirty-six this year," he said quietly. "I have nothing to show for my life, other than a few small accomplishments." He didn't dare tell her what they were. "I hadn't thought about having a family until recently. But the idea has appeal." He looked at her with real longing. "I think I would enjoy being a father."

"I don't want children," she said bluntly, hating the words even as she spoke them, because she could see his pride stinging from them.

Her tone was offensive, and it antagonized him. "I said that I wanted them," he returned coldly. "Not that I wanted them with you!"

She felt her cheeks go hot. "Sorry. I assumed..."

"Wrongly." He got up from the bed and moved away. "So we agree that this was an unfortunate accident, which we will never permit to happen again."

"Of course," she assured him.

He paused at the door. "Why would you not want children?"

Because of my health, she should have told him. Her life would be at risk from a pregnancy. Her career, too, was a sticking point—how could she raise a child and do justice to either her job or her child? But he didn't know about her career. Or her health—except for the limp. She took the coward's way out. "I have...health problems, as you may have noticed already," she reminded him quietly. "Besides, I'm still relatively young to be thinking about family life."

The pain and guilt her remarks kindled in him were shockingly brutal. He could have cursed aloud. He'd forgotten about her hip. He'd forgotten everything in the joy of having her.

"Forgive me," he said quietly. "I did not think."

She closed her eyes. "Nor did I."

"For what it's worth," he said, his accent noticeably thicker, "I am sorry."

"Not nearly as sorry as I am," she replied matter-of-factly, and with a bite in her tone.

The tension in the room was as thick as cigar smoke. He opened the door with deliberate movements and closed it behind him with a violent snap.

Glory let out the breath she'd been holding. It had been the most traumatic experience of her recent life, and not at all unpleasant. But she was in disguise. He didn't know the real Glory, and she had doubts that he'd want her at all once he did. Once he knew who she really was, the barrier between them would grow by leaps and bounds. He was a laborer. She was an educated professional. Their cultures were different, their religions were different. They were worlds apart. She couldn't give up her career that she'd worked so hard for just to eek out an existence with a poor immigrant. She wasn't even sure that he wasn't involved in some criminal pursuit. The whole situation was impossible.

She'd let her guard down and actively participated in her own seduction. Now here she was, alone and in danger and possibly pregnant. What in the world would she do if she'd conceived? He wanted a child. She didn't; not this way, with secrets separating them. He was angry that she didn't want his child. She couldn't tell him the real reason. She was living a lie, to save her life. She couldn't tell him that, either.

The tears rolled down Glory's cheek in a flood. He'd left,

she thought miserably, just in time. She wouldn't have wanted to disgrace herself by crying in front of him. She couldn't understand her own easy submission to him. Surely her past should have kept her out of reach of such an experienced man, kept her from giving in to someone who was almost a stranger. Her life was becoming far too complicated. She wished she'd never let Marquez talk her into this masquerade.

MONDAY, AFTER A QUIET and lonely Sunday during which Rodrigo wasn't even seen, she rode into town with Consuelo to get groceries. As they got out of the farm's pickup truck, Marquez, in civilian clothes, drove up in another truck and pulled in beside them. He got out, pocketing his keys and starting toward the store when he saw Glory. He pretended surprise—a good act, because he'd followed them here hoping to get a word alone with her.

"Well, if it isn't Gloryanne! How are you?" he called to Glory with a grin. "Fancy seeing you here! It's been years, hasn't it?"

Glory flushed, but hid her face from Consuelo. "Yes, it has," she agreed. "I haven't seen you since we were in high school together!" She composed herself and glanced at Consuelo. "I'll be along in a minute," she said with a smile. "I just want to catch up on Rick's life story."

"Go right ahead," Consuelo replied. She was giving Marquez an odd look. Before Glory could puzzle it out, the older woman was heading for the store.

The smile was gone immediately from both faces. Marquez, in boots and jeans and a checked blue shirt, moved closer to her. He was very solemn.

"Fuentes has someone checking you out," he said abruptly. "I don't know who, or where. You haven't mentioned anything about San Antonio down here to anyone?"

"Of course not," she faltered. Her green eyes met his dark ones. "He couldn't know I was here," she added. "The only person I've talked to at all is Rodrigo, and I'm sure he's not mixed up in anything illegal."

Marquez clenched his teeth. "I wish I could be," he said flatly. "Nobody's talking, but the police chief, Grier, let slip that Ramirez had ties to Mexico. He also had a cousin who worked for Manuel Lopez, the late great drug lord."

She fought to keep her expression from giving her away. "What else did he tell you?"

"He didn't tell me anything, Glory. I overheard him talking to one of the sheriff's men at the courthouse."

She nibbled her lower lip. "Oh, boy."

"I caught up with him later. We didn't plan it, but I suppose you know that Grier knows why you're here," he said quietly.

"Yes, he does," she replied. "But he said he'd keep an eye out for me."

"He also said he asked you to keep an eye out for visitors at the farm."

She nodded. "I can't find a safe way to contact him, though. I'm not sure if Rodrigo has listening devices in the house."

She hated having to say that, to sound as if she already suspected that Rodrigo was on the wrong side of the law. She had to try to remember that she took a vow to uphold the law, no matter how much it hurt. "Consuelo said he had all sorts of electronic devices in his room." She moved closer. "We've had two very suspicious new hires. One is a man named Castillo, who has a nasty attitude toward women. The other is Consuelo's son, Marco. He wears the tats and colors of the Serpientes gang."

"Damn!" he muttered. "I thought we'd managed to keep those devils out of our community here."

"They have links everywhere," she reminded him. "In prisons, in cities all over the world. It's a network, just like a corporation."

He leaned back against the passenger side of his truck and folded his arms over his broad chest. "This seemed like a good idea at the outset. Now I'm not too sure anymore. I didn't persuade you down here to get you killed. What if Marco brings someone with him who recognizes you? As I recall, you prosecuted two San Antonio members of that Houston gang for carjacking."

"And convicted them," she returned. She blew out a breath. "I never expected any of the gang to surface down here in Jacobsville. Well, this might be a good time for me to start packing heat."

"No."

"I can shoot," she muttered. "I used to take a .40 caliber Glock onto the police firing range and practice with it."

"Yes," he replied, eyes narrowed. "I remember. We got the windshield in the squad car replaced," he added meaningfully.

She flushed. "That was not my fault! A bird flew past and distracted me just as I started to shoot!"

"Really? What distracted you when you blew the taillight out on the sheriff's department's newest car?"

She pushed back a stray wisp of blond hair. "Listen, that deputy should never have parked his stupid car that close to the firing range in the first place!"

He wasn't buying it. "I've never seen so many cops kissing the ground in my life. All they had to do was hear your name and they started putting on Kevlar."

She laughed in spite of herself. "Okay, Okay. I'm a lethal weapon with a firearm. I admit it. But what am I going to do?"

"We need to put somebody on the farm who can protect you," he said, thinking. "I understand that there's a federal agent undercover somewhere between here and Houston, but nobody will tell me where he is or what he's posing as. If we could get word to him, he might be able to keep an eye on you."

"Long shot," she returned.

He grimaced. "Well, there's always Jon Blackhawk," he began. "He owes me a favor, and he's a fed."

"I am not working with Jon Blackhawk," she said flatly. "I don't care how sorry he is about charging his assistant with sexual harrassment."

"Maybe we can lure Marco back to the big city with the offer of a really lucrative drug run," he said then. "At least we'd have one gang member out of the picture."

"That isn't such a bad idea. Marco needs money," she said, recalling the scene in the kitchen. "He had his mother in tears, demanding money that she didn't have."

"He may be using the stuff as well as selling it," he replied. "A lot of dealers can't resist the temptation."

"It might explain the violent mood swings I'm seeing in him," she agreed.

"I know a couple of narcs in the city," he replied. "I might get word to them and see if they can flush out any information about Marco or Castillo."

"I just hope Marco isn't going to land himself in prison. Poor Consuelo!"

"She seems like a nice sort of person," Marquez replied. "Shame she has such losers for a husband and a son."

"You know about her husband?"

"I arrested him once," he said, his lips making a flat line. "She's probably going to remember that, so if she says anything to you about me, we went steady in high school. Okay?"

Her eyebrows lifted. "We did? I must have a bad case of amnesia. You'd think I'd remember something like that!"

He glowered at her. "You'd have been lucky. I was a catch in high school," he told her. "Girls couldn't keep their hands off me."

"That's not what your mother, Barbara, says," she replied smugly.

"What does my mother say?" he asked warily.

"She says you hid behind potted plants any time a girl started walking toward you."

"That was in grammar school!" he protested.

She laughed. "Really?"

He shifted his weight. "Maybe I was a little shy. But I never hid behind a potted plant."

"Is that so?"

"I might have fallen *into* a potted plant, once," he relented. "When the cheerleader captain asked me to vote for her in the class president race. She was a dish."

She couldn't stop laughing.

"It's not funny."

"Yes, it is."

He moved away from the truck. "I hate losing arguments to lawyers," he muttered. "I'm going back to work."

"What are you doing down here on a Monday?"

"I almost forgot," he chuckled. "Your boss sent you a love letter." He handed her an envelope.

"This isn't my boss's handwriting," she pointed out. "And my name is misspelled!"

"We have a mole. He doesn't like the new regime, or the new drug lord. He sent that to you via your boss. But he's only giving us information on Fuentes. That—" he indicated the envelope "—is the closest he's going to come to revealing himself as a witness. We have no idea who he is."

"Have you read this?" she asked. It was sealed, but barely.

"No. And I resent having you insinuate that I try to read

other people's mail." He stuck his hands into his jeans pockets. "Anyway, we couldn't get the steam to work ungluing it."

She laughed. "Some detective you are!"

"I'm a very good one, thanks. Read that and tell me what's in it. Then you'd better let me have it back. Even with your name misspelled, we don't want anybody locally making connections."

She slid her thumb under the seal and pulled out a small piece of lined paper that looked as if it could have come from a steno pad. "It's an address," she said, looking up at him. "And a date and time. That's all." She read it to him.

"A drop," he said at once. "A drug drop."

She handed him the note. "You could have opened it."

He shrugged as he pocketed the note. "I wanted to see how you were."

She smiled up at him. "That was nice."

"I hope I haven't just blown your cover," he said uneasily. "You were seen getting into the ranch truck and heading toward town, so I tailed you. I didn't realize Consuelo was with you until you both got out of the truck."

"Maybe she didn't recognize you," she said comfortingly.

"Let's hope so." He studied her closely, seeing the dark circles under her eyes. "Ramirez giving you a hard time?"

Her heart jumped. "No. Why do you ask?"

"Some of his friends say he's been hell to get along with since he took that job."

"He's nice to me," she lied.

"Most people are nice to you," he chided. "You're sweet."

"Tell me that the next time you see me in court with Fuentes on the spit."

"I can't wait," he chuckled.

"Me, either. If you need to get in touch with me, you can tell Chief Grier to drop by any Wednesday. Rodrigo's usually not around then."

Marquez straightened. There was something disturbing in his expression.

"What? Did I say something wrong?" she asked.

He wiped off the expression. "Nothing at all. I just had a thought. You watch your back," he added. "If you need me, call me, any time. I'm down here with mother most weekends, unless I'm on call."

"I'll remember. Thanks, Rick."

"What are friends for?" he chuckled.

CONSUELO GAVE HER A very odd look when she caught up with the older woman in the grocery store.

"You know that guy from school?" she asked.

"Yes. He was in my class," Glory said. "We went steady." She looked demure.

Consuelo turned her attention to a rack of pickling spices. "He's a cop."

"Yes, I know. He works up in San Antonio."

"He put my husband in jail," she muttered.

"Oh!"

Consuelo fell for the shocked expression. Her cold eyes

softened. "You couldn't understand how it was for me, with Marco having trouble in school and then my husband going to prison. I couldn't even afford rent. I had to do some things, to be able to buy food..." She turned away. "It was a long time ago," she said suddenly. "Don't mind me."

"I'd do anything for you that I could," Glory told the other woman. "Really."

Consuelo turned back to her. "I know you would," she said in a soft tone. "You're not still sweet on Marquez?"

Glory hesitated. "Well, not really. I haven't seen him in a long time."

"Good. That's good. Can you find me some garbage bags?"

"Sure thing."

She hobbled away on her cane. It had been a close call. Her life was starting to be a lot more complicated. Not the least of her worries was the way she and Rodrigo had parted.

EVEN THOUGH CONSUELO SEEMED to have fallen for her story about going steady with Rick, Glory was aware that the older woman was more curious about her now. She asked throwaway questions about how long she and Rick went steady and if she knew any of his fellow officers in San Antonio.

Glory had to be careful and not let it slip that she'd worked in the city. It was hard, downplaying her intelligence and not giving her education away.

Rodrigo was polite to her now, but very cool. He seemed not to be interested in her after their passionate interlude.

In fact, he was paying a lot of attention to the younger woman who'd flirted with him at the fiesta.

Glory's confidence in herself had been healthy until Fuentes's death threat had landed her at the truck farm. But divided from her profession, she found that she had no real identity as just an ordinary woman. She had no skills to speak of except that she could process fruit and make preserves. She could cook, after a fashion, but not like Consuelo could. Her homemaking skills were poor due to her impaired movement, because working with a mop or broom or even a vacuum cleaner was painful, and the aftereffects could last for days. Her blood pressure was more or less under control, but she had episodes of dizziness and headaches when she forgot her medicine. She felt almost useless around the house.

When Rodrigo started bringing his one-girl fan club, Teresa, into the house with him for the occasional meal, the way he flirted with her made Glory ill at ease. She knew that it was deliberate, because he noticed and enjoyed Glory's discomfort.

Now that she knew Fuentes was looking for her, she was under even more pressure. Her interlude with Rodrigo had caused her shame. She hadn't realized how conventional she was until she'd allowed herself to be seduced. She felt she was following in her mother's footsteps, and it bothered her. Of course, her mother had only been available to men who had money. Glory wasn't mercenary. She'd planned her life to be a solitary one. She'd fallen off the straight and narrow, and she was worrying about the consequences. Her periods were very regular. But she was now a week overdue.

It could have been stress. She hoped that it was. Her mother had been very young when she bowed to community pressure after she'd become pregnant by Glory's father. She'd married him, but she'd made him and Glory both pay. It was almost ironic that her mother's parents had died in a plane crash just a few weeks after they'd forced Glory's father and mother into marriage with their hopes to avoid a scandal.

She touched her flat belly worriedly. She'd never considered having a child. She wasn't sure her health would permit it, in the first place. In the second, she had little to do with children, and she wasn't sure that she'd be a proper mother. Her real fear was of her genetics. What if she turned out to be like her own mother, hateful and resentful and abusive to a child? The thought tormented her. It was why she'd never considered marriage and a family in the first place. She couldn't be sure. She was scarred in more ways than the purely physical. Her self-esteem was almost nonexistent.

And if she was pregnant, what would she do about it? She'd have to see her doctor before she could make any decision. If Rodrigo found out, what would he do? He was missing his former girlfriend and her child. He wanted a child of his own, a replacement for what he'd lost. But that wasn't love. It was grief, and once he had the child he might bitterly regret it. For instance, what if his girlfriend decided to divorce her husband and go after Rodrigo? Glory wouldn't stand a chance, considering the love Rodrigo betrayed when he was with the pretty blonde woman. He'd leave skid marks exiting Glory's life, if he could have the woman he really wanted and the child he adored.

She became depressed as the days passed and Rodrigo continued to ignore her. Then, one day, several things happened at once to make her position hazardous in the extreme.

First, Cash Grier showed up at her door looking somber one Wednesday morning. He asked to speak to her alone.

She followed him onto the front porch, apprehensive about the way he looked.

"What's up?" she asked quietly, wary of eavesdroppers.

He motioned her down the steps to his squad car, going slowly so that she could keep up with her cane. Then he stood so that she was facing him, so that anyone watching couldn't see their lips move.

"A trained sniper can read lips," he told her quietly. "Just in case anyone's looking, they won't be able to understand what we're saying. Marquez got in touch with his friend on the narcotics squad, who worked on a couple of his confidential informants," he said. "Fuentes has sent a killer after you."

To her credit, Glory didn't pass out. "What sort of killer?" she asked calmly.

"A professional."

She knew what that meant. She'd seen plenty of hits in the course of her work. Drug lords knew where to get the best people for that sort of job, and they didn't miss. A professional would be more than a match for most local law enforcement. On the other hand, she considered as she studied Cash Grier's stony expression, she was probably in the best small town on earth for a hit man to try to kill her. Grier here had been a government sniper. Eb Scott and Cy Parks, not to mention Micah Steele, were professional mercenaries, now retired. But Eb ran a school for counterterrorism that was known all over the country, and some of the men taking courses there would be a match for any hired assassin Fuentes cared to sacrifice.

She cocked her head and looked up at Grier. She smiled. "Finally," she murmured. "Some good news."

He stared at her without blinking. "Good news?"

"This is the worst town in America for contract killers. The only hit man who ever got into town was crippled by your wife, I hear," she said with twinkling eyes.

He laughed. "With an iron skillet," he agreed. He sighed. "Well, you've got grit. I expected at least a worried expression."

She shrugged. "We've sort of cornered the market on dangerous men in this town," she reminded him. "Look what happened to Lopez, even though he didn't buy the farm here."

"And to his replacement, Cara Dominguez," he reminded her. "None of these smugglers believe the hype about our resident mercs," he chuckled. "Their misfortune. Okay. You're not rattled. That's good. But we're taking some steps to keep you alive until you testify."

"Kevlar?" she suggested.

He studied her for a long moment, his eyes narrow as he seemed to mentally weigh the factors.

"I know some things that you don't about Jacobsville," he replied. "You're going to be safer than you'll realize. Just help us out by not going anywhere alone, especially at night."

"Don't tell me," she chuckled. "You've got snipers stationed in the pecan trees."

He laughed. "Nothing quite so visible. Just trust me."

She nodded. His reputation in police work was formidable. If he said she was safe, she was. But she wondered how it was being handled.

"You won't tell me anything even if I ask, will you?" she returned.

He grinned. "Not a word. Keeping secrets is my stock in trade."

She sighed. "Okay, then. I'll stay inside and away from the windows."

"That should do the trick until we can get enough on the hired gun to lock him up."

"You wouldn't like to tell me who he is?" she fished.

"No, I wouldn't. Not even if I knew. You're safer that way. I'll be in touch."

"Okay. Thanks."

"You're welcome."

He drove away and she ground her teeth together. One more thing, she thought, to drive me nuts. They should have left her in San Antonio and set her up in a controlled area and offered to let the hit man do his worst. Instead she was stuck here in small town America with a killer in close proximity and they said she was safe.

She threw up her hands and went back to work. She didn't share the tidbit of information with Consuelo, or Rodrigo. Neither of them had any idea what a mess her life was in. She wanted it to stay that way.

7

GLORY HATED FEELING helpless. If she was a good shot, and she had a pistol, she might have been able to defend herself. But she couldn't shoot. She wasn't whole physically, and she'd never had anyone do more than threaten to kill her. Death threats were a part of the job for most people in law enforcement and the court system. She knew judges who carried pistols to the bench under their robes and she knew some who'd survived attacks. She'd always known that if she became a prosecuting attorney, there would be the occasional threat. But this one was deadly. Fuentes didn't want to spend his life in prison. He was going to make sure that Glory didn't testify.

Cash said she was safer than she realized. She wondered if he had someone working on the farm, keeping an eye on her.

It would have helped her mental attitude a little. But a covert scan of all the workers didn't produce anyone suspicious.

She felt Rodrigo watching her as she and Consuelo sat down with him at the table to eat supper. He was astute for a man who ran a truck farm. Pity, she thought, that he was so good at management, and he'd never continued his education. She'd never asked what was the last grade of school he'd completed. Perhaps, she told herself, she didn't really want to know.

Then it hit her. What if Rodrigo was not only mixed up in the drug trade—what if he was the assassin? Her fork fell out of her fingers and hit the plate with a loud noise.

"What is it?" Rodrigo asked, frowning.

She was staring at him in utter horror. No, she told herself. No, it couldn't be! But what did she know about him, really? Only what he volunteered. He was personable, a good dancer, a hard worker and he spoke several languages. But so did a lot of criminals. He was gone every Wednesday, along with Castillo. When she'd told Cash that, his expression had closed up like a trap. Cash had said that Fuentes had sent the hit man after her, but that didn't mean the killer hadn't already been put in place for the mission. For all she knew, Fuentes might have had her tailed and tracked here to Jacobsville weeks ago. Here, where Rodrigo was close and could kill her if he was ordered to. Her heart sank deeper in her chest.

"Are you all right?" Rodrigo repeated, his accent slightly thicker as he stared at her.

"I'm getting clumsy," Glory excused her slip, picking up the fork again and smiling sheepishly. "It's peeling all those peaches. My fingers are rebelling."

Consuelo laughed. "I know how you feel! We will both be stronger than weight lifters soon, with all this exercise."

"The peach crop is almost through," Rodrigo advised them. "Only a few more days and we'll be done."

"Thank goodness!" Glory exclaimed.

He gave her a long look. "Of course, by then the first apples will be ready for picking…"

Both women groaned aloud. He only laughed.

SHE WAS WORKING IN the kitchen when Rodrigo walked in with Consuelo's son, Marco. Consuelo was hesitant, but the boy grinned and picked up his mother and whirled her around.

"I'm sorry I was short with you last time," he told the woman. "I was just having some problems, but they're all solved now. Rodrigo said I could come back, if you don't mind."

Consuelo hugged him back, tearfully. "Of course you can come back!"

He kissed her. "You're too good to me."

"Yes, I am," Consuelo replied, but she laughed.

Rodrigo was staring at Glory. He wanted to ask what was making her study him that way, but it was early morning and he had to get things organized in the fields. Sooner or later, he told himself, they were going to have to try to talk to each other. If he'd made her pregnant, he had to know. Then, choices would have to be discussed. He hoped it wasn't true. Glory had made it obvious that she didn't want a child. Or perhaps she did, but she didn't want one with a common laborer who made a living with his hands. He felt cold all over. He couldn't tell her the truth about himself. When he did, it would place even more barriers between them. He didn't want a glorified housekeeper as a wife, any more than she wanted a foreign farm worker as a husband. It was demeaning, just the same, to think she didn't want his child. She'd told him that she had health problems, and he knew her hip gave her trouble, but that was no reason for being unable to carry a child. The fact was that she didn't want the child of a common farm worker. She wouldn't admit it, but he knew just the same. It wounded his pride.

ACTUALLY GLORY WAS having more health problems by the day. But she hid it well. Fortunately she had nausea at night, rather than in the morning. She had a pretty good idea about what was causing her sudden illness, and it tormented her. She couldn't possibly have the child. She was living a lie. Rodrigo wasn't even in her own social class, and he might be a criminal. He might be the killer Fuentes had hired to put Glory out of his way. She remembered a comment her doctor had made some time ago, about her high blood pressure. Some women, he said, were fortunate enough to have their blood pressure go down when they were pregnant. But Glory's put her at high risk for a pregnancy. He said that her career was risk enough, without the addition of pregnancy. She'd assured him that she never wanted a child.

But now that had changed. She was fascinated with the reality of a child growing inside her. She'd been alone most of her life. The Pendletons were kind to her, but they weren't her family. The child would be of her own blood.

That was the most worrying thought of all. Her mother had been mentally ill, she was certain of it. Some behavioral abnormalities could be passed down from parent to child. What if the baby wasn't normal?

"What is making you so worried?" Consuelo asked one morning when Glory arrived in the kitchen with dark circles under her eyes from lack of sleep.

"Worried?" Glory thought fast. "Well, it's not exactly worry…" She poured herself some coffee and refused food. "Rodrigo hardly speaks to me lately."

"Ah." Consuelo smiled. "So that's it."

"He seemed to like me at first," Glory replied. "But lately he avoids me."

"Yes, he does." She paused. "And you are in love with him."

Glory couldn't help the sudden radiance in her face, the brilliance in her eyes behind the rounded frames of her glasses.

"I thought so," Consuelo murmured. "I could see it when you danced with him, at the fiesta. He likes you very much, but he thinks he is still in love with the pretty blonde woman. He is conflicted."

That brought Glory back down to earth. "I look a little like her, don't I?" she asked, sticking the knife in her own heart.

Consuelo grimaced.

Glory nodded. "That's what I thought, too. I remind him of her, but I'm not married to someone else."

"That may be true." She studied Glory curiously. "But on the other hand, perhaps he is beginning to feel something for you and he doesn't like it."

Glory sighed. "I guess that could be true, as well," she agreed.

CASTILLO WAS LEANING against the back door later when Glory had to go out to the warehouse for more peaches. She was wearing a pretty white sundress embroidered with yellow sunflowers. It had puffy sleeves and a full skirt. Her hair was in its usual braid. She looked young and fresh. It had been extremely hot in the kitchen and the air-conditioning unit wasn't coping well with the blazing heat. She rarely ever wore very feminine clothes. Consuelo had loaned her the dress. Thick jeans were just too hot in that kitchen.

"You know, you're not bad looking," he remarked with open lust in his small, close-spaced eyes. "I could go for you."

Glory wasn't afraid of him. Not when she knew Rodrigo was nearby, at least. She turned and looked at him without blinking. "I'm not in the market for a boyfriend, Mr. Castillo," she said flatly.

"Honey, every woman wants a man," he drawled, moving deliberately closer to her. "Even if she doesn't know it."

She backed up a step.

He only laughed. "That's it. I like a woman who pretends

she isn't interested. Go ahead and fight me, *niña*. It makes it more exciting."

He reached out and caught the front of her sundress with his forefinger, tugging it down so that the swell of her breasts was visible. She felt sick all over.

Before she could react and slap his hand away, she saw Castillo's expression suddenly change just before he went flying backward onto the ground.

Rodrigo stepped past Glory, his furious eyes on the downed man. He cursed him in Spanish and challenged him to get up and fight like a man. For a man who seemed to be calm and laid-back most of the time, Rodrigo looked amazingly dangerous now. Even Glory took a step backward when she saw his tall body tense.

Castillo fingered his bruised jaw. He was trying to hide it, but he was afraid of the taller man. Ramirez had moved like lightning. Castillo hadn't even seen the attack coming, and he was used to fights. He flushed as he dragged himself to his feet. *"Lo siento,"* he told Rodrigo. "I didn't know she was yours."

"You know now," Rodrigo bit off. His voice was very soft, but the tone was chilling. "Leave her alone."

"Sure. Sure!"

Castillo moved away without another glance at Glory.

She was trying to catch her breath and not succeeding very well. She looked up at Rodrigo curiously. His eyes were still filling with anger. His fists were clenched at his side as he turned to her.

"Thank you," she began.

"If you don't want unwelcome company, dress like a working woman, not like a debutante strolling in a rose garden," he said bluntly. His tone was crisp. Furious.

She gaped at him. "I'm wearing a sundress! It isn't even suggestive...!"

"You wear blouses and slacks or jeans on the job here," he interrupted. "I have better things to do with my days than protecting you from other men!"

"Buster, if I had a blunt object right now, you'd need protecting from me!" she shot back at him. "It's hot in the kitchen and the air-conditioning isn't working today! We called the repairman, but he hasn't come yet. So Consuelo loaned me one of her dresses, because I don't have any! Anyway, I'm not wearing baggy pants and an overcoat in my kitchen just because your men can't control their own lustful urges!"

He stepped in closer, so that she could feel the heat and power of his body next to hers. "You are getting even because I avoid you," he accused.

Her eyebrows arched. "You're avoiding me? Really? I'm sorry. I didn't notice!"

A dusky patch overlaid his high cheekbones. His eyes were black with fury. The words wounded him, and he struck back. "Do you think you were an experience no man could forget?" he asked, lowering his voice so that only she could hear him. His eyes were ice-cold. "An inexperienced, frightened innocent who didn't even know how to respond to a man's ardor?"

The insult hit home, and she couldn't hide it.

That seemed to make him even madder. "What are you doing out here in the first place?"

"We need another bushel of peaches to finish out this batch."

"I'll send Angel up with them. Anything else?"

"No, thank you." Her tone was as cold as her pride. She turned and went back into the house without another word.

HE WATCHED HER OVER the supper table. She had a small salad and a glass of iced tea, refused dessert and excused herself, all without meeting his eyes once.

"What's wrong with her?" Consuelo asked softly when she was out of the room. "Have the two of you had a fight?"

"I don't fight with employees," he returned. "The truth is that she's attracted to me and I find her unappealing. I grow weary of the heartsick looks she sends my way. She's hardly the type of woman I would choose," he added coldly. "She is uneducated and she has nothing to offer a man of experience. She has the naivete and the instincts of an adolescent. I felt sorry for her, and I was kind. She misinterpreted my compassion for affection. And," he said, finishing his coffee, "let's face it, she's no man's idea of an American beauty. Not with that long hair out of a fairy tale and those atrocious glasses she wears. No man would fall all over himself trying to seduce a woman so plain, who lacks even the most basic dress sense."

"You should not say such things about her," Consuelo

chided. "It would wound her to have you speak in such a manner."

"She will not know. Unless you tell her," he replied.

"As if I would wish to hurt her. She is a good woman."

"Good women are boring," he laughed. "I prefer mine wicked and overstimulated."

"Oh, you!"

Glory turned away from the half-closed door and made her way back down the hall, tears streaming down her pale face.

She didn't understand how Rodrigo could be so cruel after the long, sweet interlude in her bed. She'd given in without a fight. She'd responded wholeheartedly. But she was a novice, and he liked experience. She felt cheap. Used. Unwanted. She'd come down here to save her life, but her heart was being killed. Somehow, the threat of Fuentes's revenge wasn't half so painful as Rodrigo calling her plain and saying he didn't want her. He considered her uneducated—she, who'd graduated with honors from law school!

It was worse, somehow, because she was almost certainly pregnant. She didn't dare tell him now, not after what she'd overheard. She had to get Fuentes back into court and convicted so that she could stop living a lie. She wanted her old life back. She never wanted to see Rodrigo again as long as she lived!

But what about the hit man? Who would Fuentes have sent? Could it be Castillo or Marco? Could it even be Rodrigo?

She frowned as she came back to her original worry. What if Rodrigo was mixed up with Fuentes, or the killer? After all, he'd only been in Jacobsville for a little while and nobody knew very much about him. He'd hired Castillo, who was a crook of the first order. He and Castillo vanished every Wednesday. Rodrigo had ties to Mexico. He had a cousin who worked in the drug smuggling world. And the Rodrigo who'd confronted Castillo on the porch had been a man she didn't know, a dangerous man obviously used to settling problems with his fists. He could be violent. Castillo had been afraid of him. Rodrigo could be the hit man, or one of the bosses involved in drug smuggling.

She almost groaned aloud. Her life had been so simple when she was helping convict gang members and drug dealers back in San Antonio. Why hadn't Marquez left her where she was safe? At least she'd have been sure that Marquez would keep an eye on her. Down here, she had to hope that Cash Grier was telling the truth when he said he had somebody watching out for her.

She felt sick when she realized how reckless she'd been. What if her office had to prosecute Rodrigo? How would she cope with that? He'd have a great comeback—he could tell the court just how involved she'd been with him. It would damage her credibility, maybe enough to get Fuentes an acquittal. Life, she thought, was not fair.

GLORY WAS CURIOUS ABOUT where Rodrigo went with Castillo on those Wednesday jaunts. She caught a ride into town with Angel Martinez. She didn't want anyone to see her car parked in front of Barbara's Café, which was where she went as soon as Angel deposited her on the square. There, she phoned Marquez and told him about this new development.

"You should tell Grier," he replied.

"I did. Now I'm a mushroom."

He laughed. "They keep you in the dark and feed you bull…"

"Never mind," she interrupted pristinely. "Why don't you drive down here and we can tail Rodrigo and Castillo and see where they go?"

"Why should I take you along?"

"Because I'm going to be the one prosecuting the case, that's why."

"I was afraid you'd say that. When do they usually leave?"

"About five in the afternoon."

"And how are you going to get away from Consuelo long enough to ride around with me?"

"She leaves just before five every Wednesday to go to church," she said smugly. "And she takes her son with her."

There was an odd pause. "She does?"

"Yes. Isn't it curious that he'd voluntarily set foot in a church without being put in a casket first?" she returned, tongue-in-cheek.

"Maybe he walks in the front door of the church and out the back door," he mused.

"Who knows? Are you coming?"

"I'll pick you up at five. If anyone asks, we're on a hot date."

"In that case, I'll wear something conspicuous."

"Better make it something that will blend in," he countered. "You don't track people wearing flamboyant clothes."

"So much for the hot date," she murmured.

He laughed. "This isn't the time."

"That's what they all say."

"See you."

"Yes."

Barbara came up to her, frowning. "What's going on?"

Glory, who knew her, only grinned. "I'm luring your son to my house with promises of lurid wickedness."

"Hallelujah!" Barbara exclaimed. "If ever a child needed a push into seamy luridness, it's my straitlaced, puritanical son!"

"Well, it's not really that seamy," she confided in a whisper. "We're going tracking."

"Deer?" Barbara exclaimed, stunned.

"Not deer. Drug dealers."

The amused look went into eclipse. "That's dangerous territory. You should let him do that on his own."

"I can't. I'm up to my neck in this case already."

"Somebody should take Fuentes for a walk in the woods and push him down an abandoned well!"

Glory gaped at her. "You bloodthirsty cook!"

"Count on it! I hate drug dealers."

"So do I," Glory replied. "Especially Fuentes. He's more dangerous than Manuel Lopez or Cara Dominguez ever dreamed of being. He needs to go away for years and years, with no hope of parole."

"After which we can round up his smuggling ring and put them away, too."

"Exactly what I think. But first, we have to have evidence that will stand up in court."

"Spoilsport," Barbara chided.

"Yes, well, I'm an officer of the court," she reminded her. "I have to abide by the rules, even when I don't like them."

"Rick will help you get the evidence," she said.

Glory smiled. "I know he will. He's really very good at his job. But don't tell him I said so."

"I won't breathe a word."

"Thanks."

"If you ever need help, and you can't call anyone directly from the house, call me and order a sweet potato pie. I'll call Cash Grier, or Rick if he's down here, and get him right over there."

"Have you ever thought of becoming a secret agent?" Glory queried.

"All my life. But it's more fun thinking about it than doing it. At least, I think it is."

"You're probably right." She glanced out the door to the statue of old John Jacobs, the founder of Jacobsville, where the ranch pickup with Angel at the wheel stood waiting. "There's my ride. I have to go."

"What's wrong with your car?" Barbara asked.

"It's the same one I drive at home," she replied quietly.

"I keep it in the shed on the farm. I thought someone might recognize it."

"Good thinking."

"Oh, I could go into the secret agent business myself, after this," Glory said, and she wasn't really teasing. "I'll be in touch."

"Wait!" Barbara drew her to the counter, produced a sweet potato pie, bagged it and handed it to Glory. "Your cover," she said, "in case anybody wanted to know why you came in here."

"I'll see if I can find you a trenchcoat," Glory chuckled. She hugged Barbara. "Thanks."

"I'm not being altruistic. I want you to marry my son and give me lots of grandchildren," Barbara chuckled.

The mention of babies made Glory uneasy.

Barbara grimaced. "Sorry. I'm really sorry, that was uncalled for…"

"Don't be silly," Glory replied. "I'm not offended. Rick is a dish. But I have high blood pressure and I don't know if I can have a child. You see, there's never been any reason for me to ask a doctor about having children."

Barbara was noticing things that Glory wasn't aware of. The owner of a public café learned a lot about body language from observation. "Lou Coltrain is one of our best doctors, and she's still keeping secrets from grammar school. If you ever wanted to talk to a doctor in confidence, Lou would be your woman."

Glory frowned. "Why would you suggest such a thing?"

"Honey, it's a small town," she said gently. "You were dancing with that dishy manager on the farm, and from what we heard, it was so steamy between the two of you that people were dragging out fans."

Glory flushed. "Oh."

"You should remember how it is around here," Barbara continued softly. "We all know each other's business. But it's because we care about each other. You had it rough as a child, but you've turned into a fine, responsible woman. Your father would be so proud of you, Glory."

Tears stung the younger woman's eyes. She wasn't used to kindness. Not this sort, anyway.

Barbara nudged her toward the door. "Go home before you have me in tears, too. And if you want to seduce Rick, I'll loan you a hot red negligee."

Glory's eyebrows arched. "What would you be doing with a hot red negligee?"

"Hoping for an opportunity to wear it," Barbara chuckled.

Glory laughed back. The woman was truly a kind person.

"You be careful," Barbara added gently, as she went to put up the Open sign for the lunch crowd. "These guys play for keeps."

"I noticed. Thanks again."

"Any time."

GLORY DELIBERATELY IGNORED Rodrigo at lunch, talking to Consuelo about her recipe for apple butter.

He felt bad about what he'd said to her, but she'd asked

for it. She had a sharp tongue and she didn't bend. He wondered how she'd managed to fit into a temporary agency back in San Antonio with that attitude. It was as if she felt she had to be more aggressive because of her handicap. Not that the limp slowed her down. She worked as hard as Consuelo and never complained. She was as conscientious an employee as he'd ever known, and despite the physical abuse of her traumatic past, she didn't back down from the threat of a man. Castillo had been out of line.

"Remember why I hired you," Rodrigo had told the other man. "Don't make waves."

"Hell, she's pretty to look at," the man replied curtly. "Any man would try his luck."

Rodrigo's eyes had blazed at that remark. "Any man who tries his luck with Glory will end badly."

The way he said it sent chills down Castillo's spine. He held up both hands. "Hey, I understand. She's yours. I won't poach on your preserve again, I swear. I was just passing the time until we can do our job."

Rodrigo nodded. "Remember how Fuentes deals with people who mess up."

The other man swallowed hard. "Yeah."

"Back to work. I'll meet you at five to go to the warehouse."

"I'll be here."

RODRIGO GLANCED AT Glory as he left the kitchen. He saw her eyelids flicker, but she wouldn't look at him. It was just as well, he told himself. He was grieving. He didn't want to rush headlong into a relationship with a glorified cook. She had a pretty figure and he'd enjoyed her in bed. But there was more to life than sex. There was no room in his life for a simple country woman with cooking skills. He wanted a woman like Sarina, who had brains and courage. If only Colby Lane had never shown up!

He pulled out his cell phone and dialed a number. A deep voice answered.

"We're on our way," he said.

"We'll be waiting," came the reply.

He cut off the connection and dialed another number, this one local. There were two rings before it answered.

"*Culebra,*" he said in Spanish. "Snake."

"You're on."

He pocketed the phone with a smile that Castillo didn't see.

8

WHAT RODRIGO WAS EXPECTING didn't arrive on schedule. He was cursing a blue streak when the sun went down. They were in a deserted manufacturing building in Comanche Wells, a small town ten miles west of Jacobsville. The little town only had six hundred citizens. It didn't even have a policeman or a fireman, depending on the county for those services. A clothes manufacturer had tried to set up shop here and failed miserably. But the deserted building was a blessing to drug dealers. It provided a safe, defensible, private place for deals to go down.

Comanche Wells was in the center of the ranching industry of Jacobs County. Several cattle barons occupied the surrounding area and only came to town because of the feed and mill store. There was a bar, not as notorious as Shea's Roadhouse out on the Victoria highway, but it made money.

There was also a small company that manufactured computer chips. A Mexican restaurant was the only eatery and there was a single doctor and one drugstore. If there was an emergency, the ambulance had to take Comanche Wells citizens to Jacobsville General Hospital. They pulled the sidewalks in at dusk.

So now it was dark and the street that ran beside the deserted manufacturing building was bare of cars and people.

Castillo was pacing. "Where are they?" he asked furiously.

"I wish I knew," Rodrigo said tautly. "I was promised that they'd be here on schedule."

Castillo turned to him. "Yeah? Well, maybe they double-crossed you and leaked the buy to the feds."

"Not this guy," Rodrigo defended him. "He hates the feds."

"He's not alone."

"I know what you mean," Rodrigo agreed.

Castillo checked his watch. "They're fifteen minutes late!"

"They're coming a long way," Rodrigo replied calmly. He stuck his hands in his pockets and glanced at his companion. "You need to learn patience."

"The last time I was patient, two cops threw me in the back of a squad car and took me to jail," the other man said icily. He glared at Rodrigo. "How sure are you that these guys aren't going to double-cross us? That—" he indicated a briefcase sitting on an empty oil drum "—would set a petty thief up for life."

"Cross these guys and you won't have a life," he returned.

"The last dealer who weaseled on them was found in several counties."

The statement was chilling. The younger man fidgeted and stared at his watch again. "If they don't show pretty quick, we should take the stuff and get out of here. You sure they aren't cops?"

"Positive," Rodrigo assured him. "One of them is my cousin. He worked for Lopez, and then for Dominguez. If he was a cheat, he wouldn't still be in the game, would he?"

"Not with bosses like those, I guess. But Fuentes is a different sort," he added uncomfortably. "He's quick-tempered and he's left a trail of bodies across the border."

"What he pays makes it worth the risk."

Castillo glanced at him and grimaced. "Yeah. I guess so. But, still—"

He broke off as the sound of an approaching car echoed against the walls of the building. Rodrigo pulled his .45 automatic out of his belt and eased to the nearest window. He looked out covertly, and then relaxed.

"It's them," he said, putting the pistol up.

MARQUEZ WAS DRIVING HIS pickup truck when he picked Glory up at the farmhouse. He was dressed like a cowboy, in jeans and boots and wide-brimmed hat.

She got in beside him, smiling to herself. "You do blend in, don't you?" she teased.

"You have to when you're tracking people," he assured her. He grinned as he glanced at her. She was wearing the same gear he had on, except that her long hair was in a bun under a beret. "You'll blend in pretty good yourself."

"Thanks," she replied as she fastened her seat belt. "You did say nothing flamboyant."

"I did, didn't I?"

He pulled out onto the farm road that led to the highway. She noticed that he had his portable police radio along. "I thought it might be a good idea," he said when he saw her looking at it on the seat between them. "Just in case any eager beaver thinks he spots illegal traffic and tries to muscle in on my bust."

"You aren't going to arrest them?" she exclaimed, frightened for Rodrigo. "We aren't even sure that they're involved with Fuentes. Not yet, at least."

He gave her a pointed look. "I'm not working for the local law. I have no jurisdiction here."

"Oh," she said sheepishly.

"But if there's a genuine drug deal going down here, we're calling in Hayes Carson," he added, referring to Jacobs County's sheriff. "I won't let them walk."

"You may have to," she said, trying to reason with him. "It's Fuentes we want."

"We've already got Fuentes, as long as you're alive," he reminded her.

"We have him for one count of conspiracy to commit murder," she replied. "He could walk on that charge, even with my testimony. He's already walked on one drug dealing charge, but if we can link him to the drug network in this area, we can get him on an ironclad charge of conspiracy to distribute controlled substances as well. That's a federal charge and he'll do hard time."

He glared at her. "You don't have any jurisdiction here, either," he reminded her. "And your life is already on the line. If we can spook Fuentes by cutting in on his drug deal, he might back off on trying to cap you."

"Nice thought, but he doesn't have a reputation for backing off," she said. "Let him send his hired killer. Cash Grier said he's got a guy watching me."

Marquez looked worried.

"Now what's wrong?" she asked.

"Grier had a low-level thief working for him as a farm laborer for Ramirez," he said, "to get reduced time on his sentence. He talked to the D.A. about it."

"And?" she prompted.

"And the guy skipped town yesterday."

Her heart jumped. There wasn't anybody watching her. She was in more danger than ever.

"There's still the undercover fed," he said, trying to reassure her. "It's just that nobody knows exactly who or where he is."

She'd done some thinking about that. "I wonder if the undercover agent could be a woman," she said aloud.

He glanced at her. "Consuelo, you mean?"

She nodded.

"Not a chance," he replied curtly.

His tone was worrying. "What do you mean, no chance?"

He started to speak when the radio blared between them.

It gave two "ten-codes" in rapid succession. Marquez, who knew all the police in the area by their frequencies and call signs, picked it up and looked at the glowing screen.

"Damn!" he muttered.

"What is it?"

"DEA," he murmured.

"What's the Drug Enforcement Administration doing down here?" she asked, puzzled. "Do you think they're watching the farm?"

"Well, it's possible, isn't it?" he asked, frowning. "I mean, they had an agent killed down here—Lisa Parks's first husband, Walt Monroe. Another of their agents was shot, but not killed, when a huge cocaine bust went down in Houston, followed by a shootout in Jacobsville with Cara Dominguez and her gang not too long ago. They have good reason to be involved with trying to put Fuentes away."

She grimaced. "The right hand never knows what the left hand's doing," she muttered. "They play their cards too close to the chest, Rick."

"They've had to. They had a mole," he added, noting her surprise. "A very high level mole, so they had to have out-of-state DEA agents come in and handle the Houston investigation undercover. That's how they nabbed Dominguez, who kidnapped a child and was apprehended down here after the gun battle. But in this racket, there's always somebody to step into a drug lord's shoes."

"Like Fuentes," she agreed. She stared at the radio, which

had gone silent. "What do you think they're doing, monitoring or getting ready to close in?"

He thought for a minute. "I don't think they'd rush in unless there was a sizable amount of product to confiscate. You can bet that Fuentes isn't conducting a sale personally."

"Lovely thought, though, isn't it?" she sighed.

The radio crackled again. "Back off," came a low voice, a new one. "Everything's on schedule. I repeat, back off."

"Like hell!" came the terse reply in a deep, slow voice.

She and Marquez exchanged looks.

The radio went dead.

They were parked on a slight rise, behind a building, out of sight of the warehouse. A truck and a long, dark car were parked on the side street that ran alongside the structure. As they watched, two men in suits, one with a briefcase, got into the dark car and drove off. A minute later, two other men came out, also with a briefcase and dived into the pickup truck.

The two vehicles peeled out in a noisy manner, just as a third vehicle—this one an unmarked car but with blue lights going—pulled onto the street where the warehouse was located.

In seconds, all three vehicles were gone. The car with the blue lights was in hot pursuit.

"Now that was instructive," Marquez said thoughtfully.

"A drug deal went down," she said, "and if those were agents on the radio, they let it go down. Or most of them did. Somebody didn't follow orders and gave chase."

"Which indicates to me that they've got somebody on the inside," he agreed. "The law enforcement vehicle is a puzzle, though. It came in silently and with only two words of radio traffic."

"I noticed that," she said.

"I wonder who it was—local, state or federal officers." He drew in a breath. "Well, we're not going to do any good out here. I'll take you home."

"Thanks." She tried to appear normal, but she was faking it. She'd recognized one of the two men who got into the pickup truck. It was Rodrigo.

MARQUEZ WALKED HER TO the front porch, going slowly to allow for her slower progress with the cane. He'd driven around for a few minutes so that if Consuelo came home early, it would look as though Glory and Marquez were out on a date. It wouldn't do to come home too early.

"Consuelo's car isn't here," she noted.

"Probably still at church," he said, but there was something he wasn't saying out loud.

She turned to him on the porch. "What do you know about Consuelo that you aren't sharing with me?"

He shrugged. "Nothing dire," he replied. "She has a cousin who works for a trucking business in San Antonio, and he's occasionally helped with illegal drug transport. We keep him under surveillance."

"You don't think Consuelo is mixed up in this business?" she asked worriedly, because she liked the older woman.

"Of course not," he said at once. He didn't let her see his eyes.

"Thank goodness. I like her. She's been good to me," she said, smiling.

He smiled back. Good thing, he thought, that she couldn't see his eyes. "Nevertheless, watch your step here. I'm having second thoughts about pressuring you to work at the farm. I've landed you in a nest of vipers."

"Only one or two," she replied. "Thanks for looking out for me," she added. "I can take care of myself most of the time, but this isn't a normal circumstance." She sighed. "I miss my job."

"I'm sure you do. It will still be waiting when you get back there. Alive," he emphasized.

She grimaced. "Okay, I'll do what I have to." She looked up at him. "I never thought it was possible to hate fruit so much. I think I'll gag for the rest of my life every time I see a peach!"

He chuckled. "I often feel the same way, when I have to help my mother put up preserves."

"I like your mother."

"Me, too. Watch yourself."

"I will. You do the same."

He only smiled. She watched him as he got into his truck, threw up a hand and pulled out of the driveway.

She opened the door and went inside. It was dark in the hall, but she knew the layout of the house too well to worry. But as she turned toward the kitchen to get a small glass of milk to take to bed, she collided with a tall, muscular body.

She cried out, frightened. She hadn't seen or heard anything.

"Relax," Rodrigo said. He flipped the light switch and stared down at her intently. "Where have you been?"

She was still getting her breath. She felt sick, too, which would never do to let him see. She gripped her cane firmly. "I went for a ride with Rick."

He frowned. "Rick?"

"Marquez," she said, not quite meeting his eyes. "We went steady in high school. I ran into him at the grocery story recently when Consuelo and I went shopping."

There was a long, tense hesitation. His black eyes were narrow and intent on her face.

"I don't have a curfew, do I?" she asked sarcastically, to hide her anxiety. It was painful to know for sure that he was mixed up in Fuentes's drug operations. Especially in light of the possibility that she was carrying his child.

"No," he replied curtly. "No curfew. How serious is it?"

She frowned. "Is what?"

"You and Marquez."

She blinked, searching for an answer. She didn't want to put Rick in a situation where he might become a target. On the other hand, it wouldn't hurt to have Rodrigo think she had allies in law enforcement.

"We're friends," she said finally.

"Where did you go, for this…drive?" he asked slowly. And he smiled. It was the most dangerous smile she'd ever seen.

She wasn't good at pretense. She averted her eyes. "Just into town."

He knew she was lying. He'd seen Marquez's vehicle near the drop point, with two people in the cab. He couldn't figure out what Marquez was up to, unless he was dating Glory so that he had some information about Rodrigo's movements. That was disquieting. Things were at a crucial point.

"See anything interesting?" he persisted.

She looked up. "Not really."

His eyes were cold and quiet. "You don't want to put yourself into the middle of something you don't understand."

"Excuse me?"

"Marquez has enemies," he said. "He's making more by the day. You put yourself at risk just by being near him."

Her eyes widened. "You're jealous," she said pertly, trying to throw him off the track. It wouldn't do for her to blurt out anything about that warehouse or the drug deal she and Rick had witnessed.

That disconcerted him. He blinked, then scowled. "Jealous of a cop?" he scoffed.

"Hurts your ego, doesn't it?" she persisted, "that I went from you to him. Would you like to know how he compares as a lover? Ooh!"

Even in their brief intimacy, he'd never kissed her like this. He enveloped her against his tall, muscular body so that she could feel it against every inch of her own soft one. His mouth devoured hers, probing, insistent, hungry for a response. She gave him one because she couldn't help herself. He was the only man she'd ever wanted.

Her arms went under his and around him. She moaned huskily as the kiss escalated into areas of sensuality she'd never experienced.

Groaning, he backed her into the wall and pushed down against her, so that she could feel the growing evidence of his desire for her.

Her soft hands tugged at his shirt and eased their way under it, up against the warm, strong muscles of his back. She felt them ripple at her touch. Without lifting his mouth, he coaxed them to the front, to the thickness of hair on his chest while he, too, worked at fastenings. Seconds later, she felt her breasts bury themselves in that thick hair, enjoying the exquisite feel of skin on skin. In the silence of the house, the only sounds were those of ragged breathing and faint moans.

She didn't hear her cane fall. She hardly noticed when he swung her up in his arms and carried her down the hall to her room.

He locked the door behind him and fell with her onto the bed in a tangle of arms and legs and clothing that soon merged into an urgent, hard rhythm.

She felt him inside her with a sense of wonder. He was very aroused, even more so than their first time. He lost control quickly. It wasn't planned. He drove for satisfaction, groaned harshly as he felt her body arching up to accept him, pleading for more, more…more!

His last conscious thought was that she was so aroused that he wasn't sure that he could manage to satisfy her…

SHE COULDN'T STOP TREMBLING. He hadn't managed to ease the terrible tension he'd aroused in her. She felt him reach his peak and lay shivering and crying under him with her own frustration.

"Shhh," he whispered at her ear. He moved against her, very slowly, feeling her surge up to him, pleading.

"I didn't…" she choked.

"I know. Easy, *querida,*" he whispered deeply. "Easy. Move with me. Don't be so impatient. I won't stop until I satisfy you. I promise. Do what I tell you."

She had to fight to slow down. But when she did, she understood. It was frightening, the way it increased her pleasure. Every movement of his hips was sweet anguish. Every kiss against the softness of her breasts brought a wave of delight. As he moved, her long legs curled around his, feeling the power and strength of them as he shifted his weight.

"It wasn't like this, before," she whispered frantically.

"I know." He didn't sound pleased. His voice was rough. His movements were fierce, demanding. "Don't talk. Lift up to me. Hard. Hard!"

She obeyed him in a rapturous fog that denied the pain in her hip, the stupidity of letting him this close again.

"That's it," he whispered. He nipped at her shoulder as the soft noises they made grew quicker and louder. "Yes!" He caught her thigh in his hand and pulled it up. The sensations he felt were almost frightening. He felt her shudder, heard her cry of surprise as the pleasure notched up another level.

"Oh...!" she cried out, arching. "Oh! I...can't...!"

The rhythm was frantic now, not controlled or contrived. He moved up, pushed harder, harder, as a red wave of pleasure started to envelope him.

Her nails dug into him. She opened her eyes, shocked as she saw the taut, frozen contours of his face above her.

"Yes," he whispered roughly. "Watch me...!"

She couldn't close her eyes. The pleasure shook them both, convulsed them in a free-form work of art as they joined, closed and then riveted themselves into one human being.

His mouth crushed down on hers as she screamed, a husky, high-pitched helpless sign of the unbearable pleasure he was forcing her to feel. She arched, convulsed, arched again. And all the while she looked at him, letting her eyes fill with the beauty of his face, his body, as he drove into her and finally began to shudder.

"¡Dios...mio!" he cried out just as the convulsions brought him almost to unconsciousness.

She bit his shoulder helplessly. She, too, was drowning in a sea of pleasure so vast that she felt it would never end. She heard her own harsh sobs as she burst into wave after wave of delight.

But it did end. Slowly the world came back into focus, and it was over. The brief, beautiful explosion of joy was gone.

They lay together in a tangled, damp heap, shivering in the aftermath. She felt her heartbeat increase dangerously and concentrated on slow, steady breathing to bring it down. She'd never felt such sensations in her life.

He was looking at the ceiling. He hated himself for giving in once more to this weakness. She wasn't like him. She would never fit into his world. She was getting involved with a cop and his whole operation was in jeopardy. And now, out of jealousy he'd never admit feeling, he'd just doubled his chances of making her pregnant. It didn't make him feel much better to realize how much she'd enjoyed him this time. And how much he'd enjoyed her.

"Do describe how Marquez compares with me," he invited darkly.

She was trying to get her mind to work. It was sluggish. "I couldn't tell you," she confessed. "I've never slept with him."

He didn't know how he felt about that. Proud, maybe? Arrogant? He stretched, feeling his muscles ache from the tension they'd been under.

He rolled over and looked down at her. He'd tossed her glasses onto the bedside table when they'd ended up here. Her long blond hair was tangled around her flushed face. Her big, green eyes were wide and curious.

He pushed the tangled hair away from her cheek and the corner of her mouth. "You're improving."

She sighed heavily as she stared up at him. Her eyes were accusing.

"I know. It's all my fault," he murmured. He bent and kissed her softly. "I sowed my wild oats a long time ago. I'm not usually so easy to arouse."

She wanted to comment that his wild ride avoiding the police might have had a hand in his loss of control, surging adrenaline making him vulnerable, but she didn't dare.

"You could have said no," he pointed out.

"No, I couldn't," she said in a conversational tone. "You wouldn't stop kissing me long enough."

He shrugged his broad, darkly tanned shoulders. Muscles rippled there, where one of her hands was resting. "It's addictive."

She knew it was addictive. She couldn't refuse him. It was worrying, when she'd been afraid of men for most of her life and singularly unattracted to just about every man she'd ever known. Then here came this farm worker and she couldn't get out of her clothes fast enough. It was demeaning, in a way.

"Do I detect the sound of mental flogging?" he asked.

She bit down hard on a laugh that escaped anyway. "You can't expect me to be proud of the way I react to you," she pointed out. "I was happy with my life until you came along and totally uprooted it."

He traced her thin eyebrows with his forefinger. "I have noticed your lack of restraint," he commented with amusement. His eyes met hers in the dim light of the room. "We've doubled our chances of producing a child."

"I did notice."

"What do you suggest that we do about it?" he persisted.

It was a question she didn't want to answer. In fact, she didn't know how to answer it. Part of her wanted the child. Another part was scared, not only of having a child but of the hidden Rodrigo, the drug dealer who might end up in prison. Worse, she might be instrumental in helping to put him there. She'd witnessed him leave the warehouse in the company of Castillo, running from a police car. She'd have to testify.

While she was struggling with that question, the theme song from the Mexican soccer team, from the World Cup in 2006, blared out from somewhere on the floor.

"Damn!" he breathed softly.

He got out of bed, gathering up his slacks. He dug into the pocket and answered it. "Yes?"

There was a long pause.

"I know," he added.

There was another pause.

"He'd better hope he can outrun me on the way to the border," he replied. "You can tell him I said that. Yes. I'll talk to you later."

He closed the phone. Distracted, he dressed quickly and gathered up her clothing, dropping it onto the coverlet which she'd pulled up over her body.

He paused at the head of the bed and stood just looking at her. "When things settle down around here, we're going to have a long talk."

"About what?"

He sighed. "I don't really know. But if there's a child, you know we have to make decisions."

"That would be a very long shot," she lied. "I've had no symptoms of pregnancy."

He felt oddly disappointed, but he knew it was for the best. The last thing he wanted was to be tied to this woman for the rest of his life by a child he wouldn't be able to deny. Even though he wanted a child very badly, Glory was, frankly, not the sort of woman he'd want for its mother. He thought of Sarina and he felt sick all over. It was almost like commiting adultery, he reflected. He felt guilty.

"That's good," he said after a minute. He hesitated. "I never meant this to happen."

"I know. Neither did I."

He reached down and brushed his mouth gently over her damp forehead. "You were right about one thing."

"What thing?" she asked.

"I was jealous," he confessed.

He opened the door and pulled it shut behind him with quick finality.

Glory lay in the soft semidarkness thinking how easily she walked into traps of her own making.

9

THE NEXT DAY, GLORY was still flogging herself for the night before. She had to stop letting Rodrigo walk up on her blind side. She was almost certainly pregnant. She needed to talk to a doctor before she was too advanced and see just how much of a risk she would be taking if she decided to have the baby. The longer she felt the symptoms, the more attached she became to the tiny thing growing inside her. She wanted it with all her heart, regardless of the complications it would mean to her physically, as well as to her job.

Meanwhile, she noticed that Consuelo was oddly nervous. She kept pulling out her cell phone and checking to make sure it worked. In between, she worked with some distraction, once even forgetting to put sugar in the fruit they were canning.

"What's wrong?" Glory asked gently. "Is there something I can do to help?"

The older woman looked at her oddly. She grimaced. "I wish I had known someone like you many years ago," she said enigmatically. "It seemed that the whole world turned against me. I had nobody who even offered help."

Glory smiled gently. "You know I'd do anything I could for you."

That, strangely, seemed to make the older woman even more uncomfortable. Her teeth clamped tight. "Thank you," she said tightly. "But it's too late."

Before Glory could ask another question, Consuelo's cell phone rang. The woman almost popped it into the boiling fruit as she fumbled to open it. "*¿Sí?*" she said at once. She listened, winced, glanced at Glory and winced again. "*¿Lo es absolutamente necesario? ¿Estás seguro?*" She hesitated, listened, and finally said, "*Sí,*" again and hung up.

"It's something bad, isn't it?" Glory asked quietly.

"Yes," came the reply. Consuelo dried her hands and took off her apron. She wouldn't meet Glory's eyes. "I have to go out, just for a few minutes, to the store for…for more supplies. You can manage here alone, yes?"

"Of course." Glory took Consuelo's place at the stove, stirring the fruit. She forced a smile that she didn't feel. Something was very wrong, and Glory was almost certain it had to do with herself. "Don't rush. I'll be fine."

The older woman flashed her a look of utter horror. "You…you be careful, okay?" she stammered. "I won't be long."

"Okay."

Consuelo went out the door without looking back. Glory heard her car start, and then speed away.

She turned off the stove at once, her heart pounding. She wasn't sure what she knew, but she sensed danger all around her. Her job had made her more sensitive to danger, especially now. Consuelo's erratic behavior was too disturbing to ignore. She moved quickly to her room, locked her door and punched in Cash Grier's office number on her cell phone. Before it even started to ring, she heard the back door open with a slam.

"Where is she?" a young male voice demanded.

"How should I know?" another replied tersely. "Look for her!"

She hung up and dialed the emergency services number.

"Jacobs County Dispatch. May I help you?"

Glory gave her information succinctly. "I'm alone and unarmed and there are some men in the house," she said. "I think they mean to hurt me."

"Two minutes," the dispatcher said. "Stay on the line."

In the background she heard the alarm go out to local police. There was static, the dispatcher's steady, firm voice, and a clear, answering "10-76" in a deep voice, followed by a wailing siren that she heard simultaneously on the phone and outside. There must be a squad car nearby if the dispatcher said he could make it to Glory in two minutes. It was a big county.

Now if the police just made it in time...!

There were heavy footsteps, muttered curses when they tried the locked bedroom door. Glory moved barefooted to behind the door and lifted her cane over her head. If anybody managed to break in that heavy old door, she was going to get in the first blow. Damn Fuentes! She thought furiously. Damn him for a coward, sending other people to do his dirty work for him!

What sounded like a boot slamming into the door echoed in the hall, but it didn't budge. Then a shoulder hit the door, with the same result. She heard curses in Spanish and then, suddenly, furiously, gunshots went right into the door, where she would have been standing if she hadn't gotten the idea to ambush her attackers. One of the bullets shattered the wood around the doorknob and another took out the keyhole.

"Got you now, blondie!" the drawling voice carried.

But even as the door started to open, the siren grew loud and a car could be heard racing up to the porch. Her heart was racing, too. The old familiar pain came with it, stinging down her left arm. But she was full of bravado, nevertheless.

"What the hell...!" one of the voices exclaimed.

"It's the heat! She called the cops!"

"And now you can try shooting at them!" she raged.

"I'll get you next time!" a cold, angry voice in accented Spanish came through the wood. "I swear I will!"

"Like hell you will!" muttered a new, deeply drawling male voice.

There were thuds and running feet, a gunshot that sounded farther away than the hall, and then even louder thuds echoed in the hall. Then there was silence.

"Ma'am, are you still on the line?" the dispatcher asked worriedly.

"Yes," Glory assured her. "There's fighting in the hall and a gunshot outside. I'm locked in my bedroom."

"Just stay there."

"You bet!"

Another exclamation, another thud. Then silence.

There was a knock on the door. She heard the same deep voice that had answered the intruder. "Ma'am, it's the police. You okay in there?"

She didn't know whether or not to answer.

There was static outside the door and she heard the same voice come over the line when the dispatcher answered the call.

"It's really the police," the dispatcher assured her. "You can open the door now."

"Thanks," Glory said huskily. "Thank you very much."

"My pleasure."

Glory hung up the phone and opened the door, carefully. A tall, powerful looking police officer with black hair and glittery pale gray eyes was towering above her. He noted the upraised cane.

"Oops. Sorry," she said, lowering it to her side. "Sorry."

He managed a faint smile. "Going to brain the guy, huh? I don't know if it would have helped, he's so thick-skulled."

She moved out into the hall and noted, shakily, that a man was facedown on the floor with his hands cuffed behind him. She knew before they turned him over and helped him up that it was Marco.

He glared at her with hateful black eyes. "I'll be out by morning, blondie," he spat at her. "And you'll be dead by night!"

"Oh, I wouldn't bet on that," the policeman drawled.

"No, me either," his younger companion, also in uniform, agreed. He had blond hair and a nice smile. "You okay, ma'am?"

"I'm fine, thanks to both of you," she replied.

"Do you know this man?"

"Yes," she said. "He's our cook's son."

"There are bullet holes through your door there. Was he trying to shoot you?" the first officer asked.

She hesitated. She didn't dare tell them the truth. Marco knew that, and he was grinning in a sarcastic fashion.

"I don't know," she lied.

Marco only laughed. "Smart girl," he said.

The officers were looking suspicious. Glory looked past them, and Cash Grier walked in. "I just got word," he told Glory. He looked at his two patrol officers. "Take him by the dentention center. We'll charge him with aggravated assault. I'll walk her through the statement."

"I never tried to hurt her!" Marco argued. "I only wanted to talk to her."

Cash looked pointedly at the bullet holes that went through Glory's bedroom door. "Badly, apparently," he said.

"It's her word against mine," Marco said smugly. "I'll be out in twenty-four hours. I get to call my lawyer, right?"

Fuentes would have the best lawyers money could buy. Glory had never felt so frustrated. She glared at Marco. It would almost have been worth blowing her cover to charge him with attempted murder and give the reason, which would lead back to the man she was certain he worked for—Fuentes.

"Take him out of here," Cash told the officers. "I'll be along."

They walked Marco down the hall.

Glory leaned against the door facing, catching her breath. Her heart was pounding, and she had pain down her arm.

"Sit down," Cash said, easing her into a chair just inside her room. "Do you have medicine?"

She shook her head. "Not with me." It was hard to breathe. Harder to talk.

"I can call an ambulance."

She swallowed. That would complicate things even more. She concentrated on breathing steadily. Slowly the pain began to ebb. She looked up at Cash. "I'll be all right," she said softly. "This isn't the first time I've had this problem."

"It's angina, isn't it?" he asked.

She nodded. "They gave me nitroglycerin tablets," she said, pausing to breathe again. "But I'd rather do anything...than take them. They hurt my head."

He leaned against the dresser, frowning. "Knowing your medical history, I have to wonder if you're suicidal, considering your line of work."

"How odd," she mused. "That's exactly what my doctor said."

"Maybe you should listen to him. Right now, I'm all for putting you in a safe house under protective custody."

She shook her head. "If you do that, Fuentes wins. Marco missed. He thinks he'll walk. Now Fuentes will do his best to have Marco killed, too. He doesn't forgive slipups."

"You think? I'm wondering why a man as dangerous as Fuentes would send a drug-crazed teenage gang member to do a professional hit."

She felt the blood drain out of her face. She hadn't seen it. Now she realized that it was a setup. The real killer had sent Marco in to test the water, to see the reaction time of local law enforcement, to see how Glory would react.

"It was staged, wasn't it?" she asked, and horror was in her eyes.

"I think so," he replied. "A test run."

"Yes." She managed to breathe normally again. "So what do we do now?"

Cash was thinking, hard. He wasn't sure of anything, except that he wished he knew what the DEA was doing in Jacobs County. It had been one of Cash's new men, the gray-eyed one who'd rushed to Glory's aid, who'd ignored an order from the DEA to back off when a drug deal went down in Comanche Wells. Nobody knew exactly who the undercover agent was or what he was up to, and federal agencies tended not to share intel with local police unless they had to.

"What the hell is going on here?" came a familiar deep, faintly accented voice. Glory looked up and Rodrigo walked into the room. He looked at the bullet holes in the door, at Cash and then at Glory with real concern. *"Niña!"* he exclaimed gently, modifying his tone as he knelt beside her. *"¿Estás bien?"*

Her heart jumped because he'd used the familiar tense, one that Spanish-speaking people only used with loved ones or children. She met his searching black eyes and felt safe. Unthinking, she held up her arms and he went into them, enveloping her against him, rocking her, smoothing her hair. She felt tears pour out of her eyes and hated showing weakness. But she'd been scared. Really scared. Her heart was still acting up. She felt vulnerable.

"What happened?" Rodrigo asked Cash.

"It's a long story," Cash replied. "I'm not at liberty to divulge what I know."

Rodrigo's eyes narrowed. He knew this man, and his contacts. He'd been chasing a drug lord, but someone was after Glory. He didn't know why, and he knew it was useless to ask Cash. Plots within plots, he thought irritably. But at least he was used to secrets.

"Can you tell me who did this?" he asked.

"Marco," Glory murmured against his chest. "Marco did it. Poor Consuelo!"

"Where is she?" Rodrigo asked.

"She had to run to the store. She had a phone call. She looked very strange when she hung up, and she said she had to go out," Glory said, her voice muffled against the clean, nice-smelling front of Rodrigo's chambray shirt.

Rodrigo looked into Cash's eyes, and the other man knew at once who the DEA had working undercover here. He hadn't recognized Rodrigo, whom he'd only seen in the dark during a standoff with Cara Dominguez several months ago. He'd rarely seen that look in another man's face, but it was all too familiar. Rodrigo was obviously involved with Glory in some manner and he looked as if he wanted to take several bites out of Marco. He seemed fiercely protective of Glory. But Cash couldn't blow Rodrigo's cover—or Glory's. If the situation had been a little less potentially fatal, it would have been comedy. Both of them were keeping dire secrets which, apparently, they weren't willing to share with each other.

"Shhh," Rodrigo whispered at Glory's ear. "It's all right. You're safe. Nobody is going to hurt you here. Never again. I swear it."

"I was thinking of having someone come over here to work for you, just to keep an eye on her," Cash said.

Rodrigo glanced at him. "That was tried once before and it didn't work. I'll take care of her."

It was a veiled warning. When Cash searched his memory, he began to remember other things he'd heard about this agent. The man had been involved in mercenary work for many years. He was so good at what he did that there was a price on his head in almost every country on earth. For the past three years, he'd worked for the DEA out of Arizona. He'd actually gone undercover in Manuel Lopez's drug operation and helped bring the man down. More recently, he'd been instrumental in Cara Dominguez's arrest and conviction. Now he was after Fuentes. Cash knew it, but he couldn't admit it; certainly not in front of Glory.

"I was hiding behind the door when he tried to come in," she muttered, wiping her eyes as she pulled gently away from Rodrigo's comforting arms. "I was going to brain him with my cane. But he started shooting instead."

"Thank God you were behind the door instead of in front of it," Rodrigo said tersely.

"What will you do with Marco?" she asked Cash.

"Book him, lock him up and hope the judge will set bail at a million dollars."

Glory chuckled. "Oh, I think Mary Smith will do that if you ask her to. She's a renegade. She hates drug dealers."

"You know a judge?" Rodrigo asked her with narrow, suspicious eyes.

Her heart skipped. "I know of her," she said. "One of my cousins got in trouble with the law and she heard his case," she lied calmly.

"I see."

"You'll have to testify," Cash told Glory. "You're the only eyewitness I've got."

Story of my life, she thought. "I didn't see him, though," she replied sadly. "I only heard him."

"Try to get a conviction on that evidence," Rodrigo murmured absently as he examined the bullet holes. "A good defense attorney will swear that Marco came to her assistance and was falsely accused."

"But there's the gun," Glory began.

Cash ground his teeth together.

"What?" she asked.

"We didn't find a gun."

"There goes your case," Rodrigo replied dryly.

"There were two of them," Glory said. "The other one, the one who got away, probably took the gun with him when he heard the sirens. Marco was busy telling me that he'd get me next time. So you got him."

"I'll keep him as long as I can," Cash promised. "But it won't be the only attempt."

"She'll be safe here." Rodrigo repeated. He looked from Glory to Cash and back again. "I don't suppose either of you would like to tell me why my cook's assistant is attracting hired killers?"

Cash and Glory exchanged glances.

"So we play musical chairs and twenty questions, while Marco's boss plans a foolproof way to take her out, is that it?" Rodrigo asked.

"We think this was a dry run," Cash said. "To see about response time, and Glory's reaction to an intruder."

"He'll be wiser next time and hit in the middle of the night when she's asleep," Rodrigo said calmly.

"If someone would loan me a gun..." she began.

"No!" Cash said at once.

"One miserable taillight," she began hotly.

"*And* a windshield," he returned. "No gun."

Rodrigo was aware that they were talking about something they wouldn't share with him. More secrets. "We'll work out something here," Rodrigo assured Cash. His eyes narrowed. "I'd like a word with you before you leave."

Cash felt like an entrée. He knew he wasn't going to like what the man had to say. "I'll wait outside." He turned to Glory. "You sure, about the ambulance?"

She was still struggling to breathe properly. "Yes. Thanks."

Rodrigo smoothed her hair and stood up. "I won't be a minute," he told her. "Lie down. You've already had more excitement than you need."

She nodded. She moved slowly across her room, ignoring the bullet holes, and all but collapsed on the clean cover of the bed.

ON THE WIDE FRONT PORCH, Cash and Rodrigo stood facing each other like prizefighters searching for an opening.

"You'd better tell me what's going on," Rodrigo said quietly, wary of eavesdroppers.

"The same way you've kept me informed?" Cash returned coldly.

Rodrigo's black eyes narrowed. This man was intelligent, and he wasn't the sort to accept lies. "I suppose you've realized who I am, and why I'm here."

"Yes."

"That's all you're allowed to know," he replied. "I'm sorry. This isn't my operation. I have to do what I'm told."

"Can you at least tell me if what you're doing has any connection with Fuentes?"

Rodrigo nodded. "We have a mole," he said. "He's feeding us information. I had to go undercover to work out the distribution network, and it's formidable. I still have one cousin in Fuentes's employ, although Manuel Lopez had one of my cousins killed for infiltrating some years ago." He stuck his hands in his pockets. "There's a shipment of cocaine coming from Peru in about two weeks. We know how it's coming into the country, and what the destination is."

"There's an empty warehouse in Comanche Wells," Cash said easily, "and it's not where many people could notice activity at it."

Rodrigo nodded. "We met there last night." His eyes grew cold. "Someone in an unmarked squad car almost got me killed by refusing to back off."

Cash grimaced. "It's one of my new patrolmen, I'm sorry to say. He's back from overseas duty, an officer in a front combat unit and he's forgotten how to take orders. Actually he was special forces, working behind the lines."

Rodrigo nodded. "We've had a few of those sign on with us. They're valuable in the right position. But they're a liability when they don't follow orders."

"I told him so," Cash replied. "He won't do it again."

"We're still dancing around the attempted murder here," Rodrigo said.

"I noticed."

"What does she have, or know, that's important enough for someone to send a killer after her?"

Cash weighed the facts and decided that he had to level with the man somehow without giving Glory away. "She has information that could tie Fuentes to a murder. A conviction could have serious consequences on the network. Fuentes doesn't want her talking to a jury."

Rodrigo whistled. "Talk about coincidences," he mused. "And she winds up here, in the middle of a drug sting."

"Almost assassinated, as well," Cash replied.

"Fuentes wouldn't send Marco to do a job like that. Marco hasn't got what it takes for wet work. No, he was sent here so that he could be used in a dry run. Next time, Fuentes will send a professional assassin and we'll bury Glory."

"That's what I told Glory."

Rodrigo eyed him. "And the case comes up soon, I gather?"

"Yes," Cash said. "Certain people talked to the Pendletons and got Glory hired as a kitchen worker. The prosecutor in the case thought she'd be in less danger in a small town, where we could all keep an eye on her while he builds enough evidence to convince a jury that Fuentes is killing informants who rat out his drug deals."

"Marquez and you, I assume, being the people who plan to watch her?"

"I had a guy working for you who was supposed to keep me in the loop. He's gone."

"I'm still working here," Rodrigo replied. "Nothing will happen to Glory."

"You can't watch her around the clock," Cash said. "Let me help."

The other man grimaced. He felt suddenly vulnerable. He'd enjoyed Glory as a pastime, but the thought of losing her to a bullet had hit him in the gut. He couldn't bear the thought that she might be killed. Strange how much it hurt him to think of her lying dead.

"Your prosecutor should have sent a bodyguard with her," Rodrigo commented.

Cash chuckled. "That's a hoot. Whose budget would pay for it?"

"Not ours," Rodrigo had to admit. "I'm not charging them for overtime."

"You'd never get it, if your budget is like ours."

"It is. Nobody has money to spare these days." He didn't mention that he was wealthy enough to have done his job without pay. The last three years he'd worked for the DEA had been for no other reason than to be Sarina's partner.

"Okay," Cash said. "I'll have someone available to tail her if she leaves the farm. Can you cover her here?"

"Yes," Rodrigo said.

"Then maybe we can keep her alive until Fuentes goes on trial." He pursed his lips. "Marco's mother is involved in this. You know that."

"Yes," the other man said heavily. "Her husband is in federal prison. Marco just got out, and if we can prove he had a gun, it's a violation of his probation and he'll go right back in. Pity that Consuelo allowed herself to get mixed up in this."

"She'd do anything her son asked her to," Cash said. "He's all she's got."

"It's a shame."

"Yes."

"Are you going to charge her?"

Cash shifted his weight. "On what evidence? We're going to have hell even holding Marco on any charges that would stand up in court."

"The sorry little sneak," Rodrigo muttered. "I'd like to give his face a makeover."

"Not allowed. Remember, we're the good guys."

"Rearranging his face would be good," Rodrigo said pleasantly.

"You don't want to meet up with Blake Kemp in a court of law down here. He's just been appointed district attorney. Our elected one had a stroke and died. Kemp's handling the job until elections, and I bet you he'll run. He's a legal legend already."

Rodrigo whistled. "I know. Damn!"

"That's just what the lawless are saying about now," Cash chuckled. "He's hell on defendants."

"He was special forces, too, I believe, along with Cag Hart."

Cash nodded. "We're fairly blessed with ex-military around here. If you need help, I'll do anything I can."

"Thanks."

"Did you hear about your ex-partner?" Cash added.

"Sarina?"

"Yes." Cash grinned. "She's pregnant."

Rodrigo felt the words as if they were a physical blow. She hadn't said a word to him. She'd had the opportunity, at the fiesta. "It must be wonderful news for them."

"Yes. Andy Webb at the realty company told me about it. They were going to move down here; even bought Hob Downey's place to build on. But now they want to stay in Houston where the Hunters live, so they're putting the property back on the market. I suppose they're pretty much settled in Houston. I don't know how Sarina's going to keep up her DEA job, though, in that condition."

Rodrigo only nodded. He felt as if a cold, hollow place had opened up inside him.

"Well, I'll get out of here. If you need us, let me know," Cash added. "We'll put extra patrols out this way."

"Tell your new patrolman that the next time he ignores an order from me, he'll be carried feetfirst into the nearest emergency room." Rodrigo didn't smile when he said it, and his eyes were full of muted anger.

"Oh, I've already told him that," Cash replied. He grinned. "I don't tolerate disobedience, either."

"But you can thank him for being on the spot today," the Mexican added. "Even if it was a dry run, Marco's unpredictable. Glory might be dead if he hadn't been so quick. I owe him for that."

"I'll tell him."

"And what I'm doing here is still top secret."

"I knew that, too. Take care."

"You, too."

Cash drove off and Rodrigo went back inside. He felt sick all over. Sarina was pregnant. She hadn't told him. She hadn't phoned or written. Was he of so little importance to her now, after their three years of intense friendship, that she didn't even care enough to share her good news with him?

He felt lost and alone. All his dreams were dead. He was never going to be the only man in Sarina's life. It was a hard blow.

He walked back down the hall to Glory's room and paused next to her bed. Her cheeks were very flushed and she was still upset.

He sat down beside her on the bed. She reminded him a little of Sarina. But she wasn't as intelligent, or as brave. Sarina could shoot a gun and she'd faced off bad guys with him over the years. This poor shell of a woman was hiding out because she could put Fuentes on the spot in a murder. He couldn't imagine Sarina hiding from anyone.

But it wasn't fair to compare them. Sarina was in excellent health. This young woman had health problems that made her more vulnerable. He was being unreasonable because he was hurt.

He reached out and smoothed back Glory's soft hair, watching it rainbow around her flushed face. "Feeling better?" he asked quietly.

"Yes," she said huskily. "I'll be all right. You look sad."

He averted his eyes. "Perhaps I am."

"Is there anything I can do to help?"

He looked down at her with narrowed eyes and considered the one thing he could ask her that would not only help him heal, but show Sarina that he wasn't going to spend the rest of his life grieving because he couldn't have her.

"Yes," he said in a conversational tone. "As a matter of fact, there is. You can marry me."

10

"MARRY YOU?" GLORY exclaimed, and really had to fight for breath then.

"Why not?" he asked. "We're great together in bed. We like the same things. We get along well."

"But, we're not in love," she protested. She did have feelings for him, but she wasn't going to voice them. At least, not while he was still mourning his pretty blonde.

"What is love? Mutual respect and friendship seem to me to be equally important," he replied. His eyes narrowed. "You're reluctant. Is it because I earn my living with my hands, working as a laborer?"

Her eyes widened. "No, not at all," she said simply. "I admire you."

He looked surprised. "Why?"

"Because you deal with people so well, with diplomacy and tact," she began. "You never shout or demean the other workers. You go out of your way to be kind to women and children. You're honest. You don't mind hard work. And you aren't afraid of anything. That's why."

He hadn't expected a list of his character traits. He was surprised that she felt that way about him. He wasn't what he pretended to be, but she accepted him easily as if he were. For years, women—other than Sarina, of course—had wanted him for what he could give them. Here was one who thought he was poor and didn't mind. It was humbling.

"I'm flattered." His eyes narrowed as they looked into hers. "There's something else. Something you aren't telling me."

She averted her eyes.

"Come on," he coaxed.

"I heard what you said to Consuelo about me," she confessed. "That I wasn't the sort of woman who attracted you...that I was too plain..."

He pulled her into his arms and held her. "Bad temper," he muttered. "I say things I don't mean sometimes. I didn't mean that." He lifted his head and looked down at her. "I really didn't mean it."

She relaxed.

He let her back down and propped his hand beside her ear. "You don't want my children," he said quietly. His pride still stung from having her tell him that.

She grimaced. "I didn't mean that. Not really." She was still uncertain about her ability to carry a child. "I've been thinking things over, and I wouldn't mind having a child."

His eyebrows went up. His face relaxed into a radiant smile. "Truly?"

She smiled back. Her heart jumped at the expression there. "Truly."

He traced her soft mouth with his forefinger. "Then suppose you marry me?"

It was crazy. She couldn't get married; her job left her no free time. She couldn't have a child—it might kill her. But she was almost certainly pregnant already. If she could find a good doctor, who would keep close care of her, it might not be too dangerous. After all, she'd heard about Grace Carver who had a bad heart valve and she survived pregnancy when she married FBI agent Garon Grier. If Grace could do it, why couldn't Glory? Besides, with her past, she didn't want to have the baby out of wedlock. Those old-fashioned values she'd been taught early in life didn't go away easily.

"Come on," he chided.

She looked up at him and smiled. She never took risks. She was always conservative. But there was a promise of heaven in those black eyes and her heart was cutting cartwheels inside her. "Yes," she said, and refused to think of the consequences.

"Yes, what?" he teased, liking the helpless response she gave to his tender ardor.

"Yes, I'll marry you," she whispered.

His eyes flashed. Seconds later, his mouth was against

hers, hard and demanding. She wanted him. She didn't mind if he didn't have a penny to his name and she'd never be financially secure. His heart was flying. She was so like Sarina...

He pulled away from her and sat up. She looked dreamy, happy. He felt guilty because he was using her, in a way, to escape the pain of rejection. But she'd never have to know. They could stay together for a while, enjoy each other. Then, later, perhaps there would be a child. The thought was suddenly depressing. He was only kidding himself that he could be happy with a substitute, even if there was a child. She would never be Sarina, and her child would never be Bernadette. The pain was like a rope around his heart, choking him.

"When?" she asked, interrupting his thoughts.

He got up and hesitated, frowning. "When do you want to?"

She hesitated, too. He looked different suddenly. Perhaps he was having second thoughts. She should start having them; her life was in danger and she was living a lie. She had no business marrying anyone...

"Today," he said abruptly. "Right now."

"*Right now?*"

"We can be over the border in no time," he said. "Mexican weddings are binding."

Her head was swimming. Fuentes had sent a killer after her. Marco had pumped bullets through her bedroom door not a half hour ago. The real killer was still out there, and she was going off to marry a man who was probably a drug dealer, even if he wasn't a convict.

"What's wrong?" he asked gently.

She couldn't tell him all that. Not now. She looked up into his dark eyes and knew that it wouldn't matter. Whatever he was, she was already in love with him. It was far too late for second thoughts. Even if they had only a little time together, surely that was better than having no memories of love at all?

"Nothing's wrong," she lied. She got to her feet. "I'm game if you are."

He took her waist in his lean, strong hands and looked down into her soft green eyes. "You're taking me on faith," he said quietly. "I know you suspect that I'm not what I seem. We've danced around it, but I know you were with Marquez last night. And I know where you were, Glory."

She felt numb. She didn't want to have to think about his nocturnal activities. She wanted to marry him. She wanted to live with him. Her face reflected her troubled thoughts.

"You didn't know where Marquez was going, did you?" he asked slowly.

She took the opening he offered her. "No. He said we were going for a drive."

He pursed his lips. "Did he tell you why he was watching the warehouse in Comanche Wells?"

"Oh, yes," she agreed, lying through her teeth. "He said there was a deal going on to smuggle illegal immigrants into the county and hide them in that warehouse until they could be taken to safe houses."

He felt a weight lift from him. So Marquez wasn't on his case. He was working something totally different and had probably suspected Rodrigo was part of an immigrant smuggling enterprise. It made him feel less threatened.

"Rodrigo," she said gently. "You aren't getting mixed up in something that's against the law, are you?" she asked worriedly.

He sighed. He couldn't tell her the truth. "Will it help if I give you my solemn word that from now on, I'll never step outside the law?"

Her eyes were beautiful, radiant, full of dreams coming true. "Will you?" she asked and sounded breathless.

He smiled. "Yes."

"But I would have married you even if you were mixed up in something illegal, Rodrigo," she said gently. "Although I'd hope that you'd give it up, for me."

He felt like a boy on his first date. He started smiling and couldn't stop.

"I promise that I'll never hurt you. And I'll protect you from anyone who means you harm. If we're married, we can share a bedroom, and nobody will get near you at night. I'll take care of you."

Her heart flew. She smiled. Her face lit up. "I'll take care of you, too," she said impishly.

He chuckled. "You will? How kind of you."

She hugged him, impulsively, laying her cheek against his broad chest in perfect safety. "In my whole life," she said softly, "I've never felt as safe as I do when I'm with you."

That made him feel even more guilty, but he didn't let it show. He folded her close. "That's how I want you to feel."

He savored the warm contact, thinking how easily he could have lost her to Marco's insanity, could still lose her to violence. He wondered exactly what she'd seen that had put her life in danger. He meant to find out. But not today.

After a minute, he eased her out of his arms. "We'd better get going."

"What about Consuelo?" she asked suddenly, worried.

His eyes darkened. "We'll pretend she knew nothing about it and bide our time."

"Do you think she really was willing to let her son kill me?"

He looked uncomfortable. "I don't know, Glory," he said honestly. "I don't think she wanted him to."

"Neither do I. He belongs to the Serpientes gang," she added. "They don't forgive mistakes."

He cocked his head as he studied her. "No, they don't." He wondered if Marquez had told her about that. How else would she know about a big city street gang?

"He may not live long enough to face charges."

"True enough."

"Poor Consuelo."

He tugged a long lock of blond hair. "You're still concerned about last night, aren't you?" he murmured.

He meant the drug drop. She reached up and put her fingers over his hard mouth. "I don't care what you are, what you do," she said huskily. "I only know that I...I care about you, and I trust you. It won't matter. None of it will matter."

He caught his breath audibly. She thought he was a criminal and she didn't care. She wanted him, no matter what. It was very humbling.

"One day, it might," he said honestly.

"Then we'll face that day together, when it comes," she said stubbornly.

He smiled gently. "I knew you were special the first time I saw you, when you drove me up a wall joking about the can can."

"You didn't like me very much."

"Actually I did," he replied. "And I admired you. It wasn't hard to notice that you didn't let the limp keep you down. You have a strong will, and a good heart."

She wanted to ask about the blonde woman, the one he cared for. Maybe there had been a true breakup there. But she was a coward. She didn't really want to know. She'd make him love her, somehow. She knew she could, if she tried. She'd keep her secret about the baby and about her real job, and go forward day by day.

THEY WERE MARRIED IN a small chapel by the village priest. He didn't speak English, but Rodrigo's native tongue was Spanish, so they got by. She hadn't asked about rings, but Rodrigo produced one at the ceremony and slid it onto her ring finger. The wedding ring was a complex embossed band with white and yellow gold in its pattern. The companion band was equally detailed and contained a large diamond. It must have cost a fortune. She wanted to protest, but it was too late. It was a little snug on her finger. She wondered, and hated herself for it, if he'd bought that set for someone else—that blonde woman, perhaps.

"They're beautiful," she said as they drove back across the border.

"What?"

"My rings," she replied, glancing at him. "However did you get them so quickly?"

"I've had them for a few months," he said noncommittally.

She hated them. She wanted to wrench them off her hand and throw them out the window. That would never do. He was grieving for that blonde woman and her child. But if Glory could be patient, perhaps she could make him love her. Then, then, she'd ask about the wedding and engagement rings. When she could safely tell him about the child she was certain she was carrying, he might buy her a new set of rings, purchased just for her.

CONSUELO WAS IN THE kitchen when they got home. She'd been crying, and she looked sick. She jumped when the back door opened.

"You're all right," she exclaimed when she saw Glory. "I was so worried! When I got back, you were gone, and all I could get from the workers was that they heard sirens! Marco called me from the detention center and said he needed a lawyer. What for?"

Rodrigo didn't smile. "Marco put two bullets through Glory's bedroom door, trying to shoot her."

Consuelo seemed horrified. "No. Oh, no, he wouldn't hurt you. There's been a misunderstanding, that's all," she said firmly. "I know they've arrested him, but he said he was only trying to get your attention. It was the other boy who shot the gun. He said the policeman charged him with assault and accused him of firing the shots, but Marco doesn't have a gun, you know. He's on parole, so he'd have to go back to prison if he had a gun."

Talk about trying to live in dreams, Glory thought. Poor woman. She couldn't stop defending her son, even when he was caught red-handed.

"Besides, the police did not find a gun," Consuelo added. She stared at them and then, slowly, began to realize that Glory was wearing rings. Her eyes widened. "You are married!" she exclaimed.

Rodrigo smiled. "Yes. We went across the border."

"But you should have told me! I can make a cake and we can have a special supper." She was in total denial. She pushed back her wild, disheveled hair. "I must see if there are enough eggs…"

"Consuelo, not tonight," Rodrigo told her. "It has been a very long day for Glory. She isn't feeling well, after the excitement earlier."

The older woman looked at her and noticed the flushed cheeks, the haunted eyes. She grimaced. *"Pobrecita,"* she said softly. "I am so sorry. So sorry!"

Glory went forward and hugged her gently. "You don't ever have to apologize to me for anything," she said softly.

"Thank you for the thought. But I'd really rather just lie down and not think about eating right now. I'm very tired."

"Of course you are." Consuelo stepped back. For an instant, her eyes looked odd. Glory couldn't think of a word to describe them. But then, she smiled, and the look was gone. "Think what you would like to have, and I'll bring it to you later. Okay?"

"Okay," Glory said, smiling.

Rodrigo took her arm and walked her down the hall to her room, glaring at the sight of the bullet holes in the wood. "We need to move you into my room," he said.

"Not right now," she pleaded, laughing softly. "I'm sorry, but I really am tired. I just want to lie down for a few minutes."

"That isn't a bad idea. I have to check on the men and see how they're doing. Castillo was supposed to get them started after lunch, but I like to make sure. You'll be all right," he added, bending to kiss her softly on her mouth. "Put your cell phone in your pocket and call me if you need me."

"I don't know your number," she replied.

He held out his hand. She put her phone into it. He flipped it open and pulled up her phonebook, frowning when he saw the names there. "The San Antonio D.A.'s office?" he murmured.

"About the Fuentes case," she said easily, forcing herself not to react.

"Of course." What a coincidence, he was thinking, that both of them were under the gun because of Fuentes. He pulled up another screen, added his number, gave it a speed-dial number and handed the phone back to her. "I'm speed-dial number fifteen," he said, and started laughing. "You must spend a lot of time on the phone."

Hours every day when she was at work, but she couldn't tell him that. "I work for a temporary agency when I'm not cooking," she told him demurely. "I have regular clients that I work for."

He nodded. His mind was already on work. "I'll be back soon," he promised. He helped her onto the bed and kissed her one last time. "You look pretty, Señora Ramirez," he teased. Strange, how right it sounded.

She felt the same. She smiled up at him with her whole heart. "Señora Ramirez," she seconded with a sigh. She'd never expected to marry at all. Now she was married to a man who might be a drug smuggler. But she wasn't going to think about that today. She was going to savor being married to this sexy, fantastic man.

He winked at her from the door.

She closed her eyes and drifted off to sleep.

That night, she slept in Rodrigo's arms. It was the first night of her adult life that she'd slept well. He hadn't ap-proached her sexually, murmuring that she'd had too much excitement already for one day. Besides, he added, they had the rest of their lives for that particular pleasure.

GLORY WORKED IN THE kitchen with Consuelo, as usual, but the older woman was clearly distracted. Just about noon, the phone rang and she rushed to answer it.

"Marco?" she exclaimed. "Where are you? What? No. No! How could they have found it? Oh, that idiot boy, I warned you…!" She glanced at Glory. She was speaking Spanish. Glory was working away, apparently ignorant of what her co-worker was saying. "I will find an attorney to represent you. Yes, I understand. I will. I said I will, Marco! Don't worry, I'll find a way to get you out. Just do what they say for now. Yes. Yes. I love you."

She hung up, moving back to the stove where Glory was stirring the last batch of peaches.

"Bad news?" Glory asked.

"That idiot boy that Marco hangs out with had the pistol. He was the one who shot at your door, because he was drunk," Consuelo said. "Now he runs away and Marco is charged with breaking parole by owning a firearm. I could strangle that boy!"

Nothing was ever Marco's fault, Glory discerned. It was always somebody else who made the mistake and blamed Marco for it.

"You did not see who fired the gun?" Consuelo asked.

"Of course not, I was behind the door," Glory told her.

"Marco swears it wasn't him."

Glory was remembering Marco's threat, that he'd get her. She didn't want to mention it to Consuelo, or their good working relationship would be over. It did sting a little that Consuelo was taking up for her son who had tried to shoot Glory.

"They are holding Marco at the detention center. I must go and take him some money. Can you manage?"

"Yes," Glory assured her.

"There is only this last batch of peach preserves and then we have nothing to do until the apples come in, so it shouldn't be hard to finish," she added.

"I'll do fine. Go ahead and see about your son."

Consuelo took off her apron and smoothed her blouse over her slacks. Odd, Glory thought, those pants looked as if they were made of silk. So did the blouse. That was an expensive outfit to wear in a kitchen, surely?

"I won't be long," Consuelo assured her with a smile.

"Okay."

WHILE CONSUELO AND RODRIGO were out of the house, Glory phoned Dr. Lou Coltrain's office and got an appointment with her for that afternoon. Consuelo would surely eat lunch before she returned, and Rodrigo wouldn't mind cold cuts for lunch—she'd leave him a note, although she wouldn't mention where she was going.

It was a slow day at the clinic, so she got in to see Lou early. The tall, blonde woman doctor smiled at her as she came into the cubicle.

"Miss Barnes? I'm Lou Coltrain."

"Glad to meet you," Glory said. She sighed. "I would very much like for you to tell me that I'm not pregnant."

Lou's eyebrows arched. "Why?"

"It's an inconvenient time. And," she added reluctantly, "I have high blood pressure."

Lou was solemn. "How high?"

Glory told her.

"You're medicated?"

"Yes." She gave the dosage and strength of the capsules she took for the condition.

"Are you married?"

Glory flushed, and then laughed. "Yes. Just yesterday, in Mexico."

Lou hesitated. "You know, a blood test the day after you get married isn't going to be conclusive."

"It's been several weeks since my last period," Glory told her. "This amazing, sexy man came up on my blind side. I couldn't resist him then, and I couldn't refuse when he asked me to marry him. He really wants a child."

Lou pulled up her rolling stool and sat down. "What do you want?" she asked quietly.

Glory hesitated. "I thought I wanted my job and no complications. But now the complications are much more exciting than the job. My doctor and my boss sent me down here to get me away from stress and danger."

"I see." Lou was writing on a pad. "Your doctor's name and phone number?"

Glory gave it to her.

"You're taking a blood thinner as well as the combination hypertension and diuretic drug?"

"Yes."

"Any angina?"

"Yesterday," Glory replied.

"What triggered it?"

"A man shot at me through my bedroom door."

Lou stopped writing and gaped at her patient. "So that's what was going on! We heard the sirens, and somebody said that a shooter was loose on the Pendleton Farm. Did they catch him?"

"In the act," Glory replied with a smile. "One of them, at least."

"Why was he shooting at you?"

"I have evidence that a drug dealer conspired to commit murder," Glory told her. "I just have to live long enough to give it in court."

"All that and a baby…Miss Barnes, you are a wonder!"

"Señora," Glory corrected in a tone still filled with wonder. "Señora Ramirez."

Lou grinned. "I still remember the first time somebody called me Mrs. Coltrain. You don't quite get over the thrill, do you? Okay, let's draw some blood and then we'll talk."

HALF AN HOUR AND ONE emergency later, Lou walked back into Glory's cubicle, sat down and smiled.

"You have decisions to make."

"Am I?" Glory asked breathlessly.

"You are," Lou replied. "It could be a false positive this early, but considering the symptoms you're having, I doubt it. If you're thinking of a termination, this is the time to do it. If that's what you want."

"It isn't," Glory said at once. She hesitated. "There is a risk, isn't there?"

"Have you been taking the blood thinners regularly?"

Glory sat very still. "Yes. I didn't think...!"

"You need to see your own doctor," Lou said, trying not to sound as worried as she really was.

"I can't go back to San Antonio right now," Glory replied. "I'm a walking target if I do."

"Then I can refer you to a cardiologist who comes down here from Houston one day a week," she said. "She's very good. And she's due here tomorrow."

"That would be nice."

"Let her examine you and make recommendations. Then we'll all talk. Including your husband," she added. "He's part of this. You can't make such a decision alone."

"I may have to," Glory said sadly. "I haven't told him what I really do for a living, or how bad my health problems are."

"Is that wise?"

"Not really. But I wasn't thinking of getting pregnant when we..."

"That's the time you're supposed to think of getting pregnant," Lou reminded her. "Especially a high-risk case like yours."

"I messed up," Glory said, but she smiled. "I haven't had much family life." Because Lou was a sympathetic listener, Glory opened up and told her about the past, including her father's tragic fate.

Lou grimaced. "People who've had less trauma than you have are always blaming an abusive childhood for their problems. Look at you."

"I got lucky," Glory said. "Well, in some ways, at least." She stared at Lou. "I want this baby very much. Please tell me there's a chance...?"

"There's always a chance, however slim," Lou replied. Her expression was solemn. "But you need to speak with the cardiologist before you make a decision. It isn't sensible to lose your life bringing a child into the world."

"Tell that to Grace Grier," Glory said, tongue-in-cheek.

Lou laughed. "My husband did. It was useless, of course. Grace was a very determined lady."

"So am I. I graduated law school with honors," she added.

"I'm not surprised."

LOU SET UP THE APPOINTMENT for Glory. She'd have to figure some way to sneak out of the house, she told herself, to get to it without arousing suspicion. She didn't know it, but that problem was about to solve itself.

The first thing she noticed when she walked into the house was how quiet it was. No clocks ticking. No sounds from the kitchen. No water running. Nothing. It was like walking into a tomb. She wondered why her mind had come up with such an analogy as she leaned on her cane and frowned, listening.

Seconds later, the analogy slammed the door behind her.

"At last," came a familiar voice. "Finally I have you where I want you, alone, with no hope of escape!"

11

GLORY GRIPPED THE HEAD of her cane tightly in her hand. She hadn't hung around with policemen and deputy sheriffs and Texas Rangers for the past few years without learning some basic self-defense techniques. She hoped they were going to save her life, because she heard a pistol cock behind her.

"Turn around," the voice growled. "I want you to see who's killing you!"

Glory's heart was racing, but she wasn't going down without a fight. She was carrying her great-grandfather's cane, which he'd used to kill rattlesnakes. It was oiled, heavy and deadly. She leaned on the cane, as if it were painful to turn around. She moved very slowly, until she had a glimpse of fabric in the corner of her eye. Then, suddenly, she lifted the cane, pivoted quickly on her good leg, and swung the heavy cane with all her might. There was a harsh cry.

The gun, the cane and Consuelo all went flying across the floor. Glory didn't hesitate. She dived for the gun on the floor, grabbed it and aimed it at the erstwhile cook, who was still lying on the floor, trying to figure out what had happened to her.

Glory sat up, her breathing steadier now. She scooted back to the table where she'd dropped her purse and tugged it down onto the floor beside her. She felt for her phone, never taking her eyes off Consuelo, who was stirring.

She opened the flip phone with her free hand and dialed 911. When the dispatcher's voice came on the line, she gave her information very calmly and asked for assistance.

"Ma'am, is there a gun involved?"

"Yes, there is," Glory replied tightly, "and I'm aiming it at the woman who just tried to kill me."

"We'll have a unit there in no time. Please stay on the line."

Consuelo turned on the floor. She was sitting now, feeling the lump on her head that she'd sustained when Glory knocked her into the wall. She gaped at her own gun being aimed dead at her.

Glory didn't blink. "Move and you die," she told the older woman.

Consuelo began to see her predicament. "Oh, it's just you!" she exclaimed. "Thank God! I had word that someone was going to kill me!"

"Nice try," Glory replied.

"They'll believe me if I sound sincere enough," Consuelo purred. She started to get up.

"I wouldn't," Glory replied. She cocked the gun, trying to look confident when she knew she'd never hit Consuelo even if she could manage to hold the heavy thing steady enough to fire it.

The bluff must have worked, because Consuelo hesitated.

Glory was praying she wouldn't have to shoot. She'd probably hit everything in the room except Consuelo, with her bad aim. She couldn't even handle a .22, and this was a big .45 Colt automatic.

Her hand trembled holding the gun. Consuelo looked at it with increasing interest. Just as she worried that Consuelo had her pegged and was going to get up and charge her, sirens became audible and, in seconds, they came screaming up into the front yard. Car doors slammed.

Cash Grier came running in the back door, flanked by two of his officers.

"Looks like your goose is cooked," Glory told the older woman.

"It's all just a misunderstanding," Consuelo said with a shaky smile. "I had a call that someone meant to kill me and Glory came in unexpectedly."

Cash moved toward Glory. "That how it happened?" he asked her.

She handed him the .45. "Not quite. I walked in, she came up behind me and told me to turn around so that I could see who was killing me."

"That's a lie!" Consuelo exclaimed. "I had a call...!"

She stopped, while one of the other officers tugged her to her feet and handcuffed her.

"Yes, you did have a call," Cash agreed. "From Fuentes, telling you to carry out your assignment."

Consuelo gaped at him.

"Didn't I think to mention that we wiretapped your phone?" he added.

Consuelo's dark eyes flashed. She smiled coldly at Glory, showing her true colors at last. "Maybe I missed," she said, "but Fuentes will just get somebody else to collect the bounty!"

"I wouldn't bet on it," Cash told her. "We had his phone wiretapped, too."

"Brilliant," Glory said.

Cash helped her up while Consuelo was taken, still cursing, out to the squad car. "We get lucky sometimes," he said. "But then, we get problems as well. Marquez did get a warrant to wiretap Fuentes's phone," he added with a grimace. "But Fuentes has jumped bail. Nobody knows where he is."

Glory felt weak in the knees. She sat down in a chair at the kitchen table. "So Consuelo was right. He'll send somebody else."

"We've got a deal working," Cash said. "I can't tell you the details, but it involves a big shipment of a very illegal product. Fuentes has had problems with his distributors. If he loses this load, we won't have to go after him. His distributors will take him out for us."

"Can I help?" she asked.

"Sure. Don't play with guns," he said, popping the clip out of the .45. "I heard about your target practice sessions."

"Yes, well, I would have probably hit something if I'd fired that," she said, indicating the gun.

"Good thing you bluff well," he added. "You okay?"

She nodded. "You know, I came down here to get away from stress."

"We've removed the hit woman," Cash said. "And we're working on Fuentes's operation. With any luck, we'll have you back in San Antonio in no time. If you really want to go," he added. "We heard about the marriage, too," he added with a grin.

"How?" she exclaimed. "I haven't told anyone!"

Cash looked uneasy. He frowned. "Funny. I can't remember how I found out."

This was suspicious. Something was going on that she wasn't being told about.

"Who told you?" she persisted.

He was beginning to look hunted when a truck roared up out front and a door slammed. Rodrigo came in the door like a tornado. He took in the scene, dark eyes blazing with concern. His chambray shirt was stained with sweat. His black hair fell damply over his forehead. It was a hot day.

"I heard the sirens out in the fields. What happened?" he asked.

"Just a little problem with the hired help," Glory said, trying to lighten the look on his face.

"Can you translate that?" he asked, approaching her.

She shifted uncomfortably on the chair. Her hip was killing her. "When I came home, Consuelo was waiting for me with that gun." She indicated it, stuck in Cash's belt.

"Consuelo?" He looked absolutely shocked. He went down on one knee in front of Glory, his lean, warm hands stroking her arms. "Did she hit you? Were you hurt?" he asked worriedly.

It was like going to heaven. She loved that look in his eyes that was part concern for her and part fury against the person who'd threatened her. She felt safe.

"Luckily your wife is handy with this cane," Cash interjected. He lifted the cane, felt its weight and frowned. "It's heavy."

"It was my great-grandfather's," Glory told him. "Back in his day, men oiled their canes, so they were heavier and could be used for self-protection. He used to kill rattlers with that. Good thing for me it was sturdy, because it only took one swing to send Consuelo into the wall headfirst."

"My brave girl," Rodrigo said, and his eyes were warm and soft and full of pride in her.

She wanted to believe that his concern was real, she wanted it so badly. She flung herself into his arms and held on for dear life, savoring the strength of his embrace.

"You had to save yourself, again," he said ruefully. "That's twice, in a handful of days. Two times too many. I have to take better care of you, Señora Ramirez."

Cash noticed the rings Glory was wearing. "That's a pretty

set of wedding rings," he said, hoping to dig himself out of the hole he'd almost fallen into.

"Oh, you saw them," Glory remarked over Rodrigo's broad shoulder. She relaxed. So did Cash.

"I'd never have suspected Consuelo as a hit woman." Rodrigo cursed, still holding Glory close. "I should have known! If Marco was in on it, Consuelo had to be."

"She's got a rap sheet as long as my leg," Cash told him. "I gather you don't do background checks here."

"For a cook?" Rodrigo mused. "Get real."

"I noticed that she was wearing silk slacks and blouses," Glory commented. "I thought it was rather odd for working in a kitchen."

"I should have noticed that, too," Rodrigo mused.

She only smiled. She didn't want to hurt his feelings by re-marking that a farm laborer would hardly know silk when he saw it.

Rodrigo saw that look and had to fight an angry response. Of course, she wasn't supposed to know that he was any-thing other than what he pretended to be. He glanced at Cash.

"Glory will have to fill out a report, won't she?"

"Yes, if we're going to charge Consuelo. She's also going to have to fill one out on Marco—I let it slide because she was so upset. I never imagined she'd be doing two of them!"

"I don't mind," Glory told Cash. "Tell me what to do," she added, pretending that she didn't know the procedure.

Cash walked her through it, trying not to laugh.

"I'll drive her over to the magistrate's court and let her swear out warrants for mother and son," Cash told Rodrigo. "I expect you're going to be busy trying to find a new cook."

"Pronto," Rodrigo agreed, helping Glory to her feet. "We've got shipments to get out, and this is the last of the peaches. Pity Consuelo had to reveal herself now. If she'd waited a few days, it would have been great for the farm."

"I don't think the farm was exactly her priority," Glory murmured. "I'll do my part as soon as I get through helping Chief Grier lock Marco and Consuelo up for a while."

"Talk to the judge," Rodrigo advised Cash. "Try to get her to set bail upward of a million dollars on each of them."

"I'll do my best," Cash agreed.

"You're sure you're all right?" Rodrigo asked, because Glory's color was high.

"I'm just fine. A little unsettled by all the excitement, that's all," she reassured him. Her hip hurt, and her heart was beating far too fast. She hoped she wouldn't disgrace herself by passing out.

He nodded. "You'll bring her home?" he asked Cash.

"Of course."

"Then, I'll get on the phone and start looking for a cook," Rodrigo replied.

"You might try Angel Martinez's wife," Glory said. "She's a great cook, according to Angel."

He gave her a long look. "They're probably both illegal."

"You don't know that," she told him firmly.

He searched her eyes and then, finally, smiled. "All right. But if I end up in federal prison for harboring illegals, you'll have to bail me out."

"Nobody is going to need bailing out except Consuelo and her son, and you can quote me," Cash assured him with a grin. "Angel and his family are going to be just fine." Fortunately he didn't look at Glory when he said that. The two of them had called in favors to get Angel's case heard, hopefully with good results. Meanwhile, the man had three children to support, and his wife didn't work.

"What will she do with the kids?" Rodrigo asked with some concern. "None of them are older than seven. She can't leave them alone while she works over here."

"She can bring the children with her," Glory said to Rodrigo, smiling. "We'll keep them busy while we cook."

Rodrigo gave her a long look, but he didn't comment.

SHE AND CASH STOPPED by the magistrate's office, took out a warrant for Marco for aggravated assault and one for Consuelo's arrest on attempted murder. Cash added one for possession of a firearm, because Consuelo had a criminal record and wasn't allowed to own a gun. Glory filled out reports and chatted. The Magistrate was fascinated by the story, especially her foiling of the murder plot on her own.

"These drug lords are getting far too powerful," he commented. "But where there's a demand, there will be a supply. That applies to most everything, but especially drugs." He shook his head. "When I was a boy—" he looked over his glasses at her and grinned under his gray hair "—we didn't have drugs in the schools. I have to admit, I never even knew anyone who used them. But that was in the fifties. The whole world has changed since then. We watched Hopalong Cassidy and Roy Rogers at the theaters, and then Superman on black and white TV. We had wholesome heroes to emulate. It seems to me that in the modern world, far too many boys admire drug dealers, and their goal in life is to grow up and go to prison." He shook his head. "Somehow, we're losing an entire generation of productive citizens, and drugs are mostly responsible. Quick money, flashy cars, no working your way into a better job and a stiff prison sentence when you get caught. How is that appealing?"

"Don't ask me," Glory replied. "I spend most of my time helping them get into prison."

"I have heard about your record," the magistrate said with a smile. "You're a trouper, Miss Barnes." He hesitated. "I knew your father. He was a good man. It hurt us all to see him unjustly punished for something he didn't do."

"Thank you for that," she said, fighting tears. "I did clear his name, even if it was years too late. His conviction was why I studied law."

"I thought it might be. I'm glad to have had the opportunity to meet you. Now that Blake Kemp is our county D.A., you might consider coming back here to fight crime." He looked at her over his glasses again. "I could look for some silver bullets and a mask...?"

She laughed. "I could never pass for The Lone Ranger," she assured him. "I'm too short."

"Still," he said wistfully. "It's a thought."

"MOST MAGISTRATES ARE rather somber, I've found," she told Cash on the way home.

"Not Lionel," he replied. "He's the town character. I think the modern term is 'eccentric.'"

"Does he do eccentric things?"

"Depends on your point of view," Cash replied. "I suppose some people would feel uncomfortable with a wolf in the house, but he's a bachelor. I guess he can do what he pleases."

"A wolf? A real wolf?" she exclaimed.

He nodded. "She's a beauty, too. He found her on the highway and went through the usual maddening channels of bureaucracy trying to help her. Vets can't treat wild animals, you know, you have to locate a certified rehabilitator. There aren't a lot of them, and many hurt animals die while you're looking for one who will answer the phone." He glanced at her. "Most of them are so overworked that they cringe every time the phone rings. Well, anyway, Lionel took the wolf in and nursed her back to health, and then took the course that certifies you as a wildlife rehabilitator. He specializes in wolves. So he was allowed to keep the wolf, which lost a leg as the result of the accident. It could never go back into the wild, you see. He takes it around to the elementary school and gives lectures on wolves. It's a very gentle wolf. The kids love it. It's on a leash, of course. He may be eccentric but he's not crazy. All it would take is one little boy who smells strongly of bologna…"

"Oh, stop!" she exclaimed, laughing. "That's terrible!"

"It could be. But he's a responsible pet owner. He even has a city 'wolf license.'"

"Nobody gets a wolf license!" she scoffed.

"You can get one if you know the chief of police and he has ties to the city fathers." He looked suitably modest.

"Yes, but that's only because the city fathers are scared to death of you," she pointed out. "You're too dangerous for people to risk offending you."

"Why, thank you," he replied good-naturedly.

"Oh, you're a local legend all over Texas," she confided. "I understand that our state attorney general threatens people with you."

"Only federal people," he said. "And only if they make him very angry. I am, after all, his cousin."

"Really!" She was impressed.

He smiled. "I have ties to strange places," he mused. "Like one of our feds who works undercover. He's got a price on his head in every country on earth except this one. He's helped put away some of the bigger drug cartel members, not to mention running down a child killer in Central America on horseback through a jungle. Not an easy task on good days. It was pouring rain."

"Who is this madman?" she asked, laughing.

He looked odd. He cleared his throat. "Well, I never knew his name," he lied. "He was undercover, you know."

She smiled. "He must be on everyone's list of people to call in dire situations."

"He is."

"I wish you could have him come down here and take Fuentes into a jungle and do God-knows-what with him," she muttered. "He's still out there, and I'm still in his sights, figuratively speaking."

"We're working on that. Be patient. And be careful," he added quietly. "You're in some dangerous company at that farm."

Her heart jumped up into her throat. "What...do you mean?"

He cursed under his breath. He hadn't wanted to say anything, but it was better if she knew the truth. She might let her guard down and be killed. "One or two of your workers have rap sheets, mostly for physical assault. One took out a cop in Dallas and they could never prove it—he killed the one witness who saw it happen." He pulled up into the yard of the farm, cut the engine and turned to look at her. She was pale. "That cane makes a good weapon, but people will hear about how you used it. It won't work a second time. I'd like to take you out to our target range and teach you how to shoot properly." He held up a hand when she started to speak. "It's not rocket science. It can be taught. I'll send for you Saturday morning, about nine. Marquez will be home, and he's got a nice little .32 revolver that you can use. It doesn't kick as much as a .45, and it will fit your hand better."

"He tried to teach me already," she protested.

"Marquez tried to teach his mother," Cash said, glowering. "He taught her how to shoot crows."

"Excuse me?" She was shocked. Barbara, Marquez's foster mother, adored crows!

"He was explaining to her how the gun kicked and said she had to compensate. He didn't say how. She thought he meant she should hold the nose up higher when she fired, so she did, and she hit a crow. Fortunately she only singed his tail feathers. He kept going. But now they call her the Crow Crippler, and she won't touch a gun anymore."

She burst out laughing. It sounded like Rick, who wasn't the world's best instructor, even if he was enthusiastic.

"So I'll teach you," Cash replied.

"Okay. My liability insurance is paid up," she agreed. "But do make sure no squad cars park within range of the gun."

He grinned. "I'll do that. You take care of yourself. Stay close to the house, keep your cell phone in your pocket and don't go anywhere alone. Not even outside, especially at night."

She bit her lower lip. For a few minutes, she'd forgotten her predicament. "You know things that you aren't sharing."

He nodded. "I can't share them. Just watch your back. I'll have Marquez pick you up about nine Saturday morning. And don't tell him I said anything about why I'm doing the teaching, instead of him. He has a real attitude problem with authority."

She laughed. "I know. I'll keep quiet. Thanks, Chief."

"We're all in the same racket," he told her. "We have to look out for each other."

"Yes, we do."

SHE WALKED INTO THE HOUSE and closed the door, nervous and uneasy. Cash Grier knew something about someone on the property, someone with a police record who had killed a cop and was still on the run. She only knew one man who looked tough enough to do that; her husband. It was curious that he hadn't done a background check on Consuelo, or had Jason Pendleton do it. What if Rodrigo was working for Fuentes, and he was asked to kill Glory since Consuelo had flubbed it?

She felt as if her world had come crashing down on her head. Two attempts on her life, two escapes. She'd been lucky that Marco had fired into the door and not the wall. She'd been lucky that she could use her cane to deflect Consuelo's pistol. But if there was another attempt, by her own husband, what was she going to do?

She noticed that Cash hadn't mentioned that her husband could help protect her. Was there a reason for that? Did he know that Rodrigo had been involved in that drug deal in Comanche Wells; had Marquez told him?

She felt so tired. Her life had become impossibly complicated. On top of everything else, she'd forgotten to take her blood pressure pill and her blood thinner. She ground her teeth together. She was carrying a child and taking dangerous drugs that she had to have if she didn't want to end up in the hospital. If only she could go to San Antonio and see her own doctor!

Then she remembered her appointment with the cardiologist tomorrow. She was going to need an excuse to go to town. She'd manage something, if Carla Martinez worked out as the cook.

She took her medicine, hoping it wouldn't harm the tiny life inside her, and then she went back into the kitchen to work.

An hour later, Carla Martinez came to the back door with three children, two girls and a boy. The boy, Hernando, was the oldest at seven.

"*¿Podemos entrar?*" she asked hesitantly.

Obviously she spoke no English. Glory was glad that she'd studied her languages. "*Sí, entre,*" she invited with a grin. "*¡Bienvenidos! Me gusta mucho que puede ayudarme.*"

"*De nada, señora,*" she replied respectfully.

Glory showed her what needed doing, then she seated the children at the table and gave them peanut butter and cookies to eat and cups of milk to go with it, all except for the youngest girl, who was only three. She laughed up at Glory with beautiful black eyes in a perfect little face surrounded by thick, long, black hair. Glory couldn't resist. She picked the child up and carried her along to the sink where she managed to rinse dishes with one hand while she cooed to the little girl.

Rodrigo came in unexpectedly, to translate for Glory. He stopped in the doorway and watched, fascinated, the easy way she handled the child and the work. She was laughing, happy, delighted with the cuddly little girl. He thought how nice it would be to have a child. Then, abruptly, he remembered Bernadette in his arms, hugging him and asking what would she do without him? He loved the child so much. It had hurt terribly when she and her mother went to live with Colby Lane. His expression reflected his misery.

Glory sensed a presence, and turned, meeting Rodrigo's taut face and wounded eyes across the room. She didn't even need to speak. She knew what he was feeling, and why. In that moment, she knew that she'd never be able to tell him about their child. And now, she wondered if he was going to complete Consuelo's assignment and take Glory out of Fuentes's path.

He saw the odd look on her face and frowned. "Something wrong?" he asked.

She composed herself. "Nothing. We're just getting started."

"I thought you might need a translator," he began.

She laughed. "No, but thank you. I'm quite fluent in Spanish. I have to be, in my work." She could have bitten her tongue for that unwise comment.

"Your work?"

"I'm with a temporary agency," she said at once. "I have lots of clients who need someone bilingual."

"I see." He glanced at Carla and asked her, in Spanish, how things were going.

She was ecstatic about Señora Ramirez and the job. She was going to love working here.

At least someone was happy, he thought as he glanced toward Glory. She seemed different all of a sudden. Had Cash spilled the beans? He studied her intently, and then he realized that she'd be more forthcoming if she knew his secret. But something was bothering her. Perhaps she was afraid that Consuelo would make bond; or that Fuentes really would send someone else.

He didn't think the drug lord would have time. He, Castillo, and another man were going to move a shipment across the border on a makeshift pontoon bridge made of oil drums on Saturday. It was the biggest shipment Fuentes had handled, pure cocaine, and lots of it. Little did Fuentes know that his newest distributor was going to have a lot of help. Fuentes was going down. The man was scum. The young gang member who'd been feeding him information said that Fuentes had killed boys for little more than protesting his rough treatment. He had no respect for anyone around him. He'd beaten his own mother, in front of the gang member, because she'd burned his eggs. The boy said nobody wanted to work for a monster like that, regardless of how much they got paid.

He wondered how Glory was going to react when she found out the truth about his role in this operation. She was a sweet woman, but she was uneducated and unsophisticated and plain. She'd never fit into his world. He'd made a terrible mistake when he'd married her. It had been a spur of the moment thing, to spite Sarina for throwing him over. But all it had done was make him aware of how miserable he was.

He couldn't spend the rest of his life tied to this prehistoric woman. He was going to have to approach the subject of a divorce.

But first, he had to help bring down Fuentes. That might save Glory's life. When all this was over, he wanted to know how she'd gotten into this mess. Fuentes didn't send hired killers after temporary workers without good reason. She said she'd seen something illegal, but he wanted to know what. Sadly he had no time for interrogation right now. He had a job to do.

12

GLORY WENT TO SEE THE cardiologist the next day, leaving Carla in charge. She'd asked Angel to keep the children so that she could work without diversions, and Rodrigo had given him a half day. Glory had told her husband that she was due for a dental appointment in town.

Her coolness toward him had resulted in his moving into his old bedroom. He hadn't even blinked when she suggested it, because her hip was hurting and she'd keep him awake. It was a thin excuse and he saw through it at once. He noticed that she wouldn't meet his eyes. Something was wrong. He was sure it had something to do with her having seen him at the site of a drug deal. Probably Marquez, damn him, had told her that Rodrigo was a criminal. She'd denied that Marquez had told her anything, but he doubted that was true. He wished he had time to sort out his feelings for his temporary wife. He didn't. The job was his top priority at the moment. Later, he and Glory could have a long talk about their relationship. But he was certain that he wanted their marriage to end.

Glory felt guilty for deceiving Rodrigo, but deeper in her mind was the fear that her husband might be Consuelo's replacement. He was involved in drug dealing, she knew that already. It wasn't far to consider him capable of murder. She couldn't understand why she couldn't just put Rodrigo out of her mind and let Cash Grier deal with his illegal activities. It sounded easy. It wasn't. Part of her still hungered for Rodrigo, wanted him, ached to hold him. Every time she thought of the little thing in her belly, she felt sorrow like a rock inside. She didn't know what to do. Her whole life had changed since Cash Grier had made that remark about the rap sheets on people working at the farm. She knew he meant Rodrigo, and she had a horrible feeling that he was mixed up in something much more sinister than just drug dealing.

THE CARDIOLOGIST, A WOMAN, was small and energetic and brilliant. She examined Glory, had her technician perform an EKG, and then, a few minutes later, an echocardiogram. The tests allowed her to look closely at Glory's heart and make sure there weren't any blockages around her heart. When Glory related her eating habits and her determination to keep her weight down, the physician was impressed.

The only thing was the blood thinners and the medicine for hypertension that Glory had been taking, of necessity. If there were any problem with the fetus, the inability of her body to stop the bleeding could cost her the child. In fact, her medical condition could lead to early detachment of the placenta or to spontaneous abortion even without medical intervention.

"If it had been a planned pregnancy," the cardiologist said gently, "we could have prescribed alternative drugs that would present less danger to the child. However, considering the severity of your hypertension," she added sadly, "the risk to you and your child is greatly enlarged. Most physicians would recommend an immediate abortion. You could die trying to carry this child."

Glory felt sick all over as the reality of her condition hit her. She put her head down, fighting dizziness and nausea. "No," she moaned. "No, I can't. I won't." She lifted her wet eyes to the cardiologist. "You don't understand. I'm a person of faith. It goes against everything I believe...."

The other woman put a sympathetic hand on her shoulder. "I won't force you to make such a decision. But you'll have to be very closely monitored. I'll want to see you at least twice a month. I'll modify your drug therapy."

"I could stop taking the blood thinners," she said at once.

The cardiologist winced. "Considering your medical records, I can't advise that. I don't see any obvious blockages, that's true. But if your own physician was concerned about plaque or a possible clot after what he diagnosed as a mild heart attack…" She stopped. "If you'd had the heart catheterization…"

"I had too much stress on me at the time, and too busy a schedule, to agree to it," Glory said heavily. "Isn't hindsight wonderful?"

"The blood thinners would prevent a small blockage from producing a heart attack or stroke," she told Glory. "Those, as well as the blood pressure medicine with the diuretic, you must continue. As I said, I'll prescribe drugs that will be the least harmful to the child. I would prefer to send you to Houston and let them do a heart catheterization, just to make sure there are no blockages that don't show up in these tests. But this is not the time. You have too much stress already." She paused. "You want the child very much, yes?"

"Yes," Glory said at once, although she hadn't been that sure when she walked into the office. A child of her own. She could be a mother. She could have someone of her very own blood to live with and love and care for. The temptation was worth any risk. The fact that the child's father had criminal tendencies was something she forced to the back of her mind.

"Then we will do what we can," Dr. Warner assured her. "Dr. Coltrain should send you to an obstetrician."

Glory hesitated. "She wants to. But it would be too risky to see one in San Antonio, where I live," she began. "There's something very dangerous going on where I'm working. That would be another stress to add to what I'm already carrying. You see, I'm an attorney. A man I'm prosecuting for conspiracy to commit murder is trying to have me killed. I'm the only witness who heard him confess to the crime. I am hopeful that the case will resolve itself soon. In the meantime, I must avoid more worry."

"I understand. It is fortunate that you are in the very early stages of pregnancy. You can have Lou Coltrain get in touch with me if you start having more problems with the heart. I don't see any obvious problem," she added quickly. "But if your physician in San Antonio diagnosed a heart attack, we must be cautious. If you start having pain or pressure in your chest, and down your left arm or up into your jaw, especially if you also have nausea and a cold sweat, call for an ambulance at once. Don't brave it out and think you can overcome it."

Glory smiled. "I won't. I promise. I've been doing better since I came here, except for someone trying to kill me twice in one week," she added, tongue-in-cheek.

Dr. Warner's eyebrows arched. "Perhaps you might consider a less stressful profession," she said. "Your job and your physical condition are a bad mix."

"So I've been told," she replied. "But right now, I can't do much about it. It's the only job I have."

"If you need me, all you have to do is call. I can have my husband fly me down here on ten minutes' notice. He is retired now, but he flew for a major airline for many years. Now he teaches flying in Houston," she added with a chuckle.

"I'll take you up on that, if I have to. Thank you."

"I'll write the prescriptions and have them brought to the clerk's desk while you're checking out," she added. "If you have problems adjusting to the drugs, or any reactions to them, all you have to do is call. We'll find the least danger-ous ones we can. In the meantime, please try to avoid any further stress."

"I will."

A FEW MINUTES LATER, Glory climbed into her old car and started it, feeling emotional. Apparently she wasn't going to drop dead immediately, but she was under far too much stress. Living in the house with a man she no longer trusted, but whom she still loved, was her biggest problem.

The old clunker protested as she put it into gear. She missed her new car, garaged at the Pendletons's for safekeep-ing. She wouldn't drive it to work because it might become a target for disgruntled gang members she prosecuted. She loved it too much, and she hadn't dared bring it down here, where she was playing at being a day laborer. It would raise serious questions about her economic status.

At least, she thought as she pulled out of the parking lot, the baby was safe for the time being. She just had to be very careful that she didn't hurt herself. She smiled as she saw years of joy ahead with her baby.

IT WAS JUST LUNCHTIME when Glory walked into the kitchen. Carla grinned at her. Angel was sitting at the table with the three children, all of them munching cookies. The littlest girl laughed and launched herself at Glory, who picked her up and hugged her close.

"Is there enough for me, too?" she teased when she saw the huge salad on the table.

"¡Como no!" Carla chuckled. "Siéntese."

She sat, and Carla spooned salad into a bowl for her and put the bottle of salad dressing on the table, along with a fork and napkin.

"Rodrigo?" she asked, because there was no place set for him.

Carla looked worried. She and her husband exchanged a quick look.

"Has something happened to him?" Glory asked at once, horrified.

"No!" Angel lowered his voice. "No, of course not, señora," he assured her. "It is just…well, he and that Castillo and Castillo's friend climbed into the truck and drove out of town," he added. "Señor Ramirez said he and the others had an important job to do, and that they wouldn't be back until Sunday. He said to be sure and tell you to stay close to the house."

She stirred her salad without paying it much attention. Rodrigo was gone, then. She guessed that Fuentes had sent a message and her husband and his cronies went to a meeting of some sort. She had until the end of the weekend to decide what to do. Not long to arrange to protect herself from a third assassination attempt.

"Something is wrong?" Angel asked, concerned, when she didn't start eating.

She noted that several pair of eyes were watching her. She forced a laugh. "No, of course not," she lied. She tasted the salad. "Very good," she told Carla. *"Muy sabroso."* Carla smiled and turned to help her youngest daughter with a taco.

MARQUEZ DROVE HER TO the city police department's firing range on Saturday morning. He was quiet and distracted.

"You're hiding something," she accused.

He glanced at her, grinned and shrugged. "Work problems."

Her eyebrows arched. "Drug-related?" she fished.

He grimaced.

She nodded and sighed. "My husband," she muttered.

"Don't do that," he grumbled. "Prosecuting attorneys aren't supposed to be able to read minds."

"I don't. It was a logical conclusion."

"You sound very calm about it."

She turned her house key in her hands. "I would scream and pound my fists on the dash, but people might get the wrong idea if they noticed."

He laughed in spite of himself. "So they might."

She glanced at him. "Rodrigo, Castillo and the other man have gone away for the weekend," she told him.

"I know."

Her eyebrows arched. "You're tailing them."

"I am not." He turned onto the dirt road that led to the firing range. "But some friends of mine are."

She felt very old all of a sudden. "He's involved in Fuentes's operation, isn't he?"

He didn't answer.

"You don't have to protect me," she said heavily. "I recognized him when we watched the warehouse over at Comanche Wells. In fact, he even admitted to me that he was there—but not why."

"You're smart."

"Not really," she replied in a subdued tone. "I'm pregnant."

The truck almost went into the ditch, and she cried out, stunned.

"Sorry," he gritted, righting it. He stopped it in the middle of the road and looked at her, seeing the tragic expression she was no longer able to hide. "Do you love him?"

She didn't want to admit that. Her gaze fell to her lap. "Yes," she said after a minute. "I thought age brought wisdom. Not in my case."

He was frowning. "Glory, your heart…?"

"I've seen a cardiologist, and Dr. Lou Coltrain," she said quickly. "She's referring me to an obstetrician as soon as my life is out of danger from the assassin."

"But is it safe?" he persisted, frowning.

She felt the question like a knife. "I have to take blood thinners, so that I don't have another heart attack. The cardiologist said that if I have any problems with the pregnancy, that could be dangerous. She changed my drugs. I'm just starting the new ones."

"I'm so sorry," he said, and meant it.

Her hands clenched on the key. "He can't know," she said stiffly.

"Things may change for the better soon," he began.

She looked at him. "He can't know," she emphasized.

"Okay. It's your business. But if you ever need help," he added gently.

She smiled. "Thanks."

CASH GRIER WAS IN CIVILIAN clothes, his ponytail tied neatly with a string as he waited for them on the firing line.

He glanced at Marquez, who was also sporting a ponytail, then at Glory who had her hair in a neat braid. "There's always one oddball in a crowd," he noted, indicating her hairstyle.

"I am not odd," she told him. "I simply have better taste in hairstyles."

Cash scoffed. He aimed at the target and sent six rounds straight into the smallest circle.

"Showoff," Marquez muttered.

Cash grinned. "I'm the chief of police," he reminded the detective. "I have to provide a good example for my men."

"It may take a blackjack to provide a good example for Kilraven," he replied, tongue-in-cheek. "Or didn't you know that he was at the FBI office in San Antonio yesterday pumping Jon Blackhawk for information on Fuentes's distribution network?"

"He what?" Cash growled.

"Who's Kilraven?" Glory wanted to know.

"The officer who saved you from Marco the other day," Cash reminded her.

"Oh. The one who almost crashed the drug deal in Comanche Wells," she recalled.

"Exactly," Marquez added. He glanced at Cash, who looked furious. "You might as well cheer up. You hired him as your gang specialist. Gangs distribute drugs. It isn't that far a leap to investigating Fuentes."

Cash expelled the clip from his automatic violently and refilled it. "I like individual initiative, until it becomes anarchy."

"Kilraven isn't an anarchist," Marquez chuckled. "He's just used to giving orders, not taking them."

"He's in the wrong business," Cash said. "He's not a team player."

"As I recall, neither were you until you started working down here for the police department," Marquez reminded him. "If you could adjust, he can adjust. It's just that you spec ops people don't blend as easily as regular military people do. You're used to working alone or in small groups."

Cash sighed. "I guess so. He did break up a network at the local high school. He borrowed one of the DEA's drug-sniffing dogs and went locker crawling. Ticked off the board of education, and a lot of parents, but he made several arrests."

"The end justifies the means," Marquez chuckled.

Glory was about to protest that when she got dizzy and sat down hard in the grass.

"Hey, you okay?" Cash asked, concerned, as he squatted just in front of her.

"It's nothing," she said weakly. "Just a little morning sickness."

Cash bit off a bad word. He and Marquez exchanged a look she didn't see.

"He isn't to know," she told Cash. "Marquez has already promised. You have to promise, too."

"He's your husband," Cash emphasized.

She bit down on the sickness and waited until it passed. "He's working for Fuentes," she said curtly. "I'm a prosecuting attorney." She looked up. "He isn't to know that, either, no matter what."

Cash was concerned. He didn't dare tell her why. "Secrets are dangerous."

She brushed back a wisp of hair. "So I've been told. This is still privileged information."

"Okay. It's your call," Cash said finally.

She pulled herself to her feet. She couldn't use the cane and fire a pistol, so she'd left her cane in Marquez's truck. She felt pretty steady, all the same. Her hip wasn't as painful as it had been. She did very well unless she overexerted.

Marquez pulled a .32 caliber Smith & Wesson out of his belt.

"A wheel gun?" she exclaimed. "Nobody uses a wheel gun anymore!" She indicated Cash. "He's got a .40 caliber Glock. You're packing a .45 caliber Colt. And I'm going to learn to shoot a wheel gun? Why don't you give me a big rock and I can practice hitting people in the head with it!"

Cash chuckled. "Because an automatic can fail under certain conditions."

"You can shoot a Glock underwater," she informed him.

"A wheel gun won't jam," he came back. "And besides, it's small. You can fire it with one hand."

"It's a sissy gun," she persisted.

Marquez loaded it and handed it to her. "Don't argue. It's undignified."

She gave him a speaking look.

"Okay," Cash interrupted. "Let's get started."

BY THE TIME SHE DROVE away with Marquez, her hands were swollen and sore. She rubbed them.

"Nobody said I was going to have to fire the pistol with both hands, one at a time," she muttered.

"That's how the FBI teaches you to do it," he commented with a grin. "What if you get shot in your good hand? You have to be able to carry on with the other."

"I suppose so." She felt her purse. It was heavy. She had a box of ammunition that Marquez had provided, along with the pistol, sharing space with her cosmetics and wallet. She was thinking about Rodrigo and wondering if she'd have to use the pistol on him. It made her sicker.

"The sooner this case is closed, the better," he said, thinking aloud.

"When it is, my husband may be sharing cell space with Fuentes." She glanced at his worried expression. "It's true, isn't it?" she asked quietly.

He didn't dare tell her what he knew, and it hurt him. She already had all the stress she could handle, plus some.

"What do I do," she asked, "if Rodrigo calls and asks me to meet him someplace?"

"Don't go," he said.

"That's what I thought you'd say." She looked as miserable as she felt. It was ironic; for the first time in her life, she was crazy about a man, and he turned out to be a scoundrel. It wasn't fair.

"I know," Marquez said. Only then did she realize that she'd spoken aloud.

"Well, we do the job, no matter what the cost, so that we can save a few lives," she said in a low tone.

"That's the idea."

She looked out the window of the truck at the passing landscape. "I should have moved to a tropical island some-place and spent my life picking up shells on the beach."

He laughed. "That's a popular daydream around my office, too, especially when our new lieutenant goes on a rampage over budgets."

She frowned. "I thought that was what your last lieuten-ant was famous for."

"No, no," he corrected. "Our last lieutenant was a fanatic about our own spending; a real penny-pincher. No, this one goes on rampages to the city fathers about our lack of adequate funding," he said smugly. "He wants us to have better equipment and improved training. He wants me to go to the FBI school at Quanico."

"I'm impressed," she said.

"So am I. They say the course can drive people nuts, but you learn a lot there."

"They'd ruin you," she said wickedly. "You'd come back with all sorts of new ideas to improve your department and we'd find you in a ditch a few days after with a note in your mouth from your lieutenant, offering you up for adoption by any other agency that would have you."

"Spoilsport."

"Exactly who is this guy Kilraven?" she asked suddenly.

He pursed his lips. "He's the new patrol officer here."

Something in the way he said it made her very suspicious. "Oh, no," she said. "You're hiding something. Give it up."

"I'm not hiding anything," he lied.

"I'll ask Cash Grier."

"You'd have better luck asking a clam."

"Tell me. I can keep secrets."

He was amused. His eyes were dancing. "I have it on good authority," he began, "that he was sent down here from Langley…"

"Langley!" she interrupted excitedly.

"Langley," he agreed, "to flush out a potential kidnapper with ties to a government hostile to us in South America. Word on the street is that the kidnapper is very good at his job and has the perfect hostage in mind already. He thinks the hostage would bring him a lot of money from a certain federal agency to whom he is extremely valuable."

"Who?"

"Who, what?"

"Who's the potential victim?"

"We aren't sure," Marquez told her. "But we think he may be a drug agent—the same one who most recently helped shut down Cara Dominguez. He's cost the cartel over a billion dollars in the past few years."

"Wouldn't it suit them better to just kill him?" she wondered.

"I'm certain that's the idea. But they want money, and they think he can be ransomed. They'll kill him, of course, the minute they have the money."

"I thought our government didn't negotiate with terrorists."

"We don't, publicly."

She frowned thoughtfully. "There was a plot just recently to nab Jared Cameron, wasn't there?"

"Foiled by his bodyguard…"

"Tony the Dancer," she provided, grinning. "What a name!"

"It's Danzetta, actually."

"I know, but the other sounds romantic, in a thuggy way."

"It sounds like the mob, which Tony isn't part of. He's actually Cherokee."

"He's sort of dishy."

"You met him?"

She nodded. "He fed us some information about those kidnappers who got caught down here. They also had South American ties, but your D.A. didn't have jurisdiction over a federal crime. He sent them off with a federal marshal to our district U.S. Attorney for trial. They escaped."

"We heard," he replied. He shook his head. "Some case, that. Two guards were charged with aiding and abetting, but they vanished before they could be arraigned."

She glanced at him. "Big players, big money and big trouble for us. They're rumored to still be in the country."

"We heard that, too."

He pulled up at her door. "You keep that gun with you at all times," he cautioned.

"I'll have to, especially when Carla's kids are around. I wouldn't have them hurt for anything."

He smiled. "If you need help, call me, or call Cash. We'll come running."

"I will." The old depression came back. "Thanks, Rick."

He shrugged. "What are friends for?" he asked.

IT WAS A LONG SATURDAY night and a frightening evening. Rain was pouring down outside. Lightning made the trees vivid in the darkness. Its jagged, hot pattern made Glory even more nervous than she already was. Carla and Angel had gone home already, with the children. Glory was alone in the big house.

She wandered from room to room. Everything was different from her childhood. The house had been totally remodeled. Even the flooring was new. She rubbed her bare arms, feeling a chill that was probably psychological, because of the storm. Jacobsville had tornadoes. She didn't want to be caught in one when she was by herself. They'd terrified her as a child. It had been during a storm when her mother had crippled her.

There was probably a storm shelter, but she couldn't remember where it had been. Running to it outside through the driving rain and lightning was riskier than staying in the house, she thought. Either way, the weather was scary.

She wondered where Rodrigo and his partners in crime were, and what they were doing. If he got caught by the authorities, which seemed possible now, what would she do? They were on opposite sides of the law. No matter what her feelings were, she couldn't toss her whole career for a man who didn't love her.

She recalled what the cardiologist had said about her bad choice of professions. She knew the job was becoming too much for her. But what nobody understood was that the only health insurance she carried was a policy made possible through her employer. If she quit the job, how would she be able to afford to insure herself ever again?

Well, she comforted herself, if she found other employment and then had a heart attack, she could sit outside the emergency room entrance in a hospital gown holding a cup and solicit donations to pay the bill. The Pendletons would pay it, but she wanted to be independent. They'd already done so much for her. But her job was a risk. If she didn't do something, she was going to end up dead. Criminal trials were no walk in the park. Tempers flared. Sometimes it was lawyers who clashed, sometimes it was witnesses and opposing counsel. Other times, it was prosecution and defense attorneys. And once, the judge had come down hard on Glory for pushing a witness in a murder trial too far. It was no job for the timid; it was very stressful.

The thunder was louder now, and the flashes lit up all the dark corners of the house. Where was Rodrigo?

THE BIG OIL CANS WERE tied together to form a makeshift pontoon bridge across the narrow strip of river where there were no border guards, temporarily. Castillo's friend kept a lookout while Rodrigo drove the panel truck across the bridge, with Castillo on the bank, guiding the truck in its headlights. There were several hundred kilos of pure cocaine in the back. It was a haul worth a king's ransom. The three men had decided that it was safer to run it across the border like this than to risk using better equipment and more people. There had been a tunnel, but it had been discovered. This crossing area had been secured by a transfer of money, to whom Rodrigo wasn't privy. He was fairly certain it wasn't a border patrol agent or anyone in local law enforcement. Here, there was only open country that backed one of the bigger cattle ranches in the area. Rodrigo was willing to bet that someone on the ranch had been bribed to look the other way.

Castillo was grinning in the headlights. Only a few more feet. Rodrigo eased the truck over the last of the barrels and onto firm land.

"Yes!" Castillo called, raising both fists. "We've done it!"

Rodrigo stopped the truck and got out. "Easy money," he chuckled. "Help me get the drums out of the water."

"Leave them," Castillo suggested. "With what we're

getting paid for this job, we can buy more. It's dangerous to stay here too long, no matter how easy it seems."

"You're probably right," Rodrigo agreed. He signaled to the man on the bank to come down.

"I know I've asked before, but are you sure about this gringo?" Castillo added with a frown.

"Would I risk my life on someone I wasn't sure of?" Rodrigo replied.

Castillo looked at the taller man with narrowed eyes. Then he shrugged. "No. Of course not." He glanced around them again. No cars, no trucks, no airplanes or helicopters. They were having great luck.

He climbed into the cab next to Rodrigo. Then he glanced out the window and scowled. "Where's your cousin?" he asked. He jumped as he felt cold steel against his ribs.

"Just sit still and don't do anything stupid," Rodrigo said softly. His other hand lifted, carrying a portable radio unit. His thumb depressed a switch. "The wolf is at the door," he said calmly.

While Castillo was working that cryptic remark out, headlights from at least a dozen vehicles centered on the panel truck at the river's edge.

"Amigo," Rodrigo told his companion, "welcome to the land of the free and the home of the brave!"

13

GLORY WAS CHEWING HER fingernails off. Nervous tension had already jacked up her heart rate, and her breathing. She was desperate to know where Rodrigo was, how he was.

The storm was beginning to die down. Rain could be heard dripping from the eaves into the rain barrels placed there. No more flashes of light were coming in the window, although distant thunder was audible. Luckily the storm hadn't seemed to do any damage here.

She walked to the front door and looked out, feeling the .32 revolver like a rock in her jeans pocket. If only she could find out what was happening, even if it was bad news. Rodrigo might go to prison, but even that would be all right, as long as he wasn't dead. She couldn't bear the thought of never seeing him again.

The sudden jangle of her cell phone made her jump. She fumbled it out of her pocket and flipped it open. "Yes?"

"We just landed the biggest shipment of cocaine in Jacobs County history," Marquez chuckled.

"What about Rodrigo?" she asked hastily. "Was he in on it? Is he all right...?"

"We did have a little trouble," Marquez began. "They've taken him to the emergency room in Jacobsville...Glory, wait! Listen—!"

But she'd already cut him off. She grabbed her purse and scurried out the door as fast as her hip would let her. She climbed into her car, locked the doors, started it and sped out of the driveway. The phone rang again, but this time she ignored it. Rodrigo, she moaned silently. "Please, God, don't let him be dead! I'll do anything, I'll give him up, I'll walk out of his life, I'll do anything...just please spare him!"

It was so far to town, she thought frantically. This old heap of a car was okay in the city, where she only had to travel a couple of blocks to work, but it was a liability on the open road. She could barely get it to go the speed limit. She really missed her sports car. This wreck of a vehicle was expendable, and it was hardly appropriate for a race.

The darkness was almost complete. It was a moonless night. She wasn't thinking clearly. If Fuentes had a hit man after her, she was giving him the perfect opportunity to kill her. She hadn't taken any precautions at all except to lock her doors and put the pistol in her pocket. It was a stupid move. But she was thinking with her heart, and her heart wanted to see Rodrigo, to make sure he was safe. Nothing else mattered. If he was involved in the drug bust, if he'd been arrested, she'd know how to help him. If he was just still alive!

By the time she pulled into the emergency room parking lot at Jacobsville General, her heart was thumping and she could just barely get her breath. She tore out of the car, grimacing as her hip protested the stress she was putting on it. She started toward the steps and then had to retrace her path to the car. She couldn't carry a sidearm into the hospital. She locked it in the glove compartment and then went up the steps as fast as she could manage, panting and stopping to breathe halfway up.

There was a crowd in the waiting room. It was Saturday night, the busiest night. She moved in front of one of the clerks. "Rodrigo Ramirez," she said frantically. "He's my husband…!"

"Dr. Coltrain has him in cubicle three," the clerk began. "If you'll have a seat…"

But Glory had already passed her and was making excellent time. She was vaguely aware of several men standing outside the cubicle, but she didn't really look at them. She moved past the curtain and there was Rodrigo, his shirt off, looking sexy and masculine and so handsome that her heart jumped. Best of all, he was sitting up on the examination table, grinning as Lou's brother-in-law, Copper Coltrain stitched up his arm.

"Rodrigo!" Glory exclaimed.

His eyebrows arched as she ran to him and pressed close,

terrified, shaking. Her free hand smoothed over the thick, soft hair on his chest and she sighed with mingled relief and pleasure as she felt his heartbeat, reassuring at her ear.

"What are you doing here?" Rodrigo exclaimed. "How did you know?"

"Marquez phoned me," she managed. She drew back just a little, so that she could look up into his dark eyes. "Are you all right?"

He smiled. "I'm fine. It's just a flesh wound. I've had worse."

She'd been too relieved to notice the other men at first, but now she became aware of several men in uniforms and her heart sank. She knew her husband was involved in the drug world. But she wasn't the sort to run out on a sinking ship. She drew herself up proudly.

"Everything is going to be all right. We'll get you the best attorney in Texas," she assured Rodrigo in a rush. "The very best. Don't say anything that might incriminate you. In fact, don't say anything until you have legal counsel...."

She stopped because he was laughing helplessly. As she listened, she became aware that all the other men were laughing as well. She glanced behind her and belatedly recognized Police Chief Cash Grier and Sheriff Hayes Carson, DEA Senior Agent Alexander Cobb and a strange man in an expensive suit.

Cash held up a jacket. "This is your husband's, Glory," he said. Cash turned the jacket around and she read the huge letters DEA stamped in white across the back.

Her mind shut down. She frowned, staring at the jacket. Her husband had been wearing it when he was shot. Was he pretending to be a federal agent? Slowly she turned her head back to Rodrigo. He was holding out a badge. A DEA badge.

"I'm not under arrest," he told her amusedly. "I was in on the bust."

"He's the undercover narc," Cash said. "We didn't dare tell you."

She was staring at Rodrigo and feeling like an idiot. "You're the DEA agent who was undercover."

He nodded. His eyes were solemn. "I have a cousin who's managed to remain in the employ of the past two drug lords, plus this one. He got me in."

"You could have been killed," she began.

"This isn't my first walk around the block, Glory," he said in a faintly condescending tone. "My partner and I worked the Dominguez case in Houston undercover."

"Your partner...?"

"Sarina Lane," Alexander Cobb volunteered.

The blonde woman. Glory was starting to put it all together.

Rodrigo grimaced. He didn't like hearing Sarina's married name. Before he spoke his own cell phone jangled with the title song of the FIFA Soccer World Cup. He opened it and his face changed. He grinned. "Yes, we got it all," he said. He chuckled. "Are you surprised that I can work without you?" he added in an affectionate tone. "Yes. I just took a hit in the arm. A flesh wound. Nothing compared to the bullet you caught in Houston when we cornered part of the Dominguez gang in the warehouse. Yes. I'm fine. Tomorrow? That would be great! Come on down. Yes. Kiss Bernadette for me. See you tomorrow."

He hung up. Nobody had to tell Glory that the person at the end of the line had been Sarina. His partner. His working partner, whom he loved. Whom he would always love.

Glory felt weak and sick and she prayed that she wouldn't pass out at his feet from the shock.

"You should go home," Rodrigo told her, noting her high color and unsteadiness. He should be flattered that she cared so much about him, but he was a little embarrassed by the way she looked. She hadn't even brushed her hair. She looked like a farm worker, plain and uninteresting. He'd always had attractive women around him, women who dressed well and drew men's eyes. This little frump wouldn't have attracted a nearsighted pencil-pusher, much less himself. "I still have to be debriefed when the doctor finishes with me," he told her carelessly. "I'll be late."

She wanted to protest, but it would probably irritate him, in front of his colleagues. "Of course. I just wanted to make sure you were all right," she added, trying very hard to sound composed. His attitude made her self-conscious.

He nodded. "We'll talk later."

"Yes."

Marquez walked in grinning. "What a haul!" he exclaimed. "Great work, guys. Several news teams are pulling into the parking lot. Who wants to be the entrée?"

"Not me," Rodrigo said at once, "or I'll be useless in under-cover work."

"I'll talk to them," Cobb said easily. "Well, the three of us can do it," he indicated Cash and Hayes Carson. "I don't want to be accused of taking credit for something we all helped accomplish."

"That's damned kind of you," Cash chuckled.

"It's not that," Cobb mused. "I need your brother's coop-eration in a case that may have ties to San Antonio. I can't afford to offend you!"

"His brother?" the man in the suit asked.

"Garon. He's a senior special agent with the FBI in San Antonio."

"That's why the name sounded familiar," the man agreed.

"I'd better get going," Glory murmured. It wouldn't do if someone with one of the news crews recognized her, not with Fuentes still on her trail. She'd been interviewed more than once on the cases she prosecuted. She didn't need to be fingered on local TV.

"I'll make sure you get home okay," Marquez volunteered. "You don't need to be on the road at night alone. Especially not now. We don't know where Fuentes is, despite the fact that we've just confiscated his biggest load to date."

She glanced toward Rodrigo, but he was talking to Hayes Carson, and he didn't look her way. She might as well be invisible to him.

She turned, holding her head high, and walked out with Marquez.

MARQUEZ ACTUALLY DROVE behind her in his truck to make sure she got home safely.

She locked her car and walked up onto the porch. "Want coffee?" she asked him.

He hesitated. He was tired, but she looked as if she could use a friend. Her husband had been dismissive, almost as if he were ashamed of her. She deserved better, especially in her condition.

"Sure," he said, and walked into the house with her.

She served decaffeinated coffee and sliced some pound cake. They sipped coffee and munched cake in a companionable silence.

"You've been in the business long enough to know how it is with law enforcement people after busts," he said quietly. "It's the biggest high in the world. It takes time to come back down again. Meanwhile, you just want to talk until you get it all out of your system."

"Funny," she mused, "I thought that was what husbands and wives were for—to talk to."

"Rodrigo isn't your average cop," he replied. "He's done a lot of things that most of us just dream about."

She was remembering what Marquez and Cash had told her about the undercover narc who had a price on his head all over the world because he was so good at shutting down drug lords. "I guess so. That bit about him riding down an escaping child killer on horseback through the jungle in the rain was pretty impressive."

He chuckled. "That's just the frosting on the cake," he

replied. "He was with a legendary group of mercs overseas before he settled into work as a federal agent. He has a pilot's license, he speaks half a dozen languages, he's a gourmet cook and he's related to half the royal houses in Europe."

She put her coffee cup down. "Rodrigo?" she asked, surprised.

He nodded. "Both his parents were minor royals," he said. "His father was Danish and his mother was high-born Spanish. Quite a mixture."

It came as a shock. She knew nothing about the man she'd married; nothing at all.

"Why did he go into undercover work?" she wanted to know. "Most federal agents who do that get killed."

He nodded. "He has more reason than most. Lopez became infatuated with his sister, who was working in a nightclub. He forced himself on her and then killed her." He grimaced. "Rodrigo went wild. He went on a legendary drunk, crashed a helicopter and then broke into Alexander Cobb's office to get the information and equipment he needed to go after Manuel Lopez. Most people, even in law enforcement, walk wide around him. He's the most dangerous man I know."

She was beginning to realize that. "He's not domesticated."

"No. He came close to marrying his partner, but she was still in love with her ex-husband, Colby Lane. He's been linked with debutantes, movie stars, even minor royalty. But there's always a new case. He lives on adrenaline rushes. I don't think he could give up his job, even if he loved a woman…" He hesitated when he saw her face. "I didn't mean that."

"We both know he doesn't love me, Rick," she said after a minute. "He didn't want me in the emergency room. I embarrass him. I'm too plain."

"I'm sure he'd never say that to you."

She held her cup between her hands and stared down into it. "I want to go home."

"What about the baby?"

That hurt, thinking about it. "He won't want it," she said, and was certain of it. She looked up. "Get me into a safe house in San Antonio and I'll stay put until you can find Fuentes and get him off my case."

He pursed his lips. "I think the D.A. might go for that, now that we've crippled Fuentes's reputation."

"I'll phone him at home tonight," she said. "Then I'll phone you, if he says it's okay. I'd like to go tomorrow."

He frowned. "Why so quick?" he asked. Then he remembered what he'd overheard at the hospital—Sarina and her daughter would be coming down to see Rodrigo. Glory didn't want to be there when she arrived.

"I'll phone you," she repeated.

"Okay. I'll be at Mom's," he added. "I'm not on call this weekend."

She grimaced. He didn't have a lot of weekends when he wasn't on call. "Sorry."

"Hey, all I do is watch television. Mom spends most

Sundays at the nursing home after church, reading to some of the older patients."

"She's a lovely person, your mother."

He smiled. "Yes."

"Thanks, Rick," she said after a minute. "I was a little nervous being out at night alone, even with the gun."

"Where is the gun?"

"In my car," she said. "I didn't want to risk taking it into the hospital."

"Get it out of your car before I leave and keep it with you," he returned solemnly. "You're not out of the woods yet."

She sighed. "Don't I know it!"

SHE PHONED THE D.A. at home and he was agreeable to having her back on the job, in a safe house. One of the investigators would follow her to and from work and the police would put extra patrols on. But, like Marquez, he didn't think Fuentes was going to be a problem any longer. Neither did Glory. Thanks to her husband and his colleagues, Fuentes was about to have big trouble of his own over those confiscated drugs.

RICK WAS DUE AT NOON to follow her back to San Antonio. She'd sworn him to silence about her job. There was no reason to tell Rodrigo about it. He'd be back in Houston in no time, and they probably wouldn't even have to see each other again. They could get a quiet divorce and pretend they'd never met. She was so hurt by his attitude that it didn't even bother her that they were separating.

She heard him come in, in the wee hours of the morning, but she didn't have her light on, and she didn't make a sound when she heard him hesitate outside her door. He didn't open it.

The next morning, she stayed in her room until he left the house. Then she fixed herself a poached egg on toast and some coffee. She'd packed most of her things. Now, it was just a matter of waiting for Rick to follow her into the city.

She heard a car door slam and the high, sweet sound of a child's excited laughter outside.

She went to the curtained front window and looked out. Rodrigo had the little girl high in his arms, and he was laughing down into the pretty blonde woman's animated face. Watching them, Glory felt like an outsider. They were still a family, regardless of Mr. Lane's presence in their lives. She couldn't bear to see how happy Rodrigo was. She went back into her room to finish her packing.

When she was finished, she put on a pair of jeans with a pretty floppy magenta overblouse and sandals and walked out onto the porch, because Rick was due. She saw Sarina's car, but she was nowhere in sight.

She walked to the end of the porch and stopped dead when she heard voices around the corner.

"...but you're married," Sarina was saying.

"To a little country hick who dresses like a bag lady and has no social graces, or education to speak of," he said coldly. "I was ashamed to have my colleagues even see her with me last night!" He drew in a harsh breath. "She's crippled and

Fuentes wants to kill her because she's a witness to something illegal that he did. I only married her out of pity. It was the worst reason in the world." He didn't add that he'd felt a raging desire for her that he couldn't deny.

"What are you going to do, then?" came the reply.

"Whatever I have to, in order to get out of the mess I'm in."

Glory moved back away from them, feeling sick. He was ashamed of her. He married her because he felt sorry for her. She felt as if her whole life had just shattered at her feet.

She went off the porch the other way and walked blindly down to the old iron bridge that nobody used anymore, since the modern one was completed. She climbed up on the high rail and sat there, blinded by tears, hurting as if she'd been stabbed in the heart. The man she loved spoke of her with disdain, with contempt, and she was carrying his baby. She felt such a fool. How could she have thought he might come to love her? She was crippled and plain and useless to him. He thought the woman who'd worked on the farm with him was nothing but a country hick. It should have been amusing. It wasn't. Added to that, her medical condition could cost her not only her baby, but her life. It was a bleak, cold future looming ahead. Depression and melancholy settled over her like a black cloud.

She swung her legs out over the river, rushing below her over the rocks. The water was deep, there. A woman had thrown herself off this bridge back in the early 1920s and drowned because she'd caught her husband with her best friend. Sarina Lane wasn't Glory's friend, but she could understand how the dead woman must have felt. Some people had seen her on this bridge late at night, or so they said, walking along the road in a white dress. They called it the haunted bridge. But Glory wasn't afraid. She was a kindred spirit.

The rushing water was hypnotic. She wasn't really suicidal. She was just sick at heart. But something was urging her to slide closer and closer to the edge. Just a little way down, a voice nudged, and all the hurt would end. She would be free. She would never have to walk with a cane or take medicine for blood pressure or hear her husband recite her drawbacks to another woman ever again...

"Glory!"

She didn't hear Marquez at first. She didn't hear, or see him, until he caught her around the waist and dragged her down from the iron pillar.

"What the hell are you doing?" he exclaimed, steadying her against him. His face was pale. He was breathing hard. "I never thought I'd get here in time!" he added.

He must have run down the hill, she thought. But it got worse. Rodrigo and Sarina were also running down the hill, onto the bridge.

"What happened?" Rodrigo asked curtly.

"I thought she was going to j...I mean, fall," Rick corrected at once.

"I wouldn't have fallen," she told Rick without looking at the others. "I used to fish off this bridge." She still sounded dazed. "When I was a little girl, my great-grandfather would come down here with me." She smiled reminiscently. "We only had cane poles and fishing line, nothing fancy, but every Saturday when he didn't have to plow, we'd catch bass and bream for supper."

"Why were you sitting up there in the first place?" Rodrigo demanded.

She looked at him, distracted. "I've always done it," she said vacantly, "and dangled my legs over the edge."

"You could have fallen!" Rodrigo persisted hotly. He actually sounded concerned, but Glory was sure that he wasn't. After all, his own special woman was standing right beside him. He couldn't afford to let her think he was heartless about his wife.

She looked into his eyes, and her own were blazing with banked-down fury. "If I had fallen, it wouldn't have mattered to you, would it?" she asked coldly. She avoided Sarina's curious eyes and turned to Rick. "I'm ready to go when you are," she said quietly.

"Where the hell are you going?" Rodrigo asked curtly.

She couldn't bear to look at him. "I'm going home. Rick is going to follow me, just in case Fuentes hasn't been sidetracked by the loss of his product last night."

Rodrigo hadn't been thinking. Fuentes was still after her and she was going off with this detective who seemed more concerned than her husband did. He felt ashamed. "Where's home?" Rodrigo asked, scowling.

She didn't answer him. "We'd better get going. Sorry about

the work," she told Rodrigo matter-of-factly, "but I'm sure I won't be hard to replace. There are so many plain, country hicks around here who have no hope of a better life than working in someone's kitchen." She'd added that last bit deliberately, and she looked up in time to see it hit home, like a poisoned arrow. He knew then that she'd overheard him talking to Sarina. It shamed him. He hadn't meant it. Not really.

Sarina looked as if she wanted to say something, but Glory simply walked past her and Rodrigo, and kept going. Her hip was killing her, but she wasn't showing any signs of weakness to that two-legged, two-timing pit viper to whom she was still, temporarily, married.

MARQUEZ CAUGHT UP WITH her. "Are you packed?" he asked her.

"Yes. My suitcase is in the living room. I just need to get my purse and my cane."

They went inside together. She hoisted her shoulder bag and leaned a little heavily on her cane as she followed Marquez outside.

Rodrigo and Sarina were standing on the porch. Rodrigo was frowning.

"Exactly where are you going?" he asked Glory, sparing Marquez a glance as he went to put her suitcase in the trunk of her car.

Her face was bland as oatmeal as she looked at him. She was pale and unhappy, but she tried to conceal it. "That's need-to-know. You don't. Anyway, with Fuentes's operation in tatters, we think he'll be much more worried about his own life than he'll be about taking mine. You can always send flowers if I'm wrong and he puts a bullet in me," she added matter-of-factly.

Rodrigo actually flinched.

Sarina gnawed her lower lip. "We didn't get to introduce ourselves on the bridge," Sarina said quietly. "I'm…"

"Sarina Lane," Glory replied tonelessly. "Yes, I know. Mr. Ramirez speaks of you often."

Rodrigo's black eyes flashed. He didn't like her formal use of his name. But before he could speak, Marquez was back.

"I'm ready," he told Glory, pausing to nod at the couple beside her.

"Okay." She looked at Rodrigo's chin. "Thanks for letting me stay here while Fuentes was after me. I hope I won't be leaving you shorthanded."

"Carla and one of the other workers will finish up the fruit," he said stiffly. "It's only a speculative project. If it takes off, Pendleton will have to arrange for more kitchen staff to meet the demand."

"Of course," she said, and even smiled. "Well, goodbye."

Rodrigo frowned. "There will be some legalities…"

"I'll have my attorney contact you. You can file for divorce whenever you like," she said. "The sooner the better," she added bitterly. She turned, leaning heavily on the cane, and walked out of Rodrigo's life without a backward glance.

She put on her seat belt, started her car, and pulled out of the yard behind Rick's truck. She never waved. She never looked back. She just drove, even when the road became a little blurry as she pulled out of the driveway.

Sarina was frowning. Rodrigo was staring after the departing vehicles as if he were watching a movie. He was scowling, rigid.

"She heard what you said about her," she said quietly. "It must have hurt. She's proud, you call tell."

His teeth crashed together. He was remembering what Glory had said, about being shuttled into foster homes, always the child outside looking in, always the outsider, always unwanted. He didn't understand why he'd said such cruel things about her. He wasn't emotionally involved with Glory. He'd only wanted her. So why did it feel so wrong that she was leaving?

"It was an act of insanity," Rodrigo said curtly. "A divorce would be best for both of us."

Sarina was thinking. There was something odd about the other woman. She couldn't put her finger on it, but there was much more going on here than Rodrigo was admitting. He said he didn't care about Glory, but his eyes were tormented. He was pretending. Glory hadn't known him long enough to know that, but Sarina had. Not only that, she knew she'd seen Glory somewhere else, in a different setting. For some reason, San Antonio kept pulling at her mind.

So when she got back to Houston, she phoned a colleague in the San Antonio DEA office and started asking questions.

14

ALL THE EXTRA PATROLS and precautions were suddenly unnecessary for Glory's protection. She'd just moved into the safe house and was drinking her first cup of Monday morning decaf coffee when Marquez phoned.

"Guess what?" he asked.

"You won the lottery and you're running away to Tahiti?"

"That'll be the day. I called to tell you that they just found Fuentes facedown in a stream between here and Jacobsville. They didn't even bother to hide the body—it's visible from the highway."

Her heart stopped. "Say what?"

"We were right about his superior counting mistakes. This is the second big load Fuentes lost, and his organization isn't forgiving. No more chances. He's very dead."

She was sorry, even for a drug dealer to die. But it took the heat off her. "Then I'm safe?" she asked hesitantly.

"Perfectly," he replied. "Our mole in the organization said Fuentes was crazy to put out a contract on an assistant D.A. in this country without authorization, when he was already under the gun for a murder charge. Not that they don't kill attorneys, cops and journalists, but this isn't the way they operate. Anyway, the big drug lord told them to lay off you."

"Gee, I didn't get him anything," she mused.

"It was a nice present, wasn't it? Pity we can't find out who he is. Maybe the DEA will have better luck. Anyway, you can move back into your apartment whenever you like, and your boss says your paperwork is piling up, hint, hint."

She smiled. It was the first good news she'd had in a long time. "Okay. Good thing I haven't unpacked."

"Yes. I'll be over on my lunch hour to move you."

"Rick, you've done so much already..."

"You're my friend," he said simply.

"Then, thanks. I'll expect you at noon, and I'll order a pizza!"

SHE WAS STILL SQUEAMISH that night, back in her own apartment, fighting the morning sickness that seemed to get worse and last longer. She was also having some pain. She made an appointment with her physician in San Antonio and started putting together her work clothes for the next day. When she looked in the mirror, she saw the toll her experience had taken. She was pale and drawn and she looked as if she'd lost weight. But at least the pretence was over now. She could use makeup, put her contact lenses back in, wear what she liked and not have to blend in. It was a bitter thing, remembering what Rodrigo had said about her lack of culture, education and looks.

She was getting dressed the next morning when her doorbell rang. She pushed the intercom button. She wondered who it could be so early...

"May I come up?"

Her jaw clenched. "Why?" she asked, because she knew that particular feminine voice all too well.

"I need to tell you something."

For two cents, she thought, I'd ignore her. But it wasn't Sarina's fault that Rodrigo couldn't go on living without her. "Okay," she said heavily, and pressed the buzzer on the outside door.

Glory was wearing a gray suit and pink blouse, with her hair in a neat bun and makeup on, when she opened the door to her rival.

Sarina stared. "You look different."

"I have to uphold the image of the district attorney's office on the job," she said stiffly. "What can I do for you?"

Sarina's eyelids flinched. "He's not an easy man to get to know," she began. "He was still hurting from his sister's death when I was partnered with him in Arizona. He alternated between bristling and cold formality—at least, until he met Bernadette. He loves children," she said deliberately, and with a glance at Glory's belly, as if she knew that the top button of her skirt was undone because it wouldn't fasten anymore.

"You wouldn't tell him…?" Glory asked, panicking.

Sarina shook her head. "That's your business. But he should know."

"Why?" Glory asked coldly. "It won't be Bernadette."

Sarina's eyes were compassionate. "I'm so sorry," she said softly. "You won't understand, but I know how you feel. I was desperately in love with my husband when he left me for another woman, one who only wanted his money. Colby and I were apart until Bernadette was in grammar school, and that witch had convinced him that he was sterile."

Glory relaxed a little.

"Yes," Sarina replied, smiling, "I'm very much in love with my husband. All I could ever give Rodrigo was friendship. It wasn't enough. He's tenacious," she added. "It's what makes him dangerous in the field. But it's a double-edged weapon, too."

Glory's hand rested on her stomach. "I don't know if I can carry a child," she confessed. It felt good to tell someone. She'd lived with the fear for so long. "I had a slight heart attack on the job," she added slowly, seeing the sympathy in the other woman's dark eyes. "I've worked so hard to get where I am. And I'm paying the price. I have to take medicine for high blood pressure and high cholesterol, and now I have to take blood thinners as well so that I won't have a second, worse heart attack. The usual tests didn't show any blockages, but they want me to do a heart catheterization and I won't risk it while I'm pregnant. If I stop taking the blood thinners, the child will be safe, but I could die. How do I tell him all that?" she asked bluntly. "He thinks I don't want children. It isn't true. But it might be kinder to let him go on thinking it."

Sarina shook her head. "It isn't." She took a piece of paper out of her pocket and handed it to the younger woman. "That's his home address, in Houston. He's gone back there to debrief his office, and to connect some local drug smugglers with Fuentes. Go see him. Tell him."

"He won't want to know."

Sarina stared her down. "Isn't he worth fighting for?"

Glory looked down at the note in her hand. It was a forlorn hope. It would only lead to more heartache. She shrugged. "Yes," she said. "I'll go."

AND SHE DID. SHE HAD to go by the Pendletons' to get her car for the trip. The old one she drove on the job was on its last gasp.

Rodrigo lived in a gated community. It was a pretty apartment complex, very ritzy. Most of the cars in the parking lots were expensive ones. If he could afford to live here, she thought, he had more going for him than a federal agent's salary. She remembered Sarina saying that he was related to the royal houses of Europe. He was probably wealthy.

She had to show her court ID to the gatekeeper and lie about the purpose of her visit. He said that he'd have to check it with Mr. Ramirez, which he proceeded to do. But

Rodrigo wasn't in. The guard gave her racing-green Jaguar
XKE sports car a long, wistful look. It really was a beaut—
a present from her stepbrother and stepsister last Christmas.

"I'll only be a minute," she pleaded. "I have some papers
to leave with him on a case I'm trying in San Antonio."

"Oh, I see. Yes, we all heard about the happenings down
in Jacobs County," the gatekeeper said, warming to her.
"Were you in on that?"

She laughed. "Only peripherally, I'm afraid. But I will get
to try some of the coconspirators." That was a possibility, but
she made it sound as if it were the purpose of her visit.

"You go on in. He plays tennis most Saturday mornings,"
he added. "You can wait for him."

"Thanks a million."

"Sure thing."

She drove off and the guard frowned. Should he have
told her that another young lady had already gone in to see
Mr. Ramirez, and that she had a key to the apartment?

BLISSFULLY IGNORANT OF the possible complications, Glory
pulled up in the parking lot and got out, walking to the
apartment the guard had given her directions for. There was
a little Hispanic boy with a soccer ball in the green space
between the apartment buildings. She smiled at him, and
wondered if her child would be a boy.

"Do you like soccer?" the boy asked.

"Yes. I follow all the games," she replied, "and I always
watch the World Cup."

"I like Marquez," he replied. "He's captain of the Mexican team. He's a great player."

Her eyebrows arched. "Marquez?" she asked, thinking of her own Marquez, the detective.

He nodded. "We call him Rafa. I want to be like him when I grow up. Look what I can do." He bounced the ball from one knee to the other. She laughed, enjoying his skill.

She heard footsteps and turned. And there was Rodrigo, but not the man she'd known in Jacobsville. This was someone else. He was like the people Jason and Gracie invited to their social events. He was wearing an Armani suit with handmade Italian shoes. His hair was styled, not just cut, and he looked expensive and graceful…and dangerous.

"Hi, Rodrigo!" the boy called. "Want to play?"

"Not right now. Go home, Domingo," he said gently.

The boy looked from one adult to the other. "Sure." He didn't argue.

"What do you want?" Rodrigo asked bluntly.

She hesitated. She should have dressed better. She was wearing the same jeans and T-shirt she'd worn at the farm, although her hair was in a neat plait. She didn't have much makeup on. She was walking without the cane, because she didn't want pity. She tried to look comfortable.

"I wanted to tell you something," she said. She didn't know how to begin.

He smiled coldly. "Someone's been talking to you, I gather," he replied.

"Well, yes."

"And now you know that I could have afforded to buy that farm and fifty like it for cash, and suddenly those marriage vows we took have real value, no?"

Her eyes widened. "You must be joking," she began. She wasn't a Pendleton, but she was treated like one. She had a closet full of designer clothes that Gracie and Jason had forced on her. Not to mention the little Jaguar sports car she was driving.

"Joking?" He gave her a long appraisal with narrowed, contemptuous eyes. "It's no joke. Don't think you'll play on my sympathies and walk away richer. I have none for mercenary creatures like you." He was outraged that she'd tracked him here, that she was brazen enough to try to force her way into his life after they'd agreed to divorce.

"Mercenary...?" She was horrified. This wasn't what she'd expected.

Before he could say anything else, or she could come up with a reply that didn't include kicking him in the groin, his apartment door opened and a beautiful young woman with long black hair, olive skin and dark eyes called to him.

"Are you coming, Rodrigo?" she asked urgently. "I've almost burned the paella!"

"I'll be right there, Conchita," he called back.

Glory had never felt so stupid. He looked back down at her with pure revenge in his dark eyes. "She's great in bed," he drawled.

She didn't want him to see the pain he was causing. She turned away and started back toward her car. Her hip was hurting, but so was her belly. Odd, these twinges of pain. She thought about the blood thinners she'd taken for so long and hoped they weren't going to hurt the baby. The baby. Rodrigo would never know, she vowed. Never!

HE WATCHED HER WALK away with mingled fury and regret. She was proud. She'd never asked for special treatment on the farm and she had guts—she'd saved herself from both Marco and Consuelo without any help from him. He'd accused her of being after his money. Well, he told himself, she probably was. She had nothing. Could he blame her for wanting a better life?

As he mounted his steps he heard a roar and looked over the parking lot in time to see a green sports car rev out into the road. He didn't recognize the car, but he knew it couldn't be Glory's. Maybe some friend of hers had brought her. He went in to eat the paella and put Glory out of his mind.

GLORY RAN OUT OF CURSES before she left Houston. By the time she got to the expressway and was almost to Victoria, she was making them up as she went along. The pain in her belly came again. She gasped. This wasn't going away. Her own doctor was in San Antonio, and Jacobsville was much closer. Lou Coltrain knew about her condition. She decided that Jacobsville was her best bet. She hoped she could make it. She floored the accelerator.

LUCK WAS WITH HER. On the outskirts of Jacobsville, a squad car threw on its blue lights and pulled her over. She slumped over the wheel as the officer, whom she recognized from her standoff with Marco, walked to her side.

Holding his ticket book, Kilraven started to date a ticket without looking down. "May I see your license and registration, ma'am?" he asked courteously.

"The minute...you get me...to a hospital," she panted, and turned her white face up to his. "I think I'm...losing my baby," she added, and her voice broke.

"Good God!" he exclaimed.

He pulled open the door, unfastened her seat belt, and carried her, as if she weighed nothing, to the passenger side of his squad car. He put her in, gently, and fastened the seat belt. All the time, he was talking into his portable. "I'm on my way in with a pregnant woman who may be miscarrying her child," he said curtly. "Have them meet me at the emergency room entrance. There's no time to wait for an ambulance."

"Ten-four," dispatch replied. "Can you identify the patient?"

"Gloryanne Barnes," he told her immediately. "Notify Dr. Lou Coltrain."

"That's a ten-four. Dispatch clear at eleven-twenty hours."

"My...purse, and keys," she managed between bouts of excruciating pain.

He ran to get them, locking the car and racing back to get in under the wheel. He put the purse, keys inside, on the floorboard beside her, started the car and laid down rubber getting out into the highway.

"Laying drags," she managed. "They'll hang you for that."

He laughed, silver eyes flashing as he glanced at her. "You sound like a lawyer."

"I am a lawyer."

"I know."

She would have pursued that, but the pain doubled her up, in spite of the seat belt. Tears were rolling down her cheeks all the short drive to the hospital.

The rest was a blur of pain and loud voices, hands lifting her, and very soon, Lou Coltrain's gentle, calming voice. Something stung her arm. Then, peace.

When she opened her eyes again, Kilraven, the tall, good-looking policeman who'd brought her in was standing beside the bed, watching her with eyes so pale a shade of gray that they gleamed like silver against his olive complexion and jet-black hair.

"You brought me in," she murmured drowsily.

"Yes."

She touched her flat belly and started to cry silently. She knew her child was gone. She could feel the emptiness. "I lost my baby, didn't I?"

His mouth made a straight line. "I'm sorry."

She looked up at him in anguish.

"It gets better," he said stiffly. "It just takes time."

"Have you... lost a child?"

His mouth made a thin line. "Yes."

She had to fight to breathe. Her cheeks were flushed. Her heartbeat was moving the sheet that covered her.

He pushed the intercom button and said something into it, very softly. Seconds later, a nurse bustled in and checked her vitals. She grimaced.

"Just lie still," she said gently. "I'll be right back."

"What is it?" she asked the officer.

"They'll hang me if I tell you."

She studied him. "They wouldn't dare. Tell me."

His broad chest expanded under the uniform. "I think you're having a heart attack."

She nodded. "That's what…I think, too."

The nurse was back with Dr. Copper Coltrain. He checked her vitals, looked at her chart and whispered something to the nurse, who nodded and scurried out of the room.

"Heart attack." Glory murmured drowsily.

"I don't think so. An episode of angina, probably, but we'll run tests." He glared at the officer. "She can't have visitors," he said flatly.

Kilraven clasped his hands behind his back and stood at parade rest. He didn't move. His silver eyes dared Coltrain to evict him.

"He saved me," Glory protested. "I'd never have made it on my own."

Coltrain's evil expression mellowed, just a little. The nurse came back and handed him a syringe. He injected it into Glory. She managed a weak smile and everything faded away again.

THE NEXT TWO DAYS were a blur. She awoke to an ungodly noise outside her room. She recognized Sheriff Hayes Carson's deep voice cursing. She wondered if he did it often, because he was using some odd phrases.

"Crackers and milk!" Carson exploded. "I'm not serving damned divorce papers on a woman in her condition!" he was yelling into his cell phone. "You tell your damned client if he wants them served, he can come right down here to Jacobsville General and serve them himself!"

"You're disturbing the patients," Lou Coltrain chided.

"Sorry," Hayes muttered sheepishly. "It was unavoidable."

He and Lou exchanged a meaningful look. They didn't go inside and tell Glory anything. Which was a shame. Because three hours later, her husband walked into her room unannounced and stared at her as if he couldn't believe his eyes.

"What do you want?" she asked icily.

"Your sheriff refused to serve divorce papers on you." He started to pull them out of his pocket, but he hesitated. She looked worn out, heartsick, exhausted. "What the hell are you doing in here? Is it your hip again?"

Her green eyes flashed at him. "What do you care?" she asked. "You didn't even ask me why I'd come to see you. You think I'm mercenary, do you? You think money is all I want out of life."

His teeth clenched. "That's all women have ever wanted from me," he said coldly. "Except..."

"Except for Sarina," she finished for him. "But you can't have her, can you? I guess Conchita is your present consolation. Pity I didn't know that I was standing in for your ex-partner!"

His eyes darkened and he smiled coolly. His pride stung and he retaliated, "You were a poor substitute."

That was the absolute last straw. "Get out!" she shouted, sitting up. The action made her feel faint. She felt her heart racing wildly, in spite of the drugs they were giving her.

"Shall I leave the divorce papers on the table before I go?" he taunted.

"I'll tell you where to put them, and how far. Get out!" she yelled. "Get out!"

Copper Coltrain burst into the room like a redheaded tornado. "Get out of here," he said in a furious undertone. "Right now."

"I'm talking to my wife..." Rodrigo shot back.

Coltrain dragged him out of the room. "She had an attack of angina soon after she was brought in. She has extremely high blood pressure, and she's already had one heart attack before she came down here to Jacobsville!" he said icily. "Her blood pressure has been worse since she lost the baby, two days ago..."

"Baby?" Rodrigo leaned against the wall. His horrified dark eyes held Coltrain's blue ones unblinking. His olive complexion faded to the color of oatmeal. "She was pregnant?!"

"Yes." Coltrain scowled. "Surely you knew?"

Rodrigo slumped back against the wall and closed his eyes. Glory had come to Houston to tell him something, and he wouldn't let her speak. She was pregnant. She'd come to tell him about the baby. He'd sent her away, upset her. A heart attack. High blood pressure. It would be dangerous for her to have a child. He knew she was prone to attacks of faintness, but he'd dismissed it, paying more attention to her bad hip. She'd said she didn't want children. It was a lie. Her health made it life-threatening, and he hadn't even known. God forgive me, he thought. Dear God, forgive me!

"I said things to her in there," Rodrigo said heavily. "It angered me that she came to my apartment in Houston and then walked away without even talking to me. I thought she'd come to ask for money…" His eyes closed. "I knew nothing about any of this."

"For a married man, you're damned uninformed about your wife."

"I filed for divorce," Rodrigo said in a haunted tone. "My attorney said the sheriff refused to serve the papers on her, and called me. I thought maybe she was in traction for her hip…" His face was drawn. "I should be horsewhipped for what I said to her."

"An apology wouldn't be out of place."

He looked at the other man evenly. "I'm not going to upset her any more than I already have. She'll be all right?"

Coltrain nodded. "She's already under the care of a heart specialist."

"Good. Good. If she needs anything…"

"She has good insurance. We'll take care of her."

Rodrigo stood erect. He started to speak, but he only shrugged. He was ashamed of himself. Glory had done nothing to deserve such treatment from him. He'd been horrible to her, and not just today. He didn't understand himself. Not at all.

Coltrain moved away. He could read people very well. This man had no idea what was going on. Maybe it was just as well that he hadn't known, if he was divorcing Glory. Good riddance, Coltrain thought. She deserved better.

The officer who brought Glory in, Kilraven, wandered back from the canteen and watched the woman's husband staring at her door. One of the nurses had identified him to Kilraven, who was feeling anger at the man for what Hayes Carson had said.

"She's been through a lot," he told the tall, dark man. "She doesn't need any more upsets."

Rodrigo looked at him coldly. "I didn't come here to upset her. Nobody told me she'd had a miscarriage. I didn't even know she was pregnant."

The older man's silver eyes narrowed. "I heard. Pity you want to live in the past." His head jerked toward Glory's room. "That one has more grit and courage than any woman I've ever known."

"Yes," Rodrigo replied, feeling empty. "But she and I are as incompatible as any two people have ever been. She'll be better off without me."

Kilraven smiled coldly. "My thoughts exactly."

Rodrigo didn't like the arrogance in that smile, and he had to restrain his first impulse, which was to deck the man. This wasn't the place. Besides that, he was feeling particularly guilty. If he hadn't been so cruel to Glory, perhaps she wouldn't have lost his child. His child. He was responsible for its loss. Surely he could have found a kinder way to get Glory out of his life!

"I'll take care of her," Kilraven said, breaking into his thoughts. "The divorce will help her heal." His silver eyes glittered. "From what I've seen, she's never done anything in her life bad enough to deserve you as a husband."

Rodrigo's black eyes glittered as well. "She couldn't wait to replace me, could she?" he asked icily. "You're welcome to her. She would never have fit into my world."

He turned and walked away. Kilraven had made him murderously angry. Glory was still his wife. He could keep her; he didn't have to sign divorce papers. But the guilt ate away at him. His child was gone. She'd never forgive him for its loss. He'd never forgive himself.

On his way out, he almost collided with tall, handsome Jason Pendleton and his stepsister, little blond Gracie.

"Rodrigo," Jason greeted him nonchalantly. "We heard about the drug bust. Good work."

Rodrigo wasn't paying attention. He was still seeing Glory's tragic face and damning himself for his part in it. "Yes." He tried to sound interested. "What are you two doing here?"

"Visiting a family member," Jason said, scowling. "Are you all right?"

"Not really. I have to go. Good to see you both."

They watched him walk away with open curiosity.

"He's a strange man," Gracie mused.

"All men are strange," Jason said wickedly, and grinned when she flushed and laughed. "Come on. Let's see what we can do for our Glory."

GLORY TOOK A COUPLE of weeks off for tests, and to come to grips with her grief at the loss of her child. Her boss was good to her, giving her time off when she needed it and arranging for someone to cover for her when she had the heart catheterization. In the end they did a balloon angioplasty to blow out the plaque that was blocking an artery. Afterward she worked hard at her diet, took her medicine regularly and tried to convince herself that she could still manage her high-stress job despite the blood pressure that responded best to drugs when she was away from work. The doctor warned her quite bluntly that she had a congenital heart defect that had become more serious as she aged. He added that even with her lifestyle changes, she could die if she didn't find something less stressful to do for a living. It was the same old spiel, but she wasn't listening. She didn't care anymore. She'd lost her child and her husband, and the job wasn't enough to hold her to the world. But she did it with fervor and flair, going after evidence from witnesses like a bloodhound on the trail of a killer. Defense attorneys started to groan the minute she walked into the courtroom. Miss Barnes, they confided, could take rust off battleships with that tongue.

RODRIGO HADN'T PURSUED the divorce, but Glory did. She charged him with desertion and alienation of affection and irreconcileable differences and set her own attorney on him. He offered a cash settlement, which he wasn't required to do under Texas law. Glory refused hands down. He signed the papers and left the country. Nobody knew where he was.

Glory was enjoying a hostile witness on the stand in a murder trial. The man had lied about everything, especially his involvement in the crime.

"You turned state's evidence in order to receive a reduced sentence, did you not, Mr. Salinger?" she purred.

"Well, yes, but I was coerced."

She was wearing a very expensive pale gray suit with a green silk blouse the color of her eyes, and gray shoes with a short heel. Her blond hair had been cut. It curled around her delicate face like feathers. She wore contact lenses and makeup and she looked lovely. Her complexion was like peaches and cream. Her low self-image had been boosted in recent weeks by the gentle attentions of Officer Kilraven from Jacobsville, who spent his days off in the courtroom watching her work. She was one of a handful of people who knew he was the half brother of San Antonio FBI agent Jon Blackhawk. He was working undercover in Jacobsville with the help of police chief Cash Grier. Not even Glory knew on what. He was a secretive man. But he was also very masculine and he knew how to charm women. Glory had blossomed because of his interest. She wished she could encourage him, but she felt nothing more than friendship.

She glanced at him in the audience and grinned. He grinned back.

"Coerced?" she echoed the witness's statement. She moved close to him, with her file folder in her hand. "How very strange."

"What is?" he asked.

"It says here—" she indicated the file "—that you requested a meeting with the assistant prosecutor on this case—that would be me," she purred again, "and swore that you'd do anything for a reduced sentence."

He frowned. "Well, I might have said that," he agreed.

"You signed this statement in the presence of your defense attorney. That's correct, isn't it, Mr. Bailey?" she asked the defense attorney.

He got up. "Uh, well, yes..."

"Thank you, Mr. Bailey," she said, smiling. She turned back to the witness and the smile faded. Her green eyes glittered as she leaned toward the nervous man. "You will repeat the statement you gave to me, Mr. Salinger," she said with icy disdain, "or I will have you charged with perjury and I will ask for the maximum time a judge can give you in jail. Is that clear?" He hesitated. "I said," she raised her voice, "is that clear, sir?"

"Yes. Yes!" He straightened. "I saw the accused shoot the victim," he stammered.

"Saw him? Or helped him, Mr. Salinger?" She leaned forward again. "Is it not a fact that you held the gun on the victim while your friend and partner, the defendant, cut his throat from ear to ear and watched him bleed to death on the ground in front of you?!"

There was sobbing from the prosecution side of the courtroom. The victim's mother, Glory knew, and she hated to make the point so graphically, but it was necessary to force this witness to admit what he knew.

"Yes!" Salinger burst out. "Yes, yes, I held the gun on him while my partner killed him. I saw him do it. But he made me help him. He made me do it!"

"Liar!" raged the defendant.

"Order! Order in the court!" The raven-haired little judge raised her voice. The witness was now sobbing. The defense attorney was gritting his teeth. "Objection!" he called. "Objection, your honor! Leading the witness!"

"Overruled," the judge said calmly.

The defense attorney said something under his breath and glared at Glory as he sat down again.

"The defense attorney is objecting to the truth? My, my," Glory murmured.

"Another word, Miss Barnes, and I'll hold you in contempt," Judge Lenox chided.

"I'm very sorry, your honor," Glory drawled sweetly. She glanced at the defense attorney. "The prosecution rests."

"Mr. Bailey?" the judge asked the defense attorney.

The lawyer knew he'd blown it. He made a futile gesture. "The defense rests, also, your honor." His client glared at him as a deputy came to remove him from the courtroom.

"We will adjourn for lunch and resume with the summations at 1:00 p.m. Dismissed." The judge banged her gavel and stood up.

"All rise!"

Everyone else stood up.

AT THE BACK OF THE courtroom, Rodrigo Ramirez was standing with an assistant prosecutor watching the trial.

"Isn't she something?" Cord Maxwell chuckled. "A little firecracker. She's so good that defense attorneys shiver when they hear her name. She vanished for a while. Nobody knows why, but she's back now and racking up convictions the way a pool champion racks up balls. There's talk of running her for district attorney in three years."

"I can see why," Rodrigo replied. He'd started when he heard the judge call her Miss Barnes. That had been Glory's last name. But that elegant, chic woman at the prosecutor's table bore no resemblance to the pathetic woman who'd worked for him in Jacobsville. And Glory's hair had been long. Long, and beautiful.

Rodrigo had tried not to think about her, but with little success. Part of him had loved her, in spite of all his rhetoric about never getting over Sarina. He missed Glory, and he'd grieved for the child. Perhaps it would have been a disaster, if they'd remained married, but he would have kept his vows, and he would have wanted the baby. It was a shame that he hadn't let her talk to him. The guilt kept him awake at night. When he'd gone home from the hospital, he'd gone on a legendary bender. It hadn't helped the pain. Nothing had.

"They're recessing," Maxwell told him. "Let's talk to her."

Rodrigo followed him down the aisle to where the defense attorney was glaring at his opponent.

"And that's another lunch you owe me, Will." She chuckled.

"I could win cases if they'd lock you in a closet somewhere!"

"Watch it, Bailey," a tall man with silver eyes told the attorney with a grin, moving to stand beside Glory. "If you lock her up, I'll have to arrest you."

"You have no jurisdiction here, hotshot," Bailey chuckled. "And I'm not going near Jacobsville as long as you work there. Marquez has told me too much about you."

"Lies," Kilraven returned suavely. "I'm so sweet that people ask me to handcuff them when they break the law, just so they won't hurt my feelings."

"You wish," Glory laughed. "Let's get something to eat…"

"Miss Barnes?" Maxwell called.

She turned, her face radiant, and met Rodrigo's wide, shocked eyes.

15

GLORY'S GREEN EYES LOST their radiance and went cold. She glared at her ex-husband so intently that DEA Agent Maxwell had to clear his throat to divert her.

"Maxwell, isn't it?" she asked, trying to collect herself. "What can I do for you?"

"You're prosecuting one of our cases in district court," he replied. "Mr. Ramirez here is the arresting federal officer. We'd like you to depose him. He's going to be out of the country during the trial, and his testimony will be crucial to our case."

Glory didn't want to talk to Rodrigo. She averted her eyes, thinking furiously. At her side, Kilraven's big, lean hand slid over hers and clasped it firmly. She glanced up at him and smiled gently. He almost read her mind sometimes.

"The case?" Rodrigo bit off. He didn't like the other man touching Glory.

Glory turned back to him. The smile was gone. "Which case is it?"

"The accused is a man named Vernon Redding," Maxwell volunteered. He was obviously puzzled by the undercurrents. He knew nothing about Rodrigo's connection to the assistant prosecutor.

"The Redding case." She thought for a minute. "Oh, yes, the smuggling charges. Reg Barton's handling that one," she said and thought, Thank God! "He takes a late lunch, so you can probably find him at our other office in the courthouse annex right now."

"Great. We'll go over there, then. Thanks. Good to see you again, Miss Barnes."

"Yes. Same here." She didn't look at Rodrigo. Her hand was still clinging to Kilraven's.

Rodrigo wanted to say more. He was still getting used to the idea that his dowdy ex-wife was this high-powered, elegant assistant prosecutor. She'd hidden this side of her life from him. She wasn't plain and she wasn't stupid. She obviously had a law degree. She was cultured and she dressed in a manner that would make any man proud to be seen with her. She was very attractive, with her hair in that becoming style. But she hated him and had no reservations about expressing it with her eyes. He felt the chill all over.

"It was good to see you again," Rodrigo said quietly.

"Was it? Pity I can't return the compliment," she said

curtly. "I'd hoped that I'd never have to see you again as long as I lived."

He hesitated for a minute. Then, with a Latin shrug of his powerful shoulders and a quick glare at Kilraven, he turned and followed Maxwell out of the courtroom.

Glory sat down quickly. Her heart was going wild. She fought for each breath. "Get Haynes," she whispered.

Kilraven turned and walked briskly out the side door and down the hall. But he didn't have to go after Haynes, she was running toward him.

"She didn't take her medicine this morning!" she exclaimed breathlessly.

"I know."

They turned and rushed back into the courtroom. Rodrigo had stopped and gone back the minute he saw the other man rushing out of the room. He watched as Haynes shook medicine out of two bottles into Glory's hand, and Kilraven poured water from a carafe into a glass at the prosecution table.

Rodrigo frowned. She shouldn't be doing this job, he thought. It was going to kill her. He winced as he realized how far he'd fallen in his desperation to escape her. If he'd taken care of her, if he'd been kind to her, the baby might have survived and she might not be looking at him as if she'd like to see him roasting on a spit.

Kilraven looked up. Across the room, the man's pale silver eyes sliced into him. Rodrigo didn't back away from threats. But this wasn't the time to start more trouble. Glory had obviously had enough for one day.

He went back to join Maxwell. He was going to see Glory before he left town. There might be a chance, a small one, to redeem himself before he left the country. He didn't want to go away with her hating him.

HE'D MEANT TO CALL ON her at her apartment that evening, but Jason Pendleton had invited him to a party and insisted that he come. They were acquaintances. He was curious about the other man's insistence, but he didn't feel right turning him down. Jason had helped him shut down Fuentes's operation by giving him the management job at the farm. So he put on his dinner jacket and his diamond cuff links and drove his high-powered Mercedes to the family mansion.

It was gloriously lighted, inside and out. There was valet parking. He gave the liveried boy his keys and walked up the semicircular driveway past the fountain to the steps that led to the front door. There was a Jaguar XKE, racing-green, parked at the door. He recalled seeing that car before, at his apartment many months earlier. But he dismissed it. There must be dozens of the fast cars in Texas.

He was greeted by Jason and Gracie at the receiving line, and he proceeded down the hallway to the huge ballroom beyond. It was a gala evening. Thanksgiving was coming up and the house was decorated in Christmas colors. Jason mused that Gracie would put up a Christmas tree in August if she could get away with it; she loved the holiday so much. He insisted that she wait until Thanksgiving for the tree, but she'd decorated the ballroom with green and gold and red flowers and garlands, anyway.

Jason hated company, but he was working on the takeover of a computer software corporation and this was how he did business. He softened up his quarry by introducing him to Hollywood celebrities and sports stars at get-togethers like this. It was sound business.

Rodrigo accepted a whiskey on the rocks and nursed it slowly as he moved around. He came upon a young movie star who'd been his date for the premier of her second film in London. She was with a race car driver tonight, but she smiled at Rodrigo wistfully. She'd tried every trick she knew to bed him, but at the time he'd been hoping to persuade Sarina to marry him. The star was clearly attracted to her handsome escort, but she was still making eyes at Rodrigo. He lifted his glass and toasted her, but he turned away.

As he turned, he came face-to-face with Kilraven, also in a dinner jacket, looking perfectly at home among the famous few.

He frowned. There was something so familiar about this man. He didn't seem the sort to work as a patrolman for a hick police department. He noted that the other man was wearing expensive clothes and carrying a glass of what looked like iced tea.

"No whiskey?" Rodrigo asked him suspiciously.

"I don't drink."

Now he remembered. The man's aversion to alcohol was almost a mania, and it got him talked about. His dark eyes narrowed. "You were in Peru with us five years ago," he recalled with a bland smile.

Kilraven's dark eyebrows lifted. "Us?"

"Not the DEA," Rodrigo said softly.

Kilraven scowled. He stared at Rodrigo for a long time. "Laremos. You were with Laremos."

Rodrigo nodded. "You were with a paramilitary unit."

"If you advertise that," Kilraven said in a hushed tone, "you'll be wearing a rosebush and a lot of dirt by midnight."

"You wouldn't dare," Rodrigo drawled.

"Why wouldn't I dare?" came the smiling challenge.

"Because your boss and I play chess every other week. And I let him win."

Kilraven glared.

"What are you doing here?" Rodrigo asked curiously. "Do you know the Pendletons?"

"No. I know their stepsister."

"They must hide her on a closet shelf," Rodrigo murmured as he sipped whiskey. "I've never seen her."

"She was out front a few minutes ago, making sure her car was still there. I believe Gracie had asked to borrow it." He winced. "Gracie drives like she goes down steps."

Rodrigo's dark eyes twinkled a little. "Headfirst?"

"Exactly."

He frowned. "That car wouldn't be a green Jag convertible, would it?"

"In fact, it is. Racing-green is my favorite color," came a stiff, cool little voice from behind him.

He turned, and Glory was standing there, dressed in a beautiful little lacy black dress with spaghetti straps and sequins. She looked expensive and delicious, with the bodice cut just low enough to be both modest and flattering to her high, firm breasts. She was sipping brandy. Her soft blond hair curled toward her face, giving her a pixie look.

"Hello, Rodrigo," she said carelessly. "Fancy seeing you here."

"I was about to say the same thing. You never told me you were related to the Pendletons," he said coldly.

"Since when is my private life any business of yours?" she asked with an equal chill in her voice.

Her attitude pricked his temper. "Privacy is like a religion to you, isn't it, *niña?*" he scoffed. "You couldn't even be bothered to tell your husband you were carrying his child!"

"I was trying, when you began listing your new girlfriend's bedroom skills to me!" she flashed at him. "Of course, she's out of the running, too, isn't she? You're still lusting after your ex-partner!" she exclaimed. Her green eyes glittered with fury. "Remember me? The plain, crippled, stupid assistant cook that you were ashamed for your colleagues to see with you?"

He'd said that. He couldn't deny it. But he was furious that she'd brought it up. "I never said that to you!"

"You said it behind my back," she threw at him. "You didn't have the guts to say it to my face!"

"Back off," he gritted. "Nobody talks to me that way,

especially not some overzealous prosecuting attorney! I'm not in your courtroom!"

"God help you if you were," she shot back, fists clenched at her side. "I'd cut you into little pieces and throw you in the defense attorney's face!"

"I'd love to see you try it," he told her.

A crowd had gathered. The humdrum party had turned into a glorious piece of theater complete with attractive combatants. Even the movie star was listening attentively. Probably, Glory thought wickedly, to get pointers for her next argument; learn the craft from an expert.

"Why don't you go back to Houston where you belong?" she raged. "I'm sure Conchita can't wait to make you another paella lunch!"

"At least she doesn't have the tongue of a shrew and the demeanor of an ax murderer!"

"Fine talk from a glorified hit man!"

"I work for the government," he began.

"As what, an assassin?"

"Lady and gentleman," Kilraven muttered, stepping between them. "And I use the terms loosely. If you don't cease and desist, one of you is leaving in handcuffs."

"Oh, shut up!" they both shouted in unison.

Kilraven gaped at them.

They moved around him and continued.

"You lied to me from the minute you walked in my door," Rodrigo growled at her.

"It was so easy," she chided. "You believed anything I told you!"

"I felt sorry for you!"

Her face flamed. "Yes, you pitied me, didn't you? Poor, crippled Glory who…who couldn't…who…" She stopped. Her face was flaming. She was panting like a runner. She staggered.

"Oh God!" Rodrigo whispered. He moved forward, catching her up in his arms as she fell. "Get a doctor!" he shouted, and his expression went from anger to terror in a space of seconds.

"Bring her in here," Gracie said urgently, leading the way. Flighty she might be, but there was nobody cooler in an emergency. "I'll get her medicine. She keeps forgetting to take it. She'll be all right," she comforted Rodrigo, who was holding on to Glory as if he were terrified she might die in his arms. "She has these spells of angina, but they don't do damage. The heart specialist said so. They cleared the blockage with a balloon angioplasty and she's on blood thinners. Stay with her."

Gracie rushed out and spoke to the crowd gathering outside the study door. "She'll be all right. Please, leave her with us. We'll take care of her." She was also talking to Kilraven, who permitted himself to be rushed out of the room. The door closed.

Rodrigo laid Glory down on the long brocade sofa, elevating her feet on one of the pillows. He sat down beside her, feeling helpless and hating himself for bringing on this spell.

He'd done nothing but hurt her. She was fragile and big-hearted and kind. She'd loved him, and he'd been cruel to her. If she died, he'd be alone forever. Even Sarina and Bernadette would never be able to make up for the loss of Glory.

Tears stained her flushed cheeks. They were silent. Copious. He dabbed at them with a snow-white handkerchief and felt guilt like a shroud around him.

She opened her eyes and looked up at him with bridled anger.

He put his forefinger gently over her lips. "We've both said enough," he said tenderly. "I'm sorry. Sorry for everything. Especially sorry about our baby." His teeth ground together as he spoke. His jaw was rigid. "I had no right to taunt you with it."

"They think…it might have been the blood thinners," she gritted. "I had to take them. I'd already had one heart attack. They were afraid…" Tears poured down her cheeks. "I wanted my baby," she sobbed.

"*Amada,*" he whispered, and bent to kiss the tears away, so softly. "*Amada,* forgive me," he choked. "I would have wanted it, too. My poor baby." His mouth moved tenderly over her wet eyes, her nose, down to her soft, sweet mouth. He kissed it with forced brevity, groaning as it brought back exquisite memories of Glory in his arms, in his bed, loving him. "Forgive me," he groaned.

She would have. Her arms were already stealing hesitantly up and around his neck, but the door opened and Gracie burst in like a little whirlwind, with Jason at her heels. Rodrigo got to his feet, struggling for composure.

"Here." Gracie fussed, handing Glory the capsule, the tablet and the glass of water.

Glory swallowed them. "Sorry," she whispered. "I had a bad day in court. Bailey and I went head to head for the better part of three hours until we recessed for lunch. I forgot my morning medicines." She grimaced. "And then I forgot the evening dose, too."

"Careless," Jason chided, but gently. He was very fond of her, and it showed.

"Very careless," Glory agreed. "I'm sorry I embarrassed you."

"Nothing embarrasses me," Jason replied.

"Certainly not illness you can't help, baby," Gracie seconded, bending to kiss the younger woman. "You lie here for a few minutes. We'll entertain the guests. I'll tell fortunes and Jason can do a softshoe routine."

"In your dreams," Jason muttered icily.

Gracie made a face at him. She glanced at Rodrigo.

"Let him stay," Glory said unexpectedly. "We have to talk."

The other two occupants of the room exchanged worried glances. Rodrigo moved closer. "I won't upset her again," he said in a subdued tone. "I'm going out of the country tomorrow. I won't be back for a long time."

"All right," Jason said, reading Glory's sudden misery accurately. "If you need us, sing out."

"I will. Thanks." She included Gracie in that.

The Pendletons left, closing the door behind them.

Rodrigo stood over Glory, quiet and regretful. "We knew

nothing about each other," he said. "We lied and pretended. You can't build a relationship on fiction."

"I know," Glory replied heavily. "I couldn't tell you anything. I didn't know you. I was afraid at first that you were mixed up with drug smuggling, and then because Cash and Marquez couldn't tell me what was going on, I thought you were the killer Fuentes had sent after me."

He seemed surprised by the statement. "You thought I could kill you?"

She smiled in a world-weary way. "I prosecuted a teenager two months ago for beating his grandmother to death. He was high on acid and didn't know what he was doing. He's serving fifteen years. He doesn't even remember doing it. I have a low opinion of humanity. I get it from my job."

He sat down beside her again and leaned over her. "I worked as a mercenary for many years," he said. "I saw ugly things, too."

"You aren't what you seem," she replied, searching his dark eyes. "I heard about your sister. I'm sorry. Are your parents still alive?"

He shook his head. "My father raced yachts. He was lost in a storm. My mother grieved herself to death within six months. It was just the two of us, me and my sister, and an estate comparable to the gross national product of a small third-world country. I don't have to work, you see," he said cynically. "I could race yachts or go skiing in Aspen. I don't like the life-style, so I avoid it. I've spent too much of my life at the safe end of an automatic weapon. I've never wanted a settled life."

"Yes, you have," she replied. "You wanted it with Sarina."

He frowned. "Yes. I wanted it with Sarina. But it was never like that for her. She couldn't love me."

"You'll find someone, someday," she replied in a dull tone. "Someone who can live an exciting life, and go with you on adventures."

He didn't understand what she was saying.

She laughed. "I know what it is to love a job," she lied, because his acceptance of her statement gave it the ring of truth. What use would he have for a woman in her state of health, anyway? "My whole life revolves around my career. It's all I want." She didn't look up at him. That was a pity.

He got to his feet and moved away. He paused at the end of the sofa. "Will you be all right?" he asked.

"Yes. It's just the excitement," she said. The medicine was already working. She felt much better. She sat up. "They cleared out the blockage. I'm as good as I'll ever be. Well, I'll always have to take medicine, and sometimes I limp when I stress my hip too much. But, for a cripple, I do well enough."

He turned. His expression was strained. "You're no cripple," he bit off.

She only laughed. "Sure."

"Glory," he began slowly.

"Kilraven will be missing me," she said as she got to her feet. "He takes good care of me. He doesn't mind my... flaws."

"Dear God, don't talk like that! I didn't mean what I said,

Glory," he told her, desperate to correct her mistaken under-standing. "I wasn't myself."

She looked up at him with her courtroom face, the bland one that defense attorneys had underestimated so often. "You don't need to beat yourself to death over the past, Rodrigo. I'm perfectly happy with the life I have now. I'm sure you're equally happy with yours. Conchita is very pretty," she added, trying to sound as if she didn't care. "I expect she's crazy about you."

She was slamming doors in his face. He'd come face-to-face with his real fear, that he'd lose his heart completely again and suffer the same agony he'd felt when Sarina turned back to Colby Lane. He hadn't thought Glory could live with him, as he was, or cope with his lifestyle. Now he knew that she could, and he was certain they had a future. But she wouldn't even try again. He'd hurt her too badly. She'd decided that he wanted a young, strong, healthy woman, and that she was out of the running. She wasn't willing to risk her heart with him after he'd rejected it.

"I blew it, didn't I?" he asked quietly. He searched over her face, which had been radiant just for him, those eyes that had loved him, those arms that had clung to him in the darkness. He'd had all that, and he'd pushed it away.

"Don't be melodramatic," she chided, but she wouldn't look at him again. "You know you're happier without ties. Go live your life, Rodrigo. I hope you'll be happy."

"And you?" he asked bitterly. "Will you be happy?"

She raised her eyebrows. "I already am. Kilraven spoils me in every way," she added suggestively.

His sensual lips compressed. "Damn you!" he said with barely contained violence. "And damn Kilraven!"

He turned on his heel and stormed out of the room, leaving a shocked and unsettled Glory behind. When she left the study, he'd already gone home. His final words had been full of fury. She couldn't imagine why.

BEFORE HE COULD GET out the door, still seething about Glory's abrupt dismissal of him from her life, Jason Pendleton stepped in front of him. He wasn't smiling.

"Come in here for a minute," he said, indicating the living room, temporarily devoid of people.

"I'm in a hurry..."

"This won't take long."

Rodrigo composed himself with visible effort and followed the other man into the room.

Jason closed the door. He'd never looked more menacing. "What do you know about Glory?"

"Nothing, apparently," Rodrigo replied.

"Perhaps it's time you heard a few facts," the other man said curtly. "Sit down."

By the time Jason had shared the bare bones of Glory's past with him, Rodrigo was pale and sicker at heart than he'd been since his sister's death. He'd known about Glory's hip, but no more. Considering her childhood, it was amazing to him that she'd been able to respond to him in bed. It was proof, if he needed it, of how much she'd loved him.

He leaned forward, his forearms propped on his knees, his head in his hands. "She never told me any of that."

"She's very proud," Jason replied. "We've sheltered her as much as we could. I didn't want her in Jacobsville in the first place, but the D.A. convinced me that if she stayed here, we'd bury her. I don't understand why you couldn't leave her alone and let her do her job. I never thought of you as a cruel person."

"I never thought of myself that way." He lifted his head. "I wanted her. She had a quality of compassion that I'd never encountered in any woman, other than my partner, Sarina. She obsessed me."

Jason's expression gave nothing away. "The child she lost was yours, wasn't it?"

He nodded. "I knew nothing about the child until I tried to have divorce papers served on her."

"Yes. The marriage." He cocked his head. "That came as a shock."

"For me, too. It wasn't until the divorce was final that I realized what I'd given up." He shifted. "You and Gracie were at the hospital to see Glory, weren't you? I'd never seen your mysterious stepsister. I never connected either of you with Glory."

"It took us a long time to win her trust. We love her very much. No child should ever have to go through what she did."

"What about those two boys who assaulted her?" Rodrigo asked with bridled fury.

Jason pursed his lips. "Someone informed on them when they participated in a drug deal. I can't imagine who. There was tape and photos, too. They drew fifteen years each."

"Not enough, but a start," Rodrigo muttered.

"That's not all. Somehow it got mentioned to the other inmates that they'd sodomized a little girl in foster care. The last I heard, they had to live in solitary confinement for their own protection."

"My heart breaks," Rodrigo replied, but he was smiling faintly.

"What's that old saying, that God's mill grinds slowly but relentlessly? Justice is eventually served."

Rodrigo's eyes saddened. "I've already had mine. I'll spend the rest of my life grieving for what I threw away. Glory will never forgive me. I can't even blame her."

Jason's eyes narrowed. "You're in love with her."

Rodrigo's face closed up. He got to his feet. "I'm going out of the country tomorrow, to meet with my cousin over the border. He phoned me and said he has intelligence on an upcoming operation run by some ex-feds and a couple of gang members from El Salvador. They're the ones who helped set up Walt Monroe, one of our DEA agents who went undercover, so that another man could kill him." His dark eyes flashed. "We want them very badly."

Jason scowled. "Does your cousin often phone you about drug deals?"

Rodrigo shrugged. "He hasn't before, but this is a special case. I asked him to keep his eyes open when I heard that some gang members we'd been investigating were going to be in on the buy."

"One of my vice presidents was nabbed when he went over

the border to talk to some businessmen about oil invest-
ments. The government doesn't bargain with kidnappers,
but we had to. We got him out with a sizable donation, but
he'll never look the same," he added darkly. "They're helping
to finance their operations with ransom these days. You'd be
a tasty catch, especially if they found out you were instrumental in that last cocaine bust."

Rodrigo waved the concern away. "I've been at this for a
long time. I can take care of myself."

"Our hostage told us that they've got a pipeline right into
the DEA's office."

"They did have, a guy named Kennedy, but he's in prison."

"Not Kennedy," came the terse reply. "Someone else. A
great deal of money is involved. They're buying inside information. Don't share your plans with anyone in your organization."

Rodrigo frowned. This was disturbing news. "I'll check
into it," he said after a minute. Then he chuckled. "If they
do nab me, Cobb will probably offer congratulations. He
was furious that I was undercover during one of his
cleanup operations and he didn't know about it. It was his
office I ransacked after my sister was killed. We're wary of
each other."

"I heard about some of your exploits from Glory," Jason
replied. "You were all she talked about when she came back
from Jacobsville."

That only made the pain worse. He grimaced. "When
she's better, tell her I'm sorry that I brought on this attack."

His dark eyes flashed. "She seems to be attached to Kilraven lately. I don't like it."

Jason began to see the light. "She's fond of him," he told the other man. "Only fond."

There were layers of meaning in those few words. Rodrigo felt a little better. "When I get back, I'm going on the attack," he said. "Roses, chocolates, mariachi serenades, the works. Right outside the courtroom, if that's what it takes."

Jason actually grinned. "Can I tell her?"

"Better not. The element of surprise might work wonders." Rodrigo smiled, and shook the other man's hand. "Thanks. For everything."

"You should never have signed those divorce papers."

"You're telling me," Rodrigo sighed.

GLORY SETTLED BACK INTO her routine, forced herself to take her medicine more regularly and began to enjoy life again, even if it had less flavor after Rodrigo's exit. Late at night when she closed her eyes, she could still feel his lips kissing away the tears, hear him whispering "beloved" in Spanish at her ear. The only comfort she had was his fury over Kilraven. If that wasn't jealousy, she was a porcupine.

She knew he'd gone overseas. She didn't know where, or why. She hoped he wasn't risking his life in another sting. She wondered where he was. She found out unexpectedly, a week later, just a little while past Thanksgiving.

294 FEARLESS

Marquez came to her office to tell her in person. He was solemn and uneasy, and he hesitated.

"Well?" she asked, curious.

"It's about Ramirez."

Her heart jumped but she forced herself to remain calm. "He's getting married to the woman who cooks him paella?" she asked, bracing herself.

"No. He's been kidnapped," he said curtly. "He went down into Mexico on an informant's tip, and he was nabbed by Fuentes's brother."

"For ransom," she said slowly.

"Only partially for ransom," he replied. "Mostly for revenge. Glory!"

Marquez got her into a chair before she passed out. "I shouldn't have put it like that. I'm sorry," he said. "What can I do for you?"

"Get me something cold and fizzy from the machine in the hall," she said weakly. "But no caffeine."

"Right. Back in a jiffy."

She felt terrible. Rodrigo had been kidnapped. Her life was over. They might ask for ransom, but she was certain that they'd kill him anyway. It was her fault. If she'd asked him to stay, perhaps he would have. She'd wrapped herself in pride and indignation and tossed him out the door. He would die horribly. She'd never see him again. She'd be his murderer…!

No! No, she wasn't going to sit here and cry and give him up without a fight. She sat up straight. She wiped the tears away. This was no time for hysterics and self-condemnation.

That wouldn't help. Rodrigo was in trouble and she had to save him. The government wouldn't negotiate, she knew that. His own agency wouldn't be able to do anything for him. If he was to be rescued, she'd have to do it. She wasn't going to take this lying down. Those murderers weren't going to kill Rodrigo.

She picked up the phone and dialed her stepbrother. "Jason, Rodrigo's been kidnapped. I know who to send after him. I need money. They can't work for free."

"You can have a blank check," Jason replied at once. "And anything else you need."

"Thanks."

"He's family, too," came the enigmatic reply.

She hung up and looked over at Marquez, who'd just come back with a cold can of soda. He handed it to her and she sipped it gratefully before she spoke. "I need you to go to Jacobsville with me. I'm going to hire a few good men to get my ex-husband back."

His eyebrows arched. "Any particular reason for that?"

"Yes." She got up and retrieved her purse and coat from the hat rack. "We said goodbye in the middle of an argument we didn't get to finish. He's not winning by default."

She walked out the door, leaving a silently amused Marquez to follow.

16

GLORY WAS FASCINATED by the immediate agreement she got from Cy Parks, Eb Scott, and several of their colleagues when she talked to them about rescuing Rodrigo.

"He was with us in Africa," Cy said simply.

"And in the Middle East with Dutch, Archer and Laremos to protect a friend of ours who heads one of the sheikdoms near the Persian Gulf."

"Colby Lane would go in a heartbeat," Cy added. "Rodrigo saved his life."

"Not with his wife pregnant, he won't," Eb mused with a smile. "He's very protective of her."

"We've got enough people to pull it off, already," Cy remarked. "Including one very competent federal agent."

"Who?" Glory asked.

"Sorry, that's 'need to know,'" Eb said. "Just take my word for it that he's one man no kidnapper wants to tangle with."

Cy smiled down at Glory. "We'll take it from here," he said.

"I want to go with you," she protested.

He shook his head. "This is an operation for people who train constantly. You want Rodrigo alive. If you go along, and we have to watch out for you, the distraction could cost him his life."

She sighed. "Okay. I won't interfere." Her green eyes were wide and sad. "We said our goodbyes before he left, and they weren't happy ones. For the record, my stepbrother contacted you and asked you to go get Rodrigo. It's better if he never knows I was involved at all."

Cy frowned. "You were married."

Her eyes slid away. "It was an impulse that he regretted." Her tone grew cold. "He needs a woman who can share the life he leads, not one who'd hold him back and make him more bitter than he already is. He's got someone in Houston, anyway. She's young, and very pretty. I was never in the running."

Cy looked as if he wanted to argue the point, but he saw that it would do no good. "It's your call."

"Jason said to call him," she added. "He'll make arrangements for whatever sort of equipment you need." She hesitated. "You aren't going?" she worried. "You have a young son…"

He grinned. "I'd never get out of the house alive," he

agreed. "No, this is a job for younger men. He——" he indicated Eb Scott "——has a compound full of young hotheads
in his counterterrorism training unit who live for the adrenaline rush of danger. Our fed will take a team of them in to
rescue Rodrigo."

"They'll have to cross into Mexico," she began worriedly.

"Stop being a lawyer," Eb told her amusedly. "As it happens,
Rodrigo is related to some important people in the Mexican
government. I'm sure I can get permission from them, and
they will offer to help in the form of a military unit. Fuentes's
brother is in more trouble than he could imagine."

"Tell them to slug him once for me, will you?" she added.
"I've had enough of the Fuentes bunch to last me a lifetime."

"I'll make your wishes known," he promised.

She stood at the door, looking suddenly vulnerable.
"Someone will let me know…what happens?"

"Yes," Cy said at once.

She nodded. "Thanks," she added huskily.

Cy smiled gently. "You're welcome."

IT WAS PURE HELL, going through the motions at work without
having a clue what was going on down in Mexico. She knew
Cy's reputation, and Eb's. She suspected that Marquez knew
more about the operation than he let slip. She couldn't get
him to talk. She tried to call Kilraven and get him to pump
Eb for information, but he was off duty and when she called
his home, he wasn't there, either. It was frustrating, to say
the least.

She could still hear Rodrigo's furious voice, cursing both her and Kilraven. She didn't understand why. She'd thought at first that it might be jealousy, but she was having second thoughts. He'd made it obvious that he wanted no part of her. He'd called her a cripple that day he was talking to Sarina, and she overheard him. He'd said he was ashamed to have his friends see her. Words had such power, she thought sadly. They wounded the very soul. He'd denied later that he meant what he'd said, but only after he knew about the baby she'd lost. Probably his changed attitude came from guilt. Or pity. He'd said that it was no substitute for love, and he was right. She didn't want him to pretend affection that he couldn't feel. It was better if he never knew her part in his rescue, if Eb's men were able to get to him in time. Considering that Fuentes's brother blamed him for the drug lord's death, it was a very real possibility that Rodrigo would be killed long before they made ransom demands.

But if they did make demands, she considered, who would they ask to pay it? The answer was so blatant she was amazed that she hadn't thought of it. She phoned Alexander Cobb at the Houston DEA office on her lunch hour and asked him if he'd had a ransom call about Rodrigo.

"Yes," he said, stunned. "How did you know?"

"I can't say," she replied.

"We won't pay it, you know," he added apologetically. "It isn't our policy to give in to blackmail, for any reason. These criminals have kidnapped at least two federal agents in the past few months. They killed one and gave the other back in unspeakable condition."

"Federal agents?" she asked, aghast.

"They have a number of former cops and paramilitary leaders in their ranks," Cobb replied, "including one bunch called the Zetas who were in the military before they changed sides. They have pipelines into every agency that deals with drug trafficking. They try bribes first, and if those don't work, they kill to set examples. Three journalists have died for investigative reporting about the drug networks and the drug lords. One of our informers was found in the middle of a highway, dead, with a note on him saying that all potential infiltrators would be given the same treatment. You can't imagine how much we'd like to get our hands on these guys," he added.

"Yes, I can," she replied. "I really can."

"I suppose you do, since you prosecute drug cases."

"About Rodrigo…"

"I'm sorry," he interrupted. He sighed. "If there was anything I could do, believe me, I'd do it. But agency policy has my hands tied."

She felt hollow inside. Rules were rules. "I understand. Thanks anyway."

There was a pause. "The infiltrator they killed was Rodrigo's cousin," he said.

Cold chills ran down her spine. The man had helped Rodrigo shut down two other drug dealers. If they knew he was an informer, he'd probably told them, under torture, how to get to Rodrigo. But it also meant he wouldn't have any help, and it lessened his chances of survival.

"It just gets worse and worse," she said, thinking aloud.

"Some days, nothing goes right," he murmured. "For what it's worth, we do have people outside the agency negotiating. Fuentes's brother has another brother in custody in Mexico. There's a possibility that he might trade Rodrigo for the brother's release."

A faint hope began to glow inside her. "At last, a little hope," she said.

"A little is all we get. But don't give up on him," he added, and there was a smile in his tone. "A lot of people have underestimated Rodrigo, at great cost."

"I've heard about some of his exploits," she said.

"The tip of the iceberg," he replied. "He's the stuff of legends. There isn't a more dangerous man in government service. He's come back from certain-death assignments half a dozen times. Don't give up on him."

"I won't," she promised. "Not ever. Thanks."

"You're very welcome."

EVERY TIME HER PHONE rang, she jumped, always hoping it was news of Rodrigo. She couldn't concentrate on her work. She only wanted to know that he was alive, somewhere in the world. She could go on with her own life then. She'd long since given up any hope of sharing it with a man.

And then, a few days after the ordeal began, the phone rang and it was Cy Parks.

"Is he alive?" was all she could manage.

"Yes," he replied. "They worked a trade for him— Fuentes's brother."

She could have said it was a bad move, that it doubled the manpower of the surviving drug lords, but she didn't have the heart to. "He's…all right, then?" she persisted.

"Only a few bruises to show for the episode," Cy replied. "And he's mad at everybody for letting one of the Fuentes brothers out of prison. He said it to all of us, and he said it to everybody in the Mexican government that he could get to. All that, in about five languages, too." Cy chuckled. "That man has a wonderful vocabulary when he loses his temper."

"He's back in Houston?"

"Yes," he said. "Colby and Sarina Lane and their daughter picked him up at the airport. To his credit, he did stop cursing in any language except Danish in front of the child."

She had to suppress a laugh. That was like him. "Thanks, Cy," she said quietly. "And please thank the men who went in. I know what they risked. It was grand of them."

"I'll tell them you said so."

"You didn't tell him…?"

"About your part in the rescue? No. I think it was a mistake, for the record, but it's your life."

"I'm in your debt," she said, and meant it.

"We like him, too, Glory," he replied. "Take care."

"You, too."

She sat down on her sofa and stared at the opposite wall while tears of joy flowed silently down her cheeks. He was okay; he didn't die. They didn't cut him up and throw him out on a highway somewhere down in Mexico. She was so grateful that she couldn't even manage a coherent prayer. It was late and she was worn-out from the combination of a drawn-out murder trial and the mental anguish of the past few days. She pulled on an old T-shirt and a pair of sweat-pants and went to bed.

The buzzer rang. She thought she was dreaming. She glanced at the clock, blind without her contacts in, and made out fuzzy numbers. It was three in the morning. Nobody would be ringing her apartment doorbell at that hour. She pulled the pillow over her head and went back to sleep.

She felt something touch her hair. It was more than a touch. It was a caress. She was dreaming. She smiled. She smelled spicy cologne and soap. Rodrigo was always fastidi-ous. He was alive. Funny, how she remembered these things about him so vividly that he seemed to be right in the room with her. She murmured that aloud.

A deep chuckle sounded nearby.

She rolled over toward it, snuggling close to what felt like a strong forearm. It was warm and a little hairy.

"Sleepyhead."

She went still. That didn't sound like a voice in a dream. She rolled onto her back and opened her eyes. He was a little fuzzy, and she couldn't make out details. But that was Rodrigo, sitting on the edge of her bed. He was wearing a suit.

"How…?" she exclaimed.

"How did I get in?" he mused. "You forget what I used to do for a living. I have some stealth skills left."

The bedside lamp was on. He looked tired, but the hard

lines in his face had softened. There were some bruises on his jaw and a cut or two. But he was as handsome and sensual as ever. She loved looking at him.

"I pictured you in a gown, like the one you were wearing at the farm, the night I came to you," he murmured huskily.

Her heart jumped. "I rarely wear pretty things," she said.

"You do in court," he said. "I thought you were the most elegant woman I'd ever seen."

Her eyes grew sad. "Someone told you."

An eyebrow arched. "Told me what?"

"That I sent Eb Scott's men after you."

His eyes grew radiant. "You did? Even after what I'd said to you at Jason's party?"

"Damn," she muttered. She'd given herself away. "Well, if you didn't know that, why are you here?" she demanded.

"You shouldn't have been crying on Kilraven's shoulder after the party," he said in a conversational tone. "He can't keep a secret."

She felt betrayed by her best male friend. "I thought he hated you."

He shrugged. "He probably does, in his way, but I couldn't return the compliment after he threw down on three of Fuentes's best men and sent one of them straight to hell at the business end of an automatic pistol."

She sat up, pushing back her disheveled hair. She stared into his dark eyes. "Kilraven went to rescue you?" she exclaimed.

"You can't tell anyone," he replied. "But he works for

the government, too. He's handy in hostage situations. He used to work with Garon Grier on one of the FBI's hostage rescue teams."

"So that's why I couldn't get in touch with him."

He nodded. "He likes you," he replied. His dark eyes kindled. "Of course, I was grateful to him for the help. But I did tell him that if he ever touched you again, I'd hang him out to dry."

She was confused. She didn't know how to answer that. "Listen," she said gently, "you're physically fit and intelligent and rich. You can run rings around men ten years your junior. I..." She drew in a breath. "I'm never going to be able to do strenuous things. I'm in bad health. I won't miraculously find a cure. Chances are good that I won't be able to bear a child." Her eyes pleaded with his. "It would be best if you went back to Houston and married Conchita, or someone like her— someone young and strong and healthy."

He looked as if her words had been rocks, and every one had hit a tender spot. "I'll never be able to convince you that I didn't mean those things you heard me say to Sarina, will I?" he asked quietly. "I've been alone for a long time. I've done dangerous work, and enjoyed the risks. I've managed to stay out of deep relationships. Yes, I wanted Sarina and Berna-dette, but that wasn't meant to be. I had to get over the pain of losing her. And then I faced the pain of losing you, of being rejected a second time. I ran, not only figuratively, but by denying I could ever feel anything for you." He laughed coldly. "You'll never know how I felt when Coltrain told me you'd lost the baby. I'd humiliated you, tossed you out of my life, attacked you for coming to Houston to see me. The guilt was terrible. You could have died. Losing the child hurt. Losing you was…" He stopped and averted his eyes. "I got drunk. I wrecked a bar. I didn't go that far even when I knew Sarina was going back to Colby Lane with Bernadette. They actually took me off in handcuffs." He chuckled. "The judge said that next time, he'd give me public service and have me work at city beautification with a sign around my neck telling people not to feed me alcohol."

She laughed in spite of herself.

"You look pretty when you smile," he told her. His big, lean hand smoothed her disturbed hair. "I did a stupid thing. I was fuming about Kilraven's place in your life when I left San Antonio. I walked right into a trap that Fuentes's brother had set, and never saw it coming."

"I'm so glad they got you out," she said softly.

"So am I." He touched her mouth with the tips of his fingers. "It's too late for philosophical discussions, but I would like to come for you in the morning and take you for a drive. I want to show you something."

Tomorrow was Saturday. She was off. Her heart raced. "I must be dreaming," she said.

He bent and touched his mouth tenderly to hers, slowly at first, and then with a heated, desperate pressure that bent her head back onto the pillow. She clutched at his shoulders, returning the ardent caress, hearing his harsh groan as if from afar.

But he drew back quickly. "No," he said huskily. "Not now. Not like this. I'll come for you about nine. Okay?"

She was surprised, and touched, by his restraint. He seemed determined to show her that this was more than desire on his part. His eyes were saying incredible things. They made her breathless.

"Okay," she managed huskily.

He smiled, got up and moved to the door. "Until tomorrow."

He slipped out as silently as he'd arrived. She lay there, dazed, for several minutes before she turned out the light and went back to sleep.

In the morning, of course, she was sure that she'd dreamed the whole thing. The apartment house was wired so that an intruder who tried to bypass the buzzer would sound alarms.

But at nine o'clock, the buzzer sounded for real.

"Can you come down?" Rodrigo asked in a warm drawl.

"Give me two minutes!" she exclaimed, and rushed to dress.

She had on black slacks with a pink shell and sweater under her Berber coat. She wore boots with it. He was waiting in the lobby, in jeans and a sweatshirt, very relaxed and slightly windblown. He looked elegant, just the same.

He took her arm and led her out to his car, tucking her into the front seat.

"Where are we going?" she asked when he started the car and pulled out into traffic.

"It's a secret," he replied. He grinned. He looked more relaxed, and happier, than she'd ever seen him.

There was a cold wind blowing, with a few flakes of snow in it. Christmas was coming very soon. Jacobsville's main street was festooned with gaily lighted garlands that stretched over the streets. There were lights shaped like poinsettias and Christmas trees and wreaths, and Christmas trees in all the shop windows. The square had the biggest tree of all, flanked by lighted reindeer and elves, with a realistic looking Santa Claus in a sleigh.

"I've always loved this place," she commented. "Even with the bad times I had in my childhood."

"Jason told me about those, the night I left," he said quietly. "I wish I'd known, Glory."

She flushed. "It isn't something I talk about much."

"Because you don't want pity. Jason told me that, too. I've made so many mistakes with you, *amada,*" he said softly. "I hope to make up for a few of them today."

"What do you have in mind?" she asked, openly curious.

He smiled. "Wait and see."

He turned onto a side street and went a little way, and then onto another side street. He pulled into a driveway and cut off the engine.

There was a big For Sale sign in the front yard. There were trees and shrubs everywhere, and what looked like flower gardens in the middle of a semicircular driveway. The house itself was Spanish styled, with arches and a big front porch that seemed to go on forever. To the side was a stone patio

Why don't you go home and kiss your own wife while I finish trying to get mine back?"

Cash laughed uproariously. "You should marry him, Glory," he called to her. "I've never seen a man who needed coaching in social graces more. You should hear him curse!"

"I already have, thanks!"

Another squad car pulled up behind the chief's and threw on its blue lights as well. "Hey," Kilraven called to Cash, "you're obstructing traffic! Get moving or I'll ticket you!"

"Watch your mouth, Kilraven, or I'll give you school crossing duty!"

"Little kids love me!" came the laughing reply. "Hi, Glory!" he called to her. "I guess you're about to be taken off the market?"

"You can bet your life on it, Kilraven!" Rodrigo told him. He put a possessive arm around Glory to prove it. "See what you get for saving people's lives?" he teased.

Kilraven just laughed. "I wouldn't dare get married," he said. "Women would commit suicide in droves if I went out of circulation!"

"Let's go," Cash called to his man. "Sandy's made us a big pot of beef stew for lunch at the station, with homemade cornbread and real butter!"

"Race you!" Kilraven dared, pulling his head back in. He waved to the couple in front of the For Sale sign and raced past Cash onto the street. The police chief threw on his lights, and his sirens, and took off in hot pursuit.

Rodrigo looked down at Glory with his heart in his dark,

soft eyes. "Marry me," he coaxed. "I'll love you until the dark washes over me and carries me away, and the last word I whisper will be your name," he whispered.

Tears poured from her eyes. "I love you," she choked.

"And I love you," he said huskily. "I love you more than my own life."

She pressed hard against him, clinging. "I'll marry you."

"Yes."

He bent and kissed away the tears. It took a long time. He held her and rocked her in the wind, his eyes closed as he savored the newness of belonging to someone.

"You won't mind, that I can't keep up with you some of the time?" she asked, still insecure.

His lips touched her forehead. "Would you mind, if I were blind, or if I'd lost an arm, like Colby Lane?"

"Oh, no," she said at once. "You'd still be Rodrigo. And I'd still love you. More than ever."

He looked down at her tenderly. He smiled. "More than ever," he repeated. He folded her close in his arms. "Do you like the house?"

"I love it. Can we buy it and live here?"

He pulled some papers out of his inside jacket pocket and handed them to her. It was a bill of sale for the house. She looked up, awed.

He shrugged. "I wasn't sure of my chances," he confessed with a grin. "I thought if you liked the house, you might marry the owner to get it."

She grinned. "Smart thinking."

He linked his hand in hers. "I have the key, if you'd like a look inside before we apply for a marriage license."

She nuzzled his shoulder with her cheek. "Yes, I would."

He curled his arm around her and drew her along with him to the house. He grinned as he inserted the key and opened the door, letting her go in first.

There were six huge vases full of roses in the elegant, and furnished, living room. There were several boxes of very expensive chocolates piled on the sofa. And just as Glory was getting used to that surprise, a group of mariachis began playing a love song, grinning at her from behind their instruments.

Rodrigo sighed. "Flowers, candy, serenading," he said as he gave her a wicked smile. "The perfect combination for winning a woman's heart. Did I get it right?"

"Oh, yes, my darling," she laughed. "You got it right!" And she kissed him, very hard, to prove it.

In the darkest hours of her life, she'd dreamed of having a home and a loving husband and children. This seemed like a miracle. If only there could be a child, one day, she would be the happiest woman on earth despite her flaws.

He seemed to sense that sadness. He turned her to him, while the singers crooned, and tilted her face up to his. "Sometimes," he said, "all we have is faith, and hope. But miracles happen every day. Wait and see."

She smiled. It was a bittersweet hope, at best.

TWO YEARS LATER, almost to the day, she gave birth to a son, thanks to constant medical monitoring, new drugs and much prayer. Eyes brimming with tears, she looked up into her husband's radiant face and said, "Yes. Miracles do happen!"

"What did I tell you?" he teased.

They looked down at the tiny boy and saw generations of Ramirez and Barnes ancestors in that handsome small face. John Antonio Frederick Ramirez was named for two grand-fathers, one of whom was Danish, and a great-uncle.

Rodrigo kissed her. "One is enough," he said firmly. "I won't go through that fear again. I can't live if I lose you," he said.

The simple statement was so profound that it made her heart skip a beat. The truth of it was in the eyes that adored her. She reached up and drew her fingertips across his wide, sensuous mouth. "You won't lose me," she promised. "I'll stick like glue."

He drew in a long breath and relaxed. He cocked his head as he watched the tiny little boy feed at her breast and counted his blessings. He had so many!

Glory smiled to herself, secure in his love and the wonder of the years that still lay ahead. The pain of her early life had tempered her, as fire tempers steel. Her strength had carried her through the dangers she faced and, in the end, won the heart of this firebrand next to her. She thought of what she'd endured, fearlessly, and knew that what she had now was worth every single tear she'd shed, every stab of pain.

She looked down into the face of her child and felt his

tiny fist curl around her finger. It was the most beautiful day of her life. She laid her cheek against Rodrigo's broad shoulder. "I was just thinking," she murmured.

"What?" he asked, kissing her forehead.

"That my life began the day I met you," she said simply.

"Amada mia!" he breathed at her ear. "As did mine begin, when I met you."

She closed her eyes and smiled. It was, she thought, a perfect day.